THE
LAST
DISCIPLE

JAMES HOLMES

First paperback edition January 2020

Book design by Adam Hall

ISBN 978-1-7343698-1-6 (paperback)
ISBN 978-1-7343698-0-9 (ebook)

www.jamesholmesauthor.com

It is easy to go down into Hell; night and day, the gates of dark Death stand wide; but to climb back again, to retrace one's steps to the upper air — there's the rub.

— Virgil

CHAPTER I

Outside Aleppo, Syria

John Sunday was ready to kill. It was an act not uncommon to him, but one that long ago had lost its emotional resonance.

Today was different. Today he was pissed.

Under the darkness of a clouded moon, shielded from the eyes of God and radar, four black Little Bird helicopters threaded low toward their target. Sunday rode the starboard bench, his boots hanging a hundred feet over the shadowed sand. Even in the dark, he could make out tufts of desert scrub as the choppers traced the terrain like metal raptors in search of a mammalian meal.

Hours earlier, on a monitor from inside a hangar at the forward operating base near Kobani, he had watched the little blue bus, caked in desert dust, snake through what passed for a city street. The bus dodged chunks of concrete, winding streams of garbage, and husks of cars, the remnants of man's creations.

From the camera on the drone circling high above, Sunday watched as the bus pulled into the walled courtyard of the abandoned church. He could clearly tell, from the 1.8-gigapixel video twenty thousand feet up, that they were bound, their hands zip-tied behind their backs. A circle of armed men awaited them. The girls could have been Shia or Christian, perhaps Druze. They had been stolen from their families. To be raped. To be traded. To be broken, like everything else here.

Saving these girls was not Sunday's primary mission. They would have come and gone, their fates sealed, evils committed upon them, without Sunday ever stepping in. If not for Amir Taresh.

Taresh was a high-value target, like an MVP of the intelligence community's fantasy league. An upper-level smuggler and bookkeeper for Al Tariqa, a terrorist group that had dug like a dark root into the wasteland of countless wars in the Levant. Intel had identified Taresh among the men in the courtyard that late afternoon. Had watched as he approached the girls and, one by one, assessed their worth.

It was capture-or-kill for Taresh. Alive, perhaps he'd cooperate. Dead, his cell phone and any records at the abandoned church would feed the expeditionary team for months.

Via the drone's omniscient eye, Sunday watched Taresh stroll the line of girls. He paused, grabbed one by her small jaw, checked her teeth. He spoke, his words lost to the void that separated man from the indifferent machine in the clouds, and gestured toward the armed men.

The younger girls were dragged, wailing, from the group. A few of the older ones tried to save the younger ones. Some were likely sisters. There was silent screaming. Crying. Pleas for mercy fell on deaf hearts.

The seven youngest girls were taken around the back of the church, outside the wall of the inner sanctum, and forced to their knees beside a trench. They grabbed at each other, to hold each other, as their mothers had once done.

The men stepped back and opened fire.

Tiny bodies toppled into a desert ditch. Their blood soaked the grit, a sacrifice in sand that had not known moisture for an eternity.

Jesus, Sunday whispered.

They were children. Little girls. Eight, maybe nine years old.

As Sunday watched them fall, heat rushed up the back of his neck. He tasted metal in his mouth and could smell the iron in the air that would be the blood he would soon shed.

* * *

"Alpha One, Kurtz. I repeat, Kurtz," said the pilot in Sunday's headset.

The helicopter banked around the plateau, followed by three other Little Birds flying low and silent, and Sunday lowered his night-vision gear.

A ghost city emerged below, its eighty thousand inhabitants long since vanished. All that was left behind were windowed gravestones eaten by sand and time. In the green hue of the goggles, the shelled remnants of buildings flickered like phosphor phantoms.

Sunday looked over at Danny Ortz, riding starboard next to him. They'd spent years riding in like this, on the saddlebacks of helicopters. Back when their knees were young and their hearts were pure. Ortz had a five-year-old daughter stateside, and the afternoon massacre of little girls had triggered his paternal need for retribution. Opportunities for justice didn't come often with this job, and when they did, that justice was often tainted and dirty. But today... today it would be just and right.

The helicopter dropped suddenly, and Sunday's stomach rose like a butterfly tide. One of the operators hanging near the skids put his fingers to his helmet like he was tipping his hat. This was Sunday's team. Twelve total, handpicked from top-tier units, riding through the valley of darkness.

"Two minutes," said the voice in Sunday's headset. Final approach.

Instinctively he started through the checklist in his head. Routine. It was the training that had kept him alive—barely—this long. He checked his gear and reached around to make sure nothing had slipped off his belt during the flight, that the zip ties had done their job.

The four Little Birds dove in sync into the remnants of the city. The pilots threaded over the rooftops and surfed the street so low Sunday could smell the rot. Remnants of buildings passed along either side, people's homes, now just cold stone bones with memories they could not speak.

It was risky flying in so low. The few stragglers still living here had threaded extension cords back and forth like electric spider webs so they could tie into a handful of generators that powered their meager existence. Those cords could tie up the blades and send a chopper flipping and flopping.

"Thirty seconds," the pilot called out. "Everyone comes home."

Sunday looked around at his men. *Damn straight.*

The helicopter flew into the church courtyard and touched down as smooth as two fingers of forty-year-old Macallan. Sunday and the men stepped off as if they'd reached the end of an escalator, and a second later the bird was back in the sky. Another second, and the other helicopters had landed as well, and the team closed in on the church from all sides.

The men moved quickly in the darkness, darkness themselves, threading low toward the double wooden doors that led into the cathedral, weapons ready. A rear courtyard behind the cathedral led to classrooms and a parish hall. Sunday's team would have to breach the cathedral, take the second courtyard, and then clear the rooms one by one.

Sunday moved into position along the side of the door, beneath the shadow of an Eastern Orthodox cross. It was remarkable that this church still stood. Even the cross on the steeple was somehow unscathed, a darkened lighthouse eager to shine again for ships that no longer needed the light.

He tapped his helmet, and the breacher moved up, carrying a sledge hammer. With a whack of metal against metal, the sledge slammed the door handle, splintering the jamb. Sunday opened the door with a kick of his boot.

All doors open with the right key.

As the team rushed in, they were greeted by the wrath of a dozen waiting gunmen. Under the stone-cold glare of statues of Jesus and Mary, the church ignited in thunder, fire, and fog.

Sunday and his men tucked behind the stone columns and wooden pews near the back wall. The enemy gunmen were buried like termites among the thick wooden pews. Sunday scolded one sloppy enough to raise his head with a double tap from his M4 to the bridge of the man's nose, spraying blood and bone across two pews.

Sunday ducked back behind the column as bullets tore into the rock, frosting his beard with sand and stone.

"Omega," he said into the microphone near his larynx. "North wall. Need some breathing room."

"Copy, Alpha. Stand by."

Like repentant men, Sunday and the team took a knee. A moment later, an explosive charge tore through the side wall, blowing rock and stained glass across the church. One of the stone statues tumbled to the ground. Sunday's ears rang as if God Himself had spoken.

In the hanging cloud of white concrete dust, Sunday and his team moved into the aisle, picking apart the skulls of men whose brains were still deciphering the explosion. The team cleared the pews one at a time, killing men where they knelt.

Omega poured in through the hole in the side of the church, and together both teams moved toward the rear courtyard.

"Clear," Sunday said as he checked his angles and moved into the courtyard. Half a dozen doors ran along one side.

More gunshots sounded, and Sunday checked his corners. Nothing. No one was shooting at them. The shots were coming from somewhere else. Rhythmic, one after the other. Quick. Succinct.

"They're killing them."

Sunday raced toward the sound of gunfire. Edging up beside one of the doors, he peeked through a small window. He saw rows of beds, all empty.

More gunfire. Close by. One room away.

He moved quickly to the next door and peered inside. This room was much like the last, except the beds were occupied, girls bound with leather straps to the frames, and a man was moving down the line, methodically shooting the girls in the head, one by one. The girls closed their eyes, because there was safety in that darkness before the final light.

Sunday barged into the room and opened fire, killing the man before he could spin around with his AK.

He was too late. There were eleven girls here. Or had been. Now there were eleven bodies. Pillows and sheets soaking up their blood and brains.

He had failed to save them.

He had known he couldn't bring them back with him. But maybe he could have opened the door, let them free. Felt good about something for once.

Sunday stepped back into the rear courtyard. The rage, the animal inside, was slamming in its cage.

"Taresh?" he said, his teeth locked tight.

Ortz shook his head.

Sunday gestured toward the rearmost building, and the men crept through the darkness like weaponized demons. He moved quickly to the side of the door, reached out, and opened it. His men moved in low and fast.

The room glowed green through night-vision goggles. Artifacts were stacked on dining tables like it was an auction house. Old tablets. Clay pots. A part of a shield. Remnants of time, the creations of proud men who had tried to reach beyond their death.

A cry sounded from behind an open door to an adjoining room. Soft, a plea. Not to them, but to the one who held her.

"Please!" the girl sobbed.

He had a hostage.

Sunday spoke in Arabic. "Amir Taresh, you are surrounded. Surrender or be executed."

He peeked around the door, into an office.

The girl was thirteen, maybe fourteen. Long, black hair. Tear-stained cheeks. Taresh cowered behind her, pressed against the back wall, holding her tight in front of him, his gun to her temple. His eyes were wild, filled with adrenaline, flicking back and forth.

Sunday crossed the threshold, barrel extended, his finger hung on the trigger. He didn't have the shot.

"You step out that door, ten men will put a bullet through your head," Sunday said.

"You can't let him get it," Taresh pleaded.

"Get what?"

Taresh shook his head. "I should have destroyed it," he muttered. He looked up at Sunday, bags under his eyes so dark it looked like he was wearing a mask. "But I couldn't. They wouldn't let me." He started to weep. "He's coming. And there's nothing we can do."

He spoke close to the girl's ear. "*Adhhab mae Allah.*"

And then he fired. The bullet slammed through the girl's skull, tossing her brains into the wall.

Taresh lifted the gun toward his own temple, but Sunday was faster. He shot him twice in the forehead.

Sunday wasn't going to give him suicide. Fuck him.

He pulled the girl out of Taresh's arms. At least in death she could be free of this piece of shit. There was nothing more he could do. Most of her now occupied the wall.

Why kill them?

He looked over the office. Two laptops, a few cell phones, files of paperwork. Enough for months of intel. Then he checked Taresh. There was a bulge under one side of his jacket.

A bomb?

Kneeling, Sunday carefully fished the clothing open. Several sheets of blood-speckled plastic were wrapped around Taresh's waist. Sunday peeled it back with his knife.

A pair of eyes, big and round, stared back at him.

He pulled away more of the wrapping to reveal a painting of a human face. A woman. Black hair, dark eyes, lips parted with ever so slight a smile, like she knew something you did not.

Why this? In an office full of intel, why did he want a painting?

Ortz stepped into the office. "Something you need to see," he said as he glanced down at the dead girl.

He escorted Sunday into one of the classrooms. It was full of waist-high shiny steel vats.

"Gas?" Sunday asked.

"No, man." Ortz opened one of the canisters, and nitrogen fog rolled down the sides of the container like a witch's brew. He shone his flashlight into the frothy mist to reveal a collection of test tubes.

"This is how Karen and I had Jillian," Ortz said. "These are eggs. Thousands of them."

CHAPTER II

Caesarea Maritima, Israel
March, 33 CE (Common Era)

Longinus Castus closed his eyes in the warm morning sun and prayed the gods would watch over his journey. After finishing his prayer, he rose to his feet on the balcony of the prefect's home. From here the centurion could see the ships coming in, their sails like shimmering white fins on the pale-blue horizon. Past the glistening limestone lighthouse that warned sailors of the sandbars lurking beneath the waters of the Mediterranean, the boats queued in the harbor. This was a splendid seaside city, and in another life he might have been perfectly happy to stay and bask in its beauty. Instead, he turned his back on the rising sun and stepped into the darkness of the stairs.

Longinus was dreading the trip to Jerusalem. For years the Jews had been nothing but trouble, and now things had grown increasingly violent, especially after Pilate used temple funds to build an aqueduct in Bethlehem. The Jews revolted, and though the riot was put down, tensions remained high. Longinus was not looking forward to a political visit on a religious holiday for tens of thousands of desert slaves.

The centurion was a powerful man, a career soldier who had excelled on the front line, where he had shown exemplary valor and skill. He had seen many battlefields, and his arms and legs were as thick as the twisted trunks of olive trees. His fate should have been to rise through the ranks through glory in battle. Instead, the gods had devised for him a cruel jest—he had been handpicked by the general to serve as head of the auxiliary guard that protected the prefect. And as he stepped down the stairwell, he felt his career path was also destined to stay in the shadows.

Then he met her. And there had been light. When he first saw Licinia sitting on a pallet of pillows at one of the prefect's parties, what began as lust for her bosom blossomed into a loyalty he had previously held only for Rome. Even when traveling, he now found himself retreating from the soldiers so he could write to her. She had become a precious thought, and now there were whispers in his mind of a different life. A life of peace, away from all of this. Peace. And quiet.

Perhaps, one day, that life would come. But not now. Not today.

Putting the red-crested helmet upon his head, he descended into the darkness.

* * *

Jerusalem
April, 33 CE

The city was so crammed with Jews, a rider or a wagon could hardly pass. And already there was trouble. The crowds had become agitated when one particular Jew, claiming to be a messiah, returned through the gate.

Longinus couldn't have cared less about some messiah, for men boasting the ability to talk to God were nothing new on the streets of Jerusalem, and with thousands of Jews flocking to the city for the feast, this was no time for a spark. Yet this man had caused a scene at the temple and had riled the priests' tempers, and the Jews, in turn, had taken him into custody and turned to the Romans for justice. The Sanhedrin had shown up early in the morning at Pilate's doorstep at Herod's palace, demanding his ear. And Longinus was on hand, standing nearby, as Pilate listened to the priests' sleek tongues.

The Jew at the center of the storm made a pathetic case. Weak, worn, scared, he mustered only mumblings, not miracles. He was insignificant, not worthy of the priests' demands for execution. Yet the prefect acceded to the priests' demands, stating that an execution would stand as proof of Roman power, demonstrating to any other would-be Jew troublemakers that Rome indeed ruled Judea.

On the morning of the execution, Longinus walked down the long hallway of the fortress to collect the prisoner. As he approached, he heard the sound of the flagrum whipping through the air, followed by a thump as it tore into flesh. Soldiers laughed and taunted.

As the centurion stepped into the room, the soldiers pulled back and stood at attention.

The bloody Jew was on his hands and knees. Much of his dark hair and beard had been yanked out in chunks. The flagrum, which had pieces of sheep bone and metal balls attached to its thongs, had torn chunks of flesh from his back. He was naked, and had soiled himself and the stone floor.

Longinus was not a man of compassion. But the whispers in his mind again spoke to him. He raised his hand. "Enough," he said.

The soldiers nodded.

Longinus looked down at the prisoner. "On your feet!" he barked.

The Jew tried to stand, but slipped in a puddle of his own urine.

Longinus caught the bloodied Jew and helped him up. It was not a gesture of kindness. The centurion merely wanted to move forward with his day.

The prisoner looked Longinus in the eyes and spoke with slurred, tired words. "The way to me is through you," he said.

Longinus stared back at the prisoner. The man's eyes were swollen, his jaw broken, his lips split. The centurion had watched many men die. This one would be no different.

"And the way out... is through me," Longinus responded as he pushed the prisoner toward the door.

He guided the Jew down the hallway and outside, where a group of waiting soldiers placed a heavy wooden patibulum over the prisoner's shoulders. The prisoner was then escorted up the hill, his small escort, including Longinus, forcing a path through a crowd of screaming, cheering Jews who spat and cursed their own.

Atop the hill, the naked prisoner was nailed to the cross. A soldier hammered spikes into the Jew's wrists, between the radius and ulna. Blood sprayed from one wrist as the soldier tapped an artery. Finally the crucifix was raised, the Jew wailing as he was jerked violently upward.

Then began the wait. Crucifixions could take days.

The bulk of the Jews crowded atop the hill shouted curses at the false prophet, except for a small group who wept and prayed—the only living creatures apart from the flies attracted to the dying Jew who cared about his death. Among this group were two women who stared at Longinus as if they knew him. Longinus had been warned this particular group might be targeted by the others, and it was his task to keep the crowd from becoming further riled. But the morning remained without incident, and the execution proceeded faster than expected. The prisoner had already lost a great deal of blood, and he was dead by mid-afternoon.

Longinus gave the order, and the two Jew thieves hanging next to the blasphemer had their legs broken to speed their deaths as well.

Longinus took a spear from one of the Roman soldiers and walked toward the bloodied Jew. As was his duty, he thrust the point into the man's side to ensure he was indeed dead, as it would be his job to report to Pilate.

The Jew didn't respond to the jab, and when Longinus pulled back the spear, the hook of the tip snared a rib. He tugged to release it, and pulled open the gut. Blood and bile dumped from the prisoner's side onto Longinus's face. Wiping the liquid from his eyes, he spat out the Jew's rank fluids.

He went on to report that the Jew was dead.

Longinus thought nothing more of the execution. He had only one overwhelming thought: he wanted to get back home to Licinia.

CHAPTER III

Langley, Virginia
Present Day

Kat Devier pulled her thick hair back into a ponytail and sat down at the onyx-black table in an empty lab deep inside the layered labyrinth of CIA headquarters. In front of her lay a portrait of a woman with wide, round eyes.

Before she lowered the magnifying visor over her eyes, she glanced at the balloons across the room, bobbling into each other like jellyfish in the ocean. Beneath them was a half-eaten birthday cake featuring a plastic woman holding a shovel, standing on a scattering of brown sugar made to look like desert sand. Before it was cut, the cake had read "*Felix sit Natilis dies*," followed by the Roman numeral XXX. After the little office party, all that was left of the message was the rather ominous "*dies*."

The plastic woman with the shovel was supposed to be her. An archaeologist. That was what Kat was. Or used to be.

When she was at Harvard, and after graduation, she spent plenty of time on real digs. Israel. Egypt. Turkey.

And then four years ago, on a dig in Giza, she met a man, the head of their security team, needed because of the turmoil in the country at the time. He wasn't big, but he was strong. Not crazy, but controlled. He carried a gun in a holster on his hip, and, well, that was terribly attractive.

Turned out, he was a spook. A spy. The CIA was funding her dig as cover so they could get closer to the Muslim Brotherhood. And she helped him, because, well, she was an American. And besides, they were paying her bills.

Then she slept with him. That wasn't for America. Or for her bills.

It was also her first step in what would lead to a distinct change in her career. Away from archeology as she had once known it. Away from digs in exotic locations. Now she was confined to the labyrinthine depths of the CIA.

Sliding on her latex gloves and lowering her visor, she got down to work.

She knew a few things about the portrait already. It was from the first or second century BCE, or perhaps a bit later, the first or second century CE. And it was not meant to be hung on a wall. This portrait had been made to accompany the dead, to be bound to the face of a mummy, peering out for all eternity, watching the living. A common technique in the Faiyum region of Egypt at the time.

It was painted on papyrus canvas attached to wood. Even with the chipping paint, the woman's skin looked soft, the color of the warm desert sand. She had a slight part in her hair, as if groomed for the journey. Her eyes were overly large like those in a cartoon drawing, as if they'd been filled with a lifetime of vision.

The ticket indicated the mask had been found in Syria within the last week. No city or coordinates had been provided.

How'd it get to Syria? This should have been in Egypt.

It must have been moved, bought, transferred through the years.

Kat adjusted the overhead light and leaned in closer, drawn in by something that should not have been there. A pale, washed-out symbol could just be made out in the faded white of the left eye, just below the surface layer of paint:

$$יָנ$$

She jotted the symbol down in her notes and looked at it again. Then she pulled the light lower and jotted down another symbol, and another hidden between the eyes: וּבר.

These symbols made a word. And it wasn't Egyptian or Hebrew or Greek. Of course, it could have been nothing more than residue on the papyrus used as canvas. A palimpsest underneath the paint. Perhaps the face had been painted over a grocery list, an ancient lease, a contract. Sheet on top of sheet were often stacked together until it became like plaster, like papier-mâché.

Kat went to her bookshelf, pulled out a book, and flipped through the pages until she found the Aramaic word she was looking for:

ינובר: Rabbouni. My rabbi.

This wasn't a grocery list—it was a gospel. And in the Bible, there was only one person who used that word.

CHAPTER IV

Joint Base Andrews
Prince George's County, Maryland

Thick dark clouds rolled across the sky as John Sunday carried his black duffel through the parking lot of Andrews Air Force Base. It was only early November, but an early winter storm hung low on the horizon, threatening snow. A far cry from the arid temps he'd left behind. Only the cold met him. No one else. No ticker tape on the tarmac.

His beat-up Honda CRV was parked in the far corner of the lot. He kneeled by the back bumper, reached under the metal frame, and extracted a key. Opening the trunk, he tossed in his bag and pulled out a car battery. A few minutes later, he had it installed and tried the ignition. Despite three months of sitting idle, the engine finally turned over.

Jump-starting my life.

He could have afforded a better vehicle. Gotten the obligatory truck like all the other Special Forces guys he'd ever known. But why? He was never here long enough to enjoy it.

The first thing he did was hit the liquor store for a bottle of Jack—because priorities—and took out three hundred bucks from an ATM. Then he pulled onto 495, bound for a building that was home in name only. Even when he got there, he had to drive slowly and look carefully to remember which townhouse was his. Not the whole townhouse. Home was a Great English basement, but neither capitalized word in the rental ad had been accurate. The lowercase word, though, had nailed it.

He took the steps down from the sidewalk and fumbled to remember which key unlocked the front door. Inside, he flicked the switch, but no light came on. He toggled it up and down again, as if coaxing the electrons, before realizing the electricity was off. Fuck. He'd forgotten to pay the bill. He dropped his duffel on the solitary futon that made up the whole of his expansive furniture collection. Using the dim light that filtered in through a tiny window at ground level, he felt his way into the kitchen. A lone glass, an artifact from another time, sat next to the sink. He turned on the faucet to rinse the dust, but no water came out.

Fuck again. He was oh for two.

He cracked the seal on the bottle and poured, the clinging particulates and liquor now one in the glass.

He sat on the futon and stared at the white-painted brick wall. There was a small window at street level, and someone's feet passed on the sidewalk above. Below them, he sipped his whiskey, alone in the dark.

The images of the dead girls in their beds returned.

Innocent. Peaceful.

Bound. Bloody.

Tiny skulls shattered like eggs. Hair matted to blood and pillow.

He put up with the routine mental evaluations. He heard the fleet of psychiatrists who wanted him to "talk about it." But Sunday didn't. He knew what he was. What he'd done. What he'd seen. Death was never far. Try as he might to escape it, the truth was, he'd be lost if he did. This was all he knew.

And like the lights in his apartment, he could flick the switch.

But the dead children were breaking free from their box. Crawling from their beds. Stalking him in the hallways of his mind.

What if he had gotten into that room quicker? Not misjudged where the shots had come from? Maybe he could have saved at least one. What if he had taken out Taresh sooner? Gone for the shot? Gotten that girl back to her family? Maybe if he…

His cell rang. Sunday recognized the number. The voice on the other end was succinct, staccato. A man who didn't waste time.

"You back?" asked Tom Ferguson.

"Yeah," Sunday said, wondering if this meant he was getting ready to leave again.

"Ten a.m. My office."

"Yeah," Sunday replied.

"I'm bringing in Kat Devier. That a problem?"

Sunday paused. "No. No problem."

Ferguson hung up.

Despite the booze, or perhaps because of it, Sunday felt a need to get out, to get away from the dark room. Go for a walk. Get some air.

You don't have to make the call.

He ignored the whisper, grabbed his cell phone, and dialed. A number he remembered well. After four rings, a woman answered.

"You coming?" she said.

"Yeah."

"Good."

Sunday sat there in the dark, the twitch a taste on his tongue.

* * *

Sunday grabbed a wool jacket from the closet. He was too shit-faced to drive, and it was a cool night for a walk.

He headed down Sherman Avenue, near Columbia, absorbing flakes of gently falling snow that sizzled into oblivion on contact. He took a back alley that led to a dirty brick brownstone tucked in a row of similar build-ings growing together like weeds. Stepping between a cluster of overflowing garbage cans, he climbed nar-row wooden steps to a dirt-stained front door.

He knocked.

After a minute, he knocked again. Louder.

The door was answered by a woman in her late twenties. She wore only a bathrobe, and her dark hair was pulled back. Makeup covered a small sore on the side of her neck, caked like mud over a snake bite.

She smiled and put her hands around Sunday's neck. "Hey." She kissed him, wet, stale cigarette on her lips.

He'd met Lilly at the hospital where he'd been treated, and they'd discovered they had similar desires.

She took him by the hand and pulled him into the candlelit apartment. There were always candles. The flickering light was all that stood between her and total blackness.

Walking past dirty clothes and dishes in the sink, Sunday took a seat on a dingy brown couch. On a low table before him, several clear plastic bags, each containing a syringe, were fanned out like sterilized hors d'oeuvres.

One perk of being a nurse is you can steal clean supplies.

Drugs were not new to Sunday. Pills were handed out before missions to jack you up. Pills were handed out after missions to calm you down. Pills were given to you when your body hurt. When your brain hurt. And when the doctors cut back on the pills, there was always another way to get them.

Lilly went to the bedroom and returned with a little baggie of white crystals, like rock candy. She stood in front of him and let her robe fall open, revealing her breasts. Threaded beneath and between them were tattooed lilies, making it looks as if her breasts were held up by the flowers that were her namesake.

"You wanna eight?" Lilly asked.

Sunday checked his watch. It was just after nine. What time did Ferguson say he had to be in the office?

"Yeah." He reached into his pocket and pulled out a wad of cash, money that should have gone to turn on the lights and water.

She measured the ice on a piece of paper and crushed it into a fine powder. Then she prepped the syringe—meticulously. The result of that nursing school degree Momma had paid for by working overnights.

He watched her set up her gear. So clean. So neat. So orderly. Unlike the rest of her life.

She scooted closer to him on the couch, her brown nipples like arrows against his body. He took off his jacket to reveal his arm. He took a rubber tie-off from the table, wrapped it around his forearm, and opened and closed his fist, pumping the dinner bell of his blood.

Lilly folded the ice in paper and crushed it with a spoon until it was a fine powder. She pulled out the plunger on the syringe, poured in the crystals, then returned the plunger and smashed it. She pulled back thirty cc's of water in the rig, tapped it on the sides to bring out any air, and then steadied his arm on her lap.

A second later he felt the bite—and the warm river that followed.

At first, he always thought he was going to die. A feeling he knew as well as others know hunger or desire. Then his blood started to boil and his heart revved, sending the drug—and him—skyward, inward, onward.

He was thrust into a realm of the already lived. Each memory a burst, a millisecond, but somehow complete.

He was back in the muddy driveway outside the trailer. He saw his mother pulling away from his father. Preparing to abandon her own son like a child unwanted. She paused to look at him, tracks of rain beneath her eyes that he thought could be tears. But perhaps he had invented those later.

She smiled, as if to say it wasn't his fault. But perhaps that too had been conjured.

That smile lasted an eternity, but was gone in an instant. Then her little car pulled away, and he was pulled back into the house of his father, he of Old Testament wrath, a man who punished with rod and word.

A second later, maybe—how long, really, had time stopped?—Lilly leaned back and began her own needle quest. Sunday knew what that meant for her. A flash of heat would flow from the needle down to the opening between her legs. To the wetness. The animal would awaken.

She let out a soft moan.

Reaching over with hunger, Lilly unzipped John's pants. She fondled him with great intensity, then slid her mouth down over him. A few moments later, his cock primed, she shed her robe, climbed on top, and rode him with her back facing him.

Sunday watched, entranced, as her body slid rhythmically up and down. The curve of her spine, the cratered dimples over her ass flexing like mouths.

In the periphery of his vision, and the light of the flickering candles, he saw movement. Someone watching from the next room. Or a shadow moving in the corner. But the thing was... *wrong* somehow. Too big. Like a bull or an ox with a human head sitting in a chair. They were alone, and yet he felt its presence. It was prodding his mind and soul, dissecting him.

Just the drugs.

Lilly continued to grind.

Her long black hair draped down her back, but as he looked again in the flickering candlelight, he saw her skin was coated with scabs, and flakes of flesh peeled from her spine.

She increased her speed, a mad fury.

She turned her head slightly to smile back at him. Her eyes were empty sockets. The flesh on her face was purple and bloated. Her jowls hung low, and her veins were swollen like the underbelly of a fish.

"Fuck us!" she shouted like a man, and laughed.

Sunday pushed her off roughly, sending her tripping over the table and onto the floor, knocking out a candle.

"What the hell?" she shouted.

Sunday stared at her, trying to clear his head. It was just her now. Just Lilly. Her eyes too dark, her pupils too wide, but it was her.

He pulled up his pants and stumbled to the door, only vaguely aware that he was leaving. Behind him she screamed, her voice drifting, saying he couldn't leave. But she was already a hundred miles away.

As he left, Sunday swore he saw the shadow figure again in the chair. He heard its breathing.

He didn't remember the walk home.

CHAPTER V

Four Months Ago
Tal Faitha, Syria

The Khabur River was life. It flowed off the Euphrates like a vein, but its waters were truly born in deep caves and sinkholes that festered and cooled in the dark crevices of the earth. Here it flowed along limestone pavement before eventually resurfacing to serve the villages that had sprouted along its banks. It was the feeder of people, much like the religion of Christ that still acted as an oasis in this arid land.

It was in a village along the banks of the Khabur that Mara Aziz tended to her father. He had fallen ill, a tumor growing within, and she knew their time together grew short. He was dying, just as their village was dying. Their crops had shriveled around them, and she wondered if a plague had been released upon her people and the locusts would come next.

She risked her life by staying here. Her mother and younger sister had left weeks earlier, terrified Al Tariqa would come and take them in the night. Fleeing was the only way to save her sister from rape or marriage. But Mara had chosen to stay. She wanted to hold her father's hand when he looked into the eyes of his collectors.

She could not bear to let him die alone.

His cough woke him before the sun had risen. "Leave me," he said.

Mara looked upon him, this man who had carried her as a little girl on his shoulders, when he and the crops were stronger. Even in the low light, she could see the sheets were yellow with his sweat. She laid a cool cloth on his forehead. He was unable to move on his own, and it was up to her to care for him, soothe him, help him relieve himself.

"Shhh. Rest," she answered in Aramaic, the tongue of her people, the language of her Lord.

He hacked some more, pieces of him dissipating into the night air, and she wiped the bloody sputum from his lips.

When he had settled again, she returned to her bed and listened to his labored breaths. He was coughing more often now, and it kept her up most of the night. But with every wheeze and hack, she at least knew he was alive. For now.

The sound she heard next scared her even more.

The sound of trucks and gunfire.

She raced to the door to see a dozen pickups barging into the village like a storm from the desert. Men hopped off the truck beds, their guns glistening in the moonlight, and went from door to door, kicking them in as families slept.

Mara quickly closed the door. She could hide under the bed, but what about her father? Could she drag him beneath as well? They could hide there like children, joining the monster she once thought hid beneath her bed, back in the days when it was her father who protected her.

But that threat had been imaginary. She knew now that the real monsters were men.

Her father was already awake. He grabbed her hand and clutched it tight, his palms greased with sweat.

"Run," he gasped. "Please. I love you."

She held his hand, not wanting to let go, not wanting to make a decision.

The front door slammed open and two men with rifles barged in. One grabbed Mara by her hair and yanked her to her knees. The other stood over her father as if assessing whether he was worth the bullet.

Mara cowered as the first man pressed a rifle against her skull. "You want to live? You want to live?" he shouted in Arabic, though the gun was doing more speaking than him. He dragged her toward a small picture of Jesus that hung on the wall. He threw it on the floor, cracking the glass frame.

"Renounce the pig!" he shouted, gesturing with the rifle.

Mara looked toward her father.

The other man pressed the barrel of his rifle against her father's head.

"Please," she cried.

"Stomp on it! Or we will stomp on your father's head!"

"I cannot," she said, choking back tears.

The second man yanked Mara's father out of the bed. His frail body landed with a thump on the floor.

His flesh was weak, but he was still strong in her heart. Her father. Her protector.

"Do it!" the man shouted again at Mara.

All she could do was muster another "Please."

The man beside her father used his rifle butt to beat on her father's head. Then he used his boot. The rhythm of his stomping was a drum to match Mara's screams.

When it was done, and Mara's father lay dead and broken on the floor, the man next to Mara whipped out his cock. It was not for her. Instead he pissed upon the broken picture of Jesus.

Then, grabbing her by her hair once more, he dragged her out into the night.

CHAPTER VI

Langley, Virginia
Present Day

John Sunday sat a table in a windowless conference room, surrounded by highly caffeinated men in suits. Sunday was dressed in a gray army T-shirt that stank of hangover sweat. His brain felt like cotton candy on a stick.

He looked around the room at the Ivy Leaguers who toyed with people's lives from afar like the gods of Olympus. They were with the Special Activities Division, which meant Sunday was their weapon, their tool. Behind them, the American flag hung limp in the corner.

The things I've done for those colors.

At the end of the table was Sunday's boss, Tom Ferguson—CIA Deputy Director of the National Clandestine Service. He was a beef stock of a man, a former marine lieutenant colonel, more lethal in Canali than in camouflage. He was also a human contradiction. He ran ten miles a day on a treadmill, only to chain smoke. He went to church twice a week, only to order a detainee to be hung upside down and beaten until blood gushed from his ears like water from a rusted pipe.

He had also brought in Sunday when others would not. Ignored the psych results. The drug tests. The suicide attempt. Taken him in as a priest would a sinner, only to put him to work to commit more sins In the Name Of.

At the opposite end of the table was a man Sunday knew little about. David Conrad. He'd once played ball for Notre Dame, and he was said to be one of the top case officers when it came to the terrorist group Al Tariqa.

Conrad stood in front of a monitor and delivered his presentation like he was advising a group of clients on how to diversify their portfolio.

"Nineteen on site," he said, pointing to a photo of the room where the dead girls rested on pillows of blood. "Twelve inside, seven out. The girls in the beds all appear to be sixteen or older. The ones in the ditch were younger. We believe they were part of a group taken a few days ago from a Christian village outside Al-Hasakah. But they're just the latest. As you can see from satellite, there are mounds around the location, which we believe are graves. Dozens of them."

He switched to a photo of the vats of eggs.

"Which leads us to these six containers holding roughly four thousand human eggs. That confirms that a number of girls must have been brought through this facility, and their eggs extracted. Some of the girls might have been resold. Most are probably in those graves."

"Why eggs?" asked one of the men.

"There's high demand. Women who donate to clinics can get up to ten grand at a time for their eggs. China has a huge underground market for middle-class families who are faced with infertility. And then there's the stem-cell research market. A vat like this? On the black market, it could fetch three or four million."

He switched to a photo of the relics in the back room. "Let's move to the artifacts. Before Taresh got caught up in the crusade and Al Tariqa, he was an art and antiquities dealer in Berlin. That shows. He knew his stuff. We've identified items from Egypt, Mesopotamia, Persia. He'd have made a fortune on these. But there was one item that was significantly more valuable than the others."

He pulled up a photo of the painting.

"This is the portrait we found on Taresh's body. And on his hard drive, we restored a deleted email that had this photo attached." He pulled up an image of the email on the screen behind him. "It was sent to an address we had previously flagged as being linked to the Father."

At the mention of that name, the room was suddenly far more focused.

Conrad continued. "The email reads, and I quote, 'There is something beneath. Something you've been searching for. Forty million dollars, US.'"

"Bull. Shit," said another analyst. "Taresh was dreaming."

"Did the recipient make an offer?" Ferguson asked.

"He did. He agreed to the price. But before they could seal the deal, we raided the compound. Taresh knew he had something special to ask for that amount."

He gestured toward a man by to the door. "Have her come in."

The man stepped out into the hall, and a moment later a woman entered. If Sunday had been chewing gum, he would have choked on it. She looked far different from the girl he'd first met in the desert. The woman with clay stains on her crimson Harvard T-shirt. The woman he'd fallen in love with.

Now she was perfectly made up, dressed in a smart dark business suit. She cleaned up nice.

"This is Kat Devier, one of our analysts working on the piece," Conrad said.

Sunday sat up in his seat. She saw him, but didn't acknowledge him.

"Thank you," she said as she moved to plug her laptop into the jack at the end of the table. A picture of the portrait popped up behind her on the wall monitor. "Let me start with a brief history. This is a burial portrait, designed to be attached to the head of a mummy, like a picture of the dead. Based on paleographic evidence, it's late first-century CE. It's painted on papyrus—basically, any paper they could find. We don't know who the woman is in the picture, and it doesn't matter. It's what's *under* the paint that's significant."

She clicked a button to move forward to the next image. It was the woman's face again, but faded and in black and white. Littered throughout her face were pale white words.

"With infrared, you can see there's writing beneath. It's a gospel. Or at least part of one. It appears to be the Gospel of Mary."

"Jesus's mother?" asked one of the suits.

"No. Magdalene."

"Last time I checked, she doesn't have a gospel," Ferguson said.

"It could be one of the gnostic gospels. Basically, an early cross-pollination between Judaism and Christianity. There's a version of them in Coptic Egyptian, or part of them. This one, however, is in Aramaic, which is unusual."

She advanced to another image, a tighter shot of the face and words. "As you can see, we're still missing sections here around the eyes and the mouth. So what I'm about to give you is a rough translation of an incomplete text."

She cleared her throat and read:

"Rabbouni, why me? Peter is far more suited."

The Savior answered, "You are the one who tends to me. And through me, all flesh shall be tended through salvation. These are my final instructions for the birth of the way.

My death upon Golgotha will be temporary. Care for my body to my exact bidding. Take my flesh and blood across the Jordan, to the caves near Pella, where John baptized many.

When my word again sees the sun, my body shall be rekindled, the gates of this rock will be opened. And then I shall return to the kingdom of man."

Kat looked across the room. "That's all we've made out so far, but we think there are more pages beneath this one. We'll have to peel it back a layer at a time. It will be a slow go."

"What makes you think this was written by Mary Magdalene?" one of the men asked.

"Because 'Rabbouni' is the name that Mary uses in the Bible when she realizes Christ has risen from the dead and she doesn't recognize Him. And these are His instructions to her for taking care of His body. He is telling her to move His body out of the tomb."

"Are you suggesting the body of Jesus Christ is in a cave in Jordan?" asked Ferguson.

"I'm just telling you what it says," Kat answered.

"Could it be a fake?" someone asked.

"Radiocarbon dating puts the portrait at 1,980 years before present, plus or minus 60 years. Certainly within Mary Magdalene's lifespan."

Sunday knew that the men at this table cared nothing for Mary Magdalene or a lost gospel. They cared only about the Father, and whether this would give them a chance to catch him.

Sunday looked over at Kat.

She knew he was there.

And he could tell she sure as hell didn't want to see him.

* * *

When the meeting ended, the room was cleared of everyone except Ferguson, Conrad, and Sunday.

"Seven hundred and seventeen," Conrad said. "That's how many people have been killed by Al Tariqa in their last seven attacks on Christian sites. Jerusalem, Alexandria, Istanbul, Damascus, the Sudan, Athens, Rome. Four hundred and forty-three—that's how many women are missing after raids on Christian villages. No bounty on their heads. Just gone. Perhaps harvested. Perhaps shot."

"We know the numbers," said Ferguson. "What's your point?"

Conrad pointed to the picture on the screen. "This portrait is the best chance of getting to the man who's bankrolling all of it."

"If the Father is funding Taresh, why would Taresh be hitting up his boss for forty million bucks?" Ferguson asked.

"Because he got greedy. Because he knew he had something special. Taresh knew that portrait could set him up for life. That's why when it came down to it, that painting was the one thing he tried to save."

"Fifteen years we've been looking for this guy, and all we've got to show for it is a series of banking transactions," Ferguson said. "Are we just following the money again?"

"No. I think we can get the Father to surface. Get some idea who he is. He's not after the painting. He knows there's something written underneath it. Something he's been searching for, according to Taresh. That's what he really wants. What the painting leads to."

"Where are you going with this?"

"We set up a team of archaeologists in Jordan, looking for a body. Let it leak that we're digging in the desert because of evidence we found in Taresh's compound. Maybe even leak that we found something out there, even if we haven't. See who shows up to the party."

Ferguson mulled this over for a minute, then looked over at Sunday. "You got a problem with that?"

"Which part?"

"Using your ex-wife as bait?"

"No."

* * *

A half hour later, Kat still waited in the hallway outside the conference room. They had told her to wait. She'd had two cups of coffee and her foot bounced like a baby bird trying to achieve flight. She had to pee, and was just debating whether she could make it to the bathroom and back before someone came out to get her, when Conrad opened the door to the conference room.

"Come in, Kat," he said without emotion.

She stepped back into the room and stood at the foot of the table. John stared at her, and she wondered what he knew that she didn't.

"Have a seat," Ferguson said.

She pulled out a chair and sat. There was a satellite map of the western region of Jordan on the screen behind her.

"Your credentials with Harvard still good?" Ferguson asked.

She nodded. "I still teach a seminar online."

He leaned back and rolled his pen a few times between his forefinger and thumb. "If there was something out there, where do you think it would be?" he said, flipping the pen into a pointing position.

Kat stood and darted toward the map like she was answering questions on a quiz show. "Well, this is where Pella is located. John did his baptizing here along the Jordan," she said, pointing to the various locations as she spoke. "And this is the baptismal site of Jesus, here, just north of the Dead Sea. There are caves nearby, but they're tourist attractions. But *this* large area from here up to Pella, some fifty miles long... well, there could be hundreds of caves in this area. There've been a few caving expeditions along this chain, but most of it is unmapped."

"If we send you out there to look, are you going to have any problem working with John?" Ferguson asked.

She was very excited by the prospect of getting back in the field. "No," she lied.

"Good, because he and his team will be your security. They'll pose as archaeologists, and you'll report to Conrad in Amman. Get the appropriate permits through the university. We'll speed up the process and provide you with IDs. But we won't tell the Jordanians what we're looking for out there. Agency personnel only."

"Thank you, sir."

Ferguson leaned forward. "One more thing. I've been a pretty shitty Catholic most of my life, but the philosophies of Christ give me something to strive for. A place to go when my sins mount. And if the body of Jesus were to be found lying in some cave somewhere... well, that would overturn two thousand years of Christian belief. The philosophy works, in part, because He was more than a man. If that is proven not to be true…" He shifted in his chair. "Either way, I sure as hell don't want some Muslim parading the bones of Jesus Christ through the streets of Mosul."

He pointed his pen at her.

"What I'm saying to you, Kat, is there is no fortune and glory. No book deals. If you find something out there, it stays a secret. Do you understand?"

"Yes, sir."

* * *

As Kat walked across the lot toward her Mazda, there was a spring in her step and a smile on her face. That was, until she got to her car and found John waiting.

"I want you to know, I didn't ask for this," he said.

"I'm sure you didn't," she said smugly as she pulled out her keys and clicked the button to unlock the doors. She got in the car and started the engine, then paused and rolled down the window.

"Who's in charge?" she asked.

"What?"

"When we're over there? Who's in charge?"

"You head the dig. I handle security. If everything passes our safety checks, then you're free to do what you want."

"Good. You do your job and I'll do mine, and we'll get along just fine. But other than that—stay out of my way."

And she drove away, leaving John alone in her rearview mirror.

CHAPTER VII

Lanciano, Italy
39 CE

Longinus rested against the handle of his hoe and wiped the sweat from his forehead. The ground here was thick, and the clay wasn't cooperating with his blade. Longinus certainly didn't have to be out here fighting it—there were more than a hundred slaves working next to him in the morning sun—but he enjoyed a productive day of sweat.

As he took a break to look out over the olive tree seedlings in the distance, flanked by acres of more mature orchards, a cloud of dust appeared on the road leading toward the villa. Longinus watched the plume kick along the road until its source came into focus. Riders. Two dozen Roman soldiers.

Did Rome have need of him again? Though he had retired to his father's land, as a centurion he was always subject to be called back.

Setting his tool aside, he headed back toward the villa.

The riders galloped hard into the courtyard just as Longinus stepped onto the veranda. The lead man, glistening in golden plate, removed his red-crested helmet. "Longinus!" It was Tiberius, Longinus's old optio. He approached with open arms. "It has been too long, my friend."

The two men embraced.

"I see the land fights back," Tiberius said with a laugh, pointing to the dirt stains on Longinus's clothes.

Longinus smiled and brushed his dirty hands across the front of his tunic. "Yes, but in silence."

"I bring news. We must speak," Tiberius said.

Longinus's wife appeared in the entranceway. She wore a simple blue tunic, and her long black hair framed a tan, delicate face.

Longinus gestured to her. "You remember Licinia."

"*Salve*," she said. "Welcome to our home."

"The years have been far kinder to you, I see," Tiberius said with a smile, taking her hand.

"And your charms have not dulled," she replied.

"No children scampering around?"

"Not as yet. But we try. Often. An enjoyable way to pass the time." She smiled at her husband.

Tiberius cocked an eyebrow. "Indeed."

Longinus led Tiberius to the tablinum, which was rarely used. Longinus preferred to work the land rather than write letters like a pompous ass in his office.

"So how is the life of a Praetorian?" he asked as he sat behind his desk.

"A battlefield has less deceit." Tiberius took a seat and stroked the horsehair plume of his helmet. "Gaius Caligula has brought back the treason trials. He has gone mad with power."

"I'm a long way from the affairs of Rome."

"You are not far enough," Tiberius said as he ceased the grooming of his helmet.

"I have fulfilled my duties."

"You have." Tiberius paused, as if searching for words. Longinus studied his old friend's face, looking for a tell as to why he was here, but could read nothing.

Tiberius continued. "The trials are only a front. The coffers have run dry and he seeks to seize land from the wealthy." He looked up at his former superior. "Your olive farm turns a tidy profit."

Longinus leaned forward. "Are you here as my friend to serve me warning? Or do you come with an ultimatum?"

"Both."

"*Loquimini veritatem*," Longinus said. *Speak the truth.*

"I solicited Gaius on your behalf and sang of your services to Rome. Resign your property without incident and leave this place with your wife, and Caesar shall leave you be."

"And if not?"

Tiberius leaned in. "The First Cohort is less than a half day's ride. We move from villa to villa. They await my answer by midday."

"What have you brought to my home, *optio*?"

"Gaius has declared himself a god. He dresses as a woman and drags a trail of blood through the Senate. There is no reason here. No logic. Only insanity. Believe me, some of your neighbors will be run through this very day."

Longinus thought of jumping the desk, grabbing Tiberius by the hair, and breaking his neck by using the headrest of the chair to snap it backwards. But defeating the remaining soldiers on horseback outside would be difficult, even if he could rally the slaves. And it would not end there. He had tried to keep violence away from his home.

He weighed the price.

He had seen enough blood.

He stood, opened a cabinet in the corner, and fished around in a stack of scrolls until he found the one he wanted. He unfurled it, laid it on the desk, and made a few marks with a stylus.

"This was my father's land. And his father before him," he said as he handed the signed scroll to Tiberius.

"Land is plentiful," Tiberius replied. "Breath is not."

"Leave us to our affairs," Longinus said.

Tiberius rose from his chair and donned his helmet. "We return midday."

"How generous."

As Tiberius and his soldiers rode away, Longinus watched them go down the road, through the orchards that earlier that morning had belonged to him.

* * *

Licinia stood in the atrium, watching as the soldiers carried away beds and chairs, jewelry and clothing. Some of the men eyed her, yet she dared not say a word, lest it stoke their ire. Save for a few broken plates and some heavy stone statues, the house was entirely cleared. The couple's belongings were put in wagons and carted off, with the slaves trotting behind.

By dusk, she and Longinus were alone. They ate a quiet meal on the steps overlooking the orchard, dining on the olives that had come from their labors, as the sun set over the hills one last time.

That night, Licinia wept in Longinus's arms as they lay together on a mat on the floor of the domus.

"We have nothing," she said.

"We have everything," he replied, gently stroking her arm.

* * *

Longinus lay awake, restless, his mind churning. The plan was to go to Licinia's father's house in the valley, a journey of several days. It would be a humiliating trip for a centurion, a man who had spent his life fighting, not fleeing.

Eventually he drifted into a half-sleep and dreamt of a plume of swarming locusts swirling on the road ahead. He moved into the swarm, the insects crawling on his face and into his mouth, and saw then, in the road, a large, cold stone. He lifted the heavy rock covered with larvae, and beneath it was nothing but black. An eternal hole, deep and blind.

Millions of locusts burst from the hole and covered him.

He was startled awake, reaching for his sword, which lay next to him on the floor.

Someone was in the house.

While Licinia still slept, he rose quietly and moved to the atrium. There he paused in the shadows.

A half dozen soldiers, blades already in hand, were coming up the steps.

Longinus ran back to his wife. "Licinia," he whispered, shaking her. "You must hide. There are men in the house."

She was slow to stir, but when he saw her mind returned, his words were sudden and fierce. She sat up quickly and moved toward the back of the room. There were no windows, no curtains, no furniture. The best she could do was to hide in the shadows.

Longinus returned to the atrium and hid behind a column, waiting for the soldiers to pass. When the last one had gone by, Longinus stepped out, grabbed him from behind, and plunged his sword into the man's left kidney, frothing the wound with urine and blood. Longinus could smell the stale wine on him as he squealed upon the blade.

As he pulled his sword free, the others turned to face the commotion. With trained fury, Longinus blocked the next attacker's jab and pushed his blade into the soldier's exposed chest. Two more soldiers came at him, and he engaged again. Longinus deflected a strike, spun in closer, and stabbed, but the blow was low, and the blade stuck in the rib cage, snagging in the bone. It was stuck for but a moment, but it was enough. The second soldier sliced down, across the back of Longinus's calf, and his Achilles snapped.

He fell to his knees.

The remaining soldiers circled. One raised his sword high and slashed down across Longinus's shoulder, through the side of his neck, severing his mind from his arms and legs. He yelled as he slumped to the floor.

"No!" screamed his wife.

"Licinia!" he cried out. She had revealed herself.

One of the soldiers grabbed her. Longinus attempted to rise again, but his body would not respond.

"Leave her!" Longinus shouted, the words choked by the blood in his throat.

The soldier pointed his sword at Longinus. "You wish to save him?" he said.

"Please," she said.

"Then spread for us all, and we shall leave you in peace." The man placed the point of his blade at her throat.

She nodded through tears.

The man moved his blade down across her tunic, snagged it in some thread, and tore it away, revealing her naked body.

One at a time, the men took turns on top of her.

"Please," Longinus whispered, but none of his gods were near enough to hear.

When they were finished, the last soldier pulled Licinia to her knees.

"Please. Let us be," she begged.

The soldier pressed his sword to her throat again. Longinus knew then she was going to die. She looked at her husband, and he could see in her eyes that she knew it too.

"I love you," she said.

The blade tore across her neck. Longinus sobbed and screamed as she fell.

Another soldier clutched him by the back of his head, raised him up, and sawed through his throat. Longinus felt it all. Every inch of metal slicing flesh until the blade caught the backbone and the knife stopped.

Longinus closed his eyes and wondered if he would see his wife again.

Instead he was plunged alone into darkness.

CHAPTER VIII

Fairfax, Virginia
Thirteen Months Ago

Tom Ferguson sat in a room near the intensive care unit, nervously tapping his foot on the faux-wood floor. The room smelled like sterile filth— a Greyhound station laced with Lysol. And yet when the nurse had moved him here from the larger waiting room, she said this was the "nice" room. That was most certainly a bad sign.

It was four hours earlier when he'd gotten the call telling him that Sara had been in a car accident. *Accident.* That word had always struck him wrong. Were there really accidents? Or was every event the predictable result of physics and time—or perhaps the work of a spiteful god using those tools as his trade?

His daughter had only been driving for two months now, but she was a good driver. And it wasn't her fault. She had been on her way to school when a tow truck plowed through a red light and T-boned her Mercedes. Firefighters were forced to use the jaws of life to extract her. Though Tom hadn't seen the crash, visions of it played in his mind—the truck halfway through the car cabin, its cross-beam splayed through the metal like a burn.

Memories competed for his attention. Christmases. Birthdays. His daughter's triumphs. Quiet moments of them just being together. The details were fuzzy, but the joy he had felt in those moments was palpable. And beneath it, now, was panic—fear that he'd never hold his little girl again.

It had been just the two of them for some time now. Twelve years ago, Sara's mother had been diagnosed with cancer. She died shortly before Christmas. Sara was all he had left, the only umbilical to a kinder, gentler side of himself. The version of Tom Ferguson who had otherwise been devoured by a harsh world.

Tom had gotten the Mercedes for Sara specifically because it was *safe*—he wasn't trying to raise her high school street cred. But still, a driver's-side hit, with minimal protection between the door and the driver… that was bad. Particularly when the vehicle plowing into you was a tow truck.

When it comes to physics and time, size matters.

He didn't think he could compete with a spiteful god.

The door swung open, and a doctor stepped in. He was young, maybe thirty. He tried to act older, but his baby face betrayed him.

Before the man even spoke, Tom knew. He knew.

"I'm sorry," the doctor said. "We did what we could…"

The doctor used more words. Details. Explanations. But Tom heard none of it. He had been stripped of the only thing left that he cherished. And only one thought repeated in his mind.

My own sins brought this down upon my head. The wrath of God for what I have done in the name of country.

He felt his knees buckle. The theft of the only thing left he cherished. He crumpled into the plastic orange chair, and his insides felt like they were being peeled away with a scalpel. It was his dying.

* * *

Tom sat in the hospital chapel, hollowed by exhaustion and grief. On the wall before him hung a stained-glass image of Jesus. The Son of God stood on blue shards of glass water, His disciples looking on in awe.

Tom hadn't been in a chapel since Linda's cancer. That was when he rejected God. Because God had done nothing.

And now, what was this? Punishment?

He mentally cursed the Christ before him.

There were soft footsteps at the door, and another man took a seat in the pew behind him. The man whispered a prayer beneath his breath. What language was that? Italian?

Then a pause. A silence.

"Mr. Ferguson."

Tom turned around. The man sitting behind him was in his late thirties, handsome, and dressed in an Armani suit. But it was the eyes that caught him. They were crystal-green like Irish hills after a spring rain.

"My name is Silas Egin. I'd like to help you."

Tom said nothing. Was this man another doctor?

"We can bring your daughter back to life."

Tom froze. What the fuck? Was this some kind of sick joke? He barely restrained himself from leaping over the pew and tearing the guy's fucking head off.

"*What* did you say?" he barked, the marine in him surfacing.

"We can bring Sara back," the man repeated.

Tom's jaw tightened. "Get the fuck away from me."

"Mr. Ferguson, I understand your disbelief, but what I say is true. I apologize for coming so soon, but time is of the essence. Go. See her. See her face. Hold her cold hand. And know that there *is* a way for you to be with your daughter again." He pulled out a business card and set it on the pew. "Call this number, and they will give you instructions."

He turned to slide out of the pew, then turned back. "You have come here, yes? For a reason?" He gestured toward the stained-glass window. "He has heard you. He has delivered the way."

He left the chapel, leaving Tom alone again. Completely, utterly alone.

CHAPTER IX

Fifty Miles Outside Pella, Jordan
Present Day

Kat lifted the flap on the army tent that had been her home for the last two weeks and stepped outside. She slipped on her mud-caked caving boots and looked out across the stone valley. The soft pink hues of the early-morning sun kissed the desert rocks just as they had for hundreds of millions of years before humans were here to view it.

And of course, *he* was there—standing on the ridgeline, watching over the campsite, as he had done every morning. In Egypt, that behavior had made her feel safe.

But things had been different in Egypt. He had been different then. She had been different.

He'd asked her out many times before she ever said yes. She was in Egypt to work, not to get caught up with GI Joe. But eventually she succumbed to his big pearly grin. "Dinner, no breakfast." Those were her words.

"Never think of it," he had said.

And so they dined at a little café near the base of the pyramids under a ridiculously full moon. He was funny. And fun. And handsome. And sometime after the sixth glass of wine, they ended up in a room on the top floor of the Four Seasons, making love near the balcony, with the curtains blowing, the pyramids watching through the window, the Nile reflecting upon them both.

He ended up buying her breakfast after all.

She'd felt protected when she was with him. Safe. And she liked that feeling when she went to bed at night. Knowing that someone was watching over her. Someone who would take care of her if things went to hell.

But then… he didn't.

Why didn't he?

They'd been able to avoid each other in the States in the build-up to the trip over here. He didn't show up until the morning they took off for Jordan. And for the two weeks they'd been on site, they'd each treated the other like a leper. He did what she said when it came to running the camp and what caves to explore, and she followed his instructions for security. They were numb, professional. She hated that about him—his ability to go cold. So she played her role of "bitch" just as well.

The resulting tension was so thick it was probably visible to the satellites in low-Earth orbit that sporadically passed overhead.

Switching to work mode, she grabbed a rolled bundle of papers and laid them on a foldout table—3D laser-scanned cross-sections of an underground cavern they'd found the day before. The cavern was seventy feet down, accessible only via a long, narrow slit, and it was her job to plan how they would tackle it.

Still, even as she planned out the day, her gaze continued to drift to the ridgeline, where John scanned the horizon with a pair of binoculars. She cursed herself for thinking about him at all, for having any feelings toward him after what he did.

* * *

John scanned the horizon as the sun started to rise. In the distance, a twisting column of bats clogged the sky, returning to their rocky womb in the earth.

He lowered his binoculars and looked down at the campsite. She was up early, already going over the day. He watched her as she pulled her hair into a ponytail and unfurled some maps. In his mind, he could smell her again. That soft, sweet smell on her skin when she first woke in the morning. Like cotton.

It was that softness that had attracted him to her in the first place. That, and her joy. She was always smiling, a big cheeky grin that lit up her whole face. She had been so happy when they first met. He was happier then, too. Funny, even. They would laugh together. Sometimes tears would even run down her face because she was laughing so hard.

But now that joy had been consumed, and in its place guilt rose up like puke in the back of his throat. The sins of the past lurked in his mind, a dark box just waiting to be opened.

Even here, in the peace of the sunrise, he could hear it again.

The screaming.

* * *

Fairfax, Virginia
Two Years Ago

Sunday couldn't remember where he lived. He drove up and down the same block for five minutes. In his defense, all the units looked the same. What number? 3452? Or 4532? He'd been gone six weeks and couldn't remember. Fuck.

He'd been gone his whole life.

He finally decided on a unit and pulled over. Fumbling around in the glovebox, he grabbed a bottle of pills, because despite the booze, his back was on fire. He downed the pills with a swig of spit and grabbed his black duffel.

He knocked, because he couldn't get the key right, and to be honest he still wasn't entirely sure he was standing at the right door.

She answered.

For a moment he just stood there, frozen in the doorway of their little apartment in Fairfax. After traveling seven thousand miles, he couldn't travel another seven inches to make contact.

Then finally, he stepped forward and hugged her. Awkwardly. It felt obligatory. A chore. It wasn't that he didn't want to see her, he just... he couldn't feel anything yet. Couldn't focus on this place. Coming back, rekindling. He assumed it was this way for her too, though she never let on either way.

He pulled back. It was always he who broke the hug first. She watched him silently as he moved into the apartment. Their apartment.

She could probably smell the booze on him. Like cologne brewed in a barrel in Tennessee. She was probably wondering if he needed to drink just to come home. Just to see her.

And maybe he did.

He saw the empty bassinet in the corner. Saw that she'd been getting ready. Of course she had. While he was away, she was preparing for the baby. *Their* baby. It still seemed a foreign concept to him. Something happening to someone else, far away.

He passed the bassinet and went to the kitchen cabinet, where he fished around for the bottle.

When she first told him she'd gotten pregnant— no, that wasn't fair; he'd *gotten* her pregnant—he said he would do the right thing. And he did. He did do that. He bought her a ring, he kneeled down in the little kitchen, and he proposed.

A week later, they were married.

And three days later, he was off again.

Always away. Always to some far corner of the world he could never talk about.

Even now, back once more, with a pregnant wife awaiting him and an expectant bassinet in the corner, his mind was in Afghanistan.

The raid had gone to shit. He'd held a man in his arms as he died. Terry Baxter. Sunday repeated the name. *Terry Baxter.* He had pounded on his bloody chest, coated like crimson mud, in an effort to drum life back into him. He'd held Terry and scooped his eyeball back into the remnants of his skull like he was putting a marble back in a box.

Then the man's other eye popped open, and with that one good eye, Terry stared past Sunday. Past everything. Looking somewhere beyond.

"They're coming. Oh my God. I'm sorry…"

Terry had seen something in those final seconds. Or maybe it was just a lack of oxygen to his brain. And Sunday held his dying breath in his hands before it was released into the universe to become… nothing.

Terry Baxter had been only twenty-three years old. A kid, with a mom and a dad, a little brother, a young girlfriend who desperately wanted to become a young wife.

Army Master Sergeant Terry Baxter.

KIA in Nerkh.

A place no one could find on a map even if they had a map to get there.

He suddenly realized Kat was making small talk. Asking him about the flight. He responded with some grunts that echoed in the cabinet. He hoped she hadn't dumped the bottles, flushed the pills the military doctors were all too happy to prescribe him. The ones that made his muscles blend into the cushions of the couch. She knew this was his fight. His battle. She had faith that he was a warrior, and that he would rise to the fight.

He knew she'd been hoping that the baby would give him focus. But that was as foolish as thinking that buying a new house would fix your marriage. Same problems, new appliances. A baby wouldn't change who he was. Who he had become. There was something loose inside, and he was afraid it could never be fixed.

He had been trained to kill. To do horrible things. He did what he was ordered to do, and as a consequence, he had developed a moral flexibility that troubled her, with her sensible Catholic upbringing. How many dead were locked away in the place he dared not go, the corner room where madness and evil things stain the walls with their sin?

"I do what has to be done," he'd told her once. "So that people get to make good choices."

That was his justification. Bad things have to be done to give the rest of us a chance to do good. Kill a terrorist? That saves a planeload of nice families on their way to vacation in Orlando. One man dead at Sunday's hand, and some kid gets to buy a Mickey balloon instead of putting on an oxygen mask as his plane plummets thirty thousand feet.

Someone must wield the knife that draws the blood.

But Kat... she didn't have to be a part of that. So why did she stay? Sometimes he felt like he was a stray she had brought home, and she was trying against all odds to take the street out of him. And it was only a matter of time before the street dog bit her.

She said she believed he was a good man. He hoped she meant it. He needed her to. He needed someone to believe that. Because he couldn't do it himself.

And now... well, now she stayed because they were going to have a baby. Which was the worst reason to stay.

"Do you want to go out?" she asked. "We could—"

"No." He collapsed onto the couch and turned on the TV.

* * *

The pills had dulled his mind to a pillow, but he still noticed she was wearing the little sundress that had drawn his eye when he first saw her in Egypt. The dress used to fit like a petal hanging on a flower. Now it was tight like an overstuffed sausage. She rubbed her hands around her belly as if warming the baby within.

He should be pleased. She was carrying his child.

Why couldn't he just appreciate this life? Why did the battlefield call to him even when he was here?

What did you see, Terry?

Later that night, they made love. Or more precisely, had sex. And then he slept next to her, snoring like a homeless drunk passed out in a public library.

* * *

He woke in the night to the sound of screaming.

He didn't know whose at first.

Then he realized it was his.

"Fuck you! Fuck you!" he was shouting. His voice was so loud and booming it scared him. It reminded him of his father.

It took him a few seconds to recognize where he was. This place. This room. The white wispy curtains in the window.

And then he looked down.

He was on top of her, his hands tight around her throat. Her face was pale as bone.

How long?

How long had he been choking her?

He released her and leaned down, put his ear to her mouth.

She wasn't breathing.

Oh God.

"Kat?" he cried, like a child who'd broken his favorite toy. A child trying to crawl back into the arms of a mother who had long ago rejected him.

"Baby?" he called again, this time with intent, as if the force of his voice could summon her from the beyond.

He leaned down over her and parted her lips, the tart of the night's sleep on her mouth, the bitter of her dying, and exhaled deeply into her lungs. He started chest compressions. It was the second time this week he'd made this same desperate attempt to stave off death.

She didn't move.

He continued pumping, the springs of the bed responding with a mocking squeak to remind him of the times of fleeting bliss they'd shared here.

Suddenly she seized, a dead woman ejected. She gasped, gagged, choked.

He rolled off her and sat on the edge of the bed, breathing hard.

She turned away, trying to catch her own breath, like she'd just run a marathon in her underwear.

He rose from the bed and stood against the far wall like a wounded animal. And in the moonlight of the ghost curtains, he sobbed. Sobbed for his sins. Sobbed for the man he had become. For the break inside him. Sobbed because he knew there was no fixing it.

CHAPTER X

When Kat woke the next morning, he wasn't there. No note. Nothing. The closet still had his clothes in it. She thought, optimistically, he'd just gone to get her breakfast. Like old times.

But deep down, she knew. Knew he was gone.

That afternoon, the bleeding came. She went to urinate, and there was a streak. Pinkish at first. Then dark crimson like a red warning scream.

And she felt more scared than she'd ever been. So small. She needed him now, more than ever. Her man.

Why doesn't he answer his cell?

Bleeding is normal, she told herself over and over. But that evening, it was worse. She urinated, and the bowl was a revolting soup of frothy, bubbling blood.

And then the contractions came.

* * *

Sunday sat in his truck, the nine-millimeter in his lap. Next to him, riding shotgun, was a half-empty bottle of Jack.

He had parked at a construction site where he could watch the setting sun cast shadows over the wood-frame skeletons of future apartment buildings. A light rain fell, providing just enough water to make even the dirty bulldozers and cranes start to look clean again.

He placed the gun between his teeth so he could feel the little hole of the barrel with his tongue. He screamed in the hollow of the driver's seat. The gun was so tight in his fingers that his knuckles turned white.

You don't deserve to live, motherfucker. Not after the things you've done. The people you've killed. And now Kat. You hurt her because you can't love, you piece of shit. All you can do is kill. She deserves better.

Do it.

DO IT!

But another voice, a whisper of reason, spoke in the back of his brain.

Suicide doesn't pay.

If he pulled the trigger and blew the back of his skullcap clean into the back seat, it would be Kat and the baby who would suffer. They'd get no insurance money. He'd be no better than a deadbeat dad who just took off one day with a stripper from Vegas. That would be his level of pathetic. One last selfish act. One final act of cruelty.

Kat and the baby will suffer.

He grabbed the bottle of pain pills from the glove-box. Two years earlier, he'd been shot in Iraq. Once in the arm, blowing off a solid chunk of triceps. Another in the side, shattering two ribs. And a third in his leg, splintering his femur. The guy who shot him had wiped his bullets in shit, so when the rounds tore into Sunday's body, they spread that stinking filth like a plague throughout his bloodstream.

Now he opened the bottle and dumped the pills in his hand. Eleven little white soldiers.

Can I make it look like an accidental overdose? How many pills would look "accidental"? If I mix them with enough booze, would five do it? Would that look like too many? Or would it be too few and I wake up a vegetable?

He decided on six pills, a nice even number. He put them in his mouth. He knew if he chewed them it would go faster, so he bit down and felt the acidic talcum burst on his tongue. He washed them down with a giant swig of liquor, then went ahead and sucked down the rest of the bottle.

And he waited.

The sun began to disappear, the storm clouds winning. The rain fell with more intensity, the drops pattering loudly on the roof of the truck. A soothing sound. A good sound to die by.

Pitter, patter, pitter…

Another sound in the distance. A squeal of tires. A thud.

He turned, slowly, his mind in a fog, and looked through the rain-streaked rear window.

Just outside the construction site was a car. Stopped right in the middle of the road. The driver got out, walked to the front bumper, knelt. Then he stood and darted back into the car, backed up, and peeled off down the slick road.

Sunday's mind drifted once more beyond the rain-drops, out through the glass. His eyes fluttered. The pills. Six had been enough.

Had he seen something else in the road? Something... blue? The driver had hit something. A clump of cloth. Yes.

He let his eyes close. It didn't matter now.

A cry. A faint moan. It mixed with the distant drums of the rain on the roof.

God damn it. Let me die.

He was fading, his arms and legs melting into the upholstery.

Somehow he resurrected himself long enough to push himself out the door. Standing there in the rain, water rolling down his face, he could see better now. Hear better.

The cloth in the road.

It was crying.

Like an ice skater he slid through the mud, his movements languid and slow. He stumbled into the road, stood over the small body, face-down, wearing a blood-splattered blue winter coat.

"Can you hear me?"

Sunday's words were slow. His mouth was disconnected from his brain.

He knelt, reached out, and slowly, gently rolled the body over.

A little boy. No more than ten years old.

One side of the child's face was bloody, broken. Caved in.

Sunday leaned in to feel for a pulse.

It was there. Weak. Fading. A dying pump on the dam between this world and nothingness.

He reached into his pocket for his phone. He would call the police.

The battery was dead.

They all were.

There was no one else around. He had picked this spot so he could die in peace.

Fuck.

The child moaned. He wasn't dead yet.

And Sunday saw them all, summoning him, the brothers of the battlefield, the ones he must bring home. His inner drill sergeant woke, and for a moment, the drugs coursing through him were held at bay by a dull blade of adrenaline.

He carefully scooped up the child. The boy's wet, bloody jacket smeared across his T-shirt.

Somehow he made it back to the truck. He laid the boy in the passenger seat and got back behind the wheel. He was in no condition to drive. He drove anyway.

He was moving through a tunnel. All around the edges of his vision the darkness pressed in, trying desperately to strangle his sight forever.

He took a corner, and the child shifted and groaned.

"It's okay. You'll be okay," Sunday said.

The child's breathing was labored. He'd probably broken a rib or two, and the bones had now speared a lung.

How far was the hospital? Ten miles? A thousand? He was remote-piloting his body. He struggled to hold on to the steering wheel, his fingers fuzzy caterpillars.

Finally he turned down a recognizable road toward the hospital.

"Almost there."

The little boy groaned, then whispered, his voice so faint Sunday almost didn't hear it.

"John…"

Did he say my name?

It had to be a hallucination. The pills.

When he looked back at the boy, the child was sitting upright, staring at him, half his face caved in, his eyes all white.

"God. Sees," the boy whispered, his voice a rasp that hung in the air like frost.

The truck nearly hit a median, and Sunday corrected before looking back at the child. The boy was leaning against the passenger's side window. His lips weren't moving.

Sunday spun the truck into the emergency room roundabout and opened the driver's-side door. He tried to move around to the passenger side, but his legs were like someone else's, and he folded to the ground like a snuffed-out cigarette.

"We're gonna get you some help, okay?" said a man's voice. "Gurney!"

"Child," Sunday mumbled. "In truck." He could barely form the words.

"There's a kid in there!" the voice shouted.

Sunday cracked his eyes open. A man in scrubs was hovering over him. A woman raced to peer into the cab of the truck.

Before Sunday succumbed to darkness, he heard the woman's words.

"There's no one here," she said.

* * *

As Kat drove herself to the hospital, she repeated "You're okay" like a shaman's chant. But she wasn't okay. She collapsed in front of the nurse's station as she was filling out paperwork in the ER. From there she was in and out of consciousness.

They rushed her into the operating room. She remembered the lights overhead, a nurse over her, telling her everything would be fine, one of the lies the living tell the dying because deep down they know what's coming.

God, please. Please help me. Please save my baby.

Again she was out.

When she woke again, they had delivered it.

But there was no sound.

No sound.

God, please.

She demanded to see it.

No, they said.

"Show me my baby!" she screamed.

And then, there it was. Presented like a pale crystal ball, laid upon her bare chest.

Tiny. Blue. Eyes closed. She could see his tiny little fingers and toes. He was no bigger than a coffee mug in her palms. Still warm.

He had been molded inside her from the clay of her womb.

And as they took him away, she cried.

No. She had *cried* when she fell off her bike as a child. This was something different. Gut-wrenching. Soul-crushing. A hollowing inside, a ripping of the sinew from her heart. She had failed to create, and from within her it had been, but could not be.

She had never felt so alone.

CHAPTER XI

Fifty Miles Outside Pella, Jordan
Present Day

Three clicks east of the archaeologists' campsite, Silas Egin lay low and watched through a pair of one-hundred-millimeter binoculars. He was practically invisible, having plucked the surrounding scrub and threaded it into his ghillie suit with botanical precision.

He heard their conversations in his ear, courtesy of a laser microphone that fired an infrared beam and absorbed sound from two miles away. He was also linked into their radio transmission traffic, and he could even read their text messages and emails on their phones. He knew that a CIA shrink was hounding John Sunday for treatment for a possible dissociative disorder. He knew that Danny Ortz's daughter was graduating kindergarten in Virginia and that Ortz sent her big emoji hearts, a pathetic substitute for his failure to be there in person. He knew that Kat Devier spent her evenings reading on her tablet—either a Coptic translated copy of the Gospel of Mary, or a biography of Mary Magdalene that contended she was the first disciple.

In this way, Egin was their god. A technological superior, like Pizarro or Cook in paradises lost.

Now he looked around at the low scrub and the Jordan burbling nearby. This was a place of peace, of calm. Was this the valley where the Lord had walked? Where He now waited to be found again? The place Egin's own father had sought for so long?

Tangled in the corners of Egin's nest was a mass of spiny hawthorn that reminded him of Christ's crown. Its dying yellow fruit spewed forth a pungent smell of rot to attract pollinators—a symbol that from death, there can be life.

He'd been in this spot for three days now. Three days on his belly, except when he had to take a piss, which allowed him to briefly roll onto his side to whip out his cock. He'd changed his diet a week and a half earlier to prevent having to take a shit, but nevertheless, he now felt the pushing in his belly, and he doubted he'd make it until nightfall. In another seven or so hours, he'd have to just shit himself.

He eyeballed the radar system tucked in the ridgeline on the outskirts of their camp. Their false sense of security, like a blanket carrying smallpox. The radar was capable of detecting a crawler a mile out and a vehicle at five. But the radar, like their laptops and radio communication equipment, contained invisible code that fed back into Egin's computer, allowing him to pull up whatever he wanted whenever he wanted it. An advantage of having worked with the very people who had supplied it all.

Egin could even remotely shut down their entire system if he chose. They would be left blind, and he, along with the others hidden in this valley, would strike.

* * *

By mid-morning the team had set up their gear, and the sound of hammers echoed through the valley as they banged their metal bolts into the rock. The opening to the cavern was a five-foot hole at the base of a cliff, tucked under a granite outcropping. It had been hidden from satellite imagery, a secret like so many that lie below the feet of men. The cavern itself was even better hidden, another seventy feet down through a throat flossed with rocky teeth.

Because of all the rock in the way, cave-to-surface communication was impossible without stringing cable, so they were forced to use a system similar to one first used to communicate across trenches during World War I. Sunday's backpack held a small yellow portable radio system developed by British cavers. It looked like a '70s-era CB used by big-rig truckers.

From there Sunday checked the smaller radio on his shoulder, which would be used within the cave itself.

"Radio check," he said, looking over at Kat.

She idly squeezed the trigger of her own radio, looking annoyed that he had spoken. "Copy," she said.

She strapped a harness between her legs, put on her helmet, adjusted the headlamp, and attached the rope to the anchor that was bolted into the rock above the shaft. After locking her carabiners, she double-checked that the rope was loaded. She grabbed a handful of flaked-out rope and tossed it behind her into the mouth of the cave, and the rope was fed through the belay with precision.

As Sunday watched her, he finished prepping his own gear. He was the one who had taught her to rappel—years ago, early in their relationship. They'd gone climbing together in New Mexico and Arizona, and she was a quick study. She was never afraid to learn something new. To be brave. Another reason he'd been drawn to her.

And her butt had looked great in the little blue spandex shorts she wore.

"On line," Kat shouted. She stepped backwards, kicked off ever so slightly, and abseiled like a spider down a silk line.

Sunday watched as she was slowly swallowed by the darkness.

* * *

The light bounced in triangle shards around the crooked shaft as Kat descended. The sound of her own breathing echoed off the rocks and came back to her in the stony silence. She continued to drop, carefully. Twenty, forty, sixty feet down. Granules floated in her lamplight as the cave sent out particulates to greet her.

Then she touched down on the cave floor, a plume of dust rising around her boots. She paused to check the yellow oxygen meter hanging on her hip, then turned to shine her headlamp around in the darkness.

She was in a small chamber, no more than ten feet wide. It was just a hole in the ground.

She checked it and saw it was empty. She was just about to call to the surface and let them know she was coming back up when she felt it—a wisp of cold air. It fluttered across her neck, and she turned, half-expecting to see something pass. She looked up, but because the shaft twisted and turned, she couldn't see any light at the top.

Alone in the darkness of the pit, she thought she heard a whisper.

Here.

She turned again, searching for the source. Somewhere there was a flow of air, hissing as it passed through an opening in the earth.

She unhooked from the line and moved toward the end of the small space. That was when she saw it: another opening, about three feet wide, tucked low beneath a rock. It didn't make any sense. The shaft hadn't shown up on her maps. It wasn't supposed to be here. She got onto her hands and knees and peered in with her lamp. It was a slender shaft. She'd have to crawl in on her belly.

As she scanned with the light, she caught a glimpse of something passing quickly across the tunnel. An animal's leg? No. That was impossible.

But it looked like a hoof.

She stretched into the hole, an Eve searching for fruit. As she aimed her light ahead of her, she looked for movement, hoping not to see something furry—or hooved—crawling toward her.

There was a noise in the darkness. A scurrying.

Kat wriggled back out quickly. The sound hadn't come from the shaft, it had come from above.

John was coming down a line toward her. He touched down like a tethered astronaut returning to the cargo hold of the space station, then radioed back up to the surface.

"Topside, pretty tight down here. You're gonna have to stay put."

"Copy that," said Danny, his voice hollow and distant.

John then looked over at Kat, who was still on her hands and knees in front of the opening. "Seriously?" he said.

"I can fit." She started to slide into the shaft once more. "There an opening on the other side—I can feel the air."

"If you get stuck…"

"You'll save me," she said as she crawled in headfirst.

Behind her, Sunday shook his head. He'd walked into a fight. He kneeled and watched her scurrying away from him. He was going to say something. Tell her that he was too big to go in there and pull her back out if she got stuck. But he said nothing, and just let her go.

* * *

The tunnel squeezed her with stone fingers, and she had to wriggle her hips and think skinny thoughts. An inch at a time, she gripped her fingernails into the rock and pulled herself through. The shaft was only about ten feet long, but by the time she got to the end of it the rock had torn her T-shirt and scraped her back, drawing blood, the first moisture here in an eon.

Finally she emerged from the other side—pulling her body out as if being birthed from a stony uterus—and stood.

She was in another chamber, this one part of a much bigger cave. A huge mound of collapsed rock lay in a far corner. She was under the mountain now, looking at what had once been—perhaps some ancient opening to the surface that had long ago collapsed from geologic shifts and had been buried by rock, the earth concealing its sins.

The radio crackled on her shoulder. "You all right?" John asked, his voice a fading dream.

"Yeah," she replied.

She felt for the breeze again. It passed across her, a whisper, and the hairs on her arms stood at attention, as if her body's primitive warning system knew something her conscious mind did not.

But that wasn't all she felt. She had a sudden and distinct sense that she was not alone.

Someone was watching.

And tapping.

Whatever it was, it was circling her, its... hooves?... striking the rock like a horse clicking down a cobblestone street.

Could there be goats down here?

She scanned with the lamp, but the cave was wide, and the darkness absorbed the light as if feasting on the photons. She could only light a few feet around her.

I'm imagining it.

She moved forward slowly, careful to mind her step. If she stumbled or twisted an ankle, she'd have to drag her injured body back through that shaft. And if she stepped off a sharp drop, she wouldn't be dragging her injured body out of here at all.

As if listening to her fears, an abyss appeared mere inches in front of her boot tips, deep, dark, and eternal. She'd been moving so carefully, looking so closely— how could she have gotten so close before seeing that?

She shone her light into the chasm, but it answered with only black.

But she heard something that seemed to be coming from below.

A breeze?

No. More like whispers. A flurry of them. Moving over each other like water moccasins.

She felt suddenly certain that a conversation was happening deep down in the darkness.

The cave was talking about her.

She spun around, her beam her only chronicler. Without it all would be lost and there would be no more. This time her lamplight landed square on a series of scratches on one wall. Scratches. Or scribbles?

Carefully stepping back from the abyss, she moved toward the wall. There, etched in the feldspar, was a letter 'T'. She was sure it wasn't just a natural feature of the rock. It had been scraped at, worn down by an animal's claws rather than time.

Was it a T? The Greek letter tau?

No. It was the true cross, the one used in traditional Roman crucifixion.

She shone her light at the floor below the cross, and there she saw it. Tucked into a small recess in the cave wall, standing like a cold sentinel over the abyss, was a clay cylinder, about knee-high. Its lid was sealed with mud.

The Egyptians sealed the tops of jars with linen and mud. They'd also stamp the mud with a mark.

Kat kneeled and leaned in closer with the light.

There it was. That same squat letter T.

The jar was too small to hold bones. Certainly not the bones of an entire man. She reached out and touched the pot. Through her gloves, it was cold. She held the clay jar, certain this was the first time it had been touched by human hands in two millennia.

She clicked her radio.

"I… I found something." She sounded out of breath even though she'd done nothing physically straining. "A sealed clay jar with a cross on it. Tell the surface team. We're going to need to lift it out."

* * *

Egin watched the team around the hole. Then he heard the words through his earpiece, which was dialed into the frequency of their radio.

"Topside, you copy?"

"Copy Ground."

"Uh, we've got something here. Some kind of clay jar with a cross on it. We're gonna need a basket."

"Copy that."

Egin ran his tongue across the dry chap of his lips. He reached to his throat and activated the microphone strapped like a noose to his larynx. His voice was hoarse, having gone unused for days.

"They found something."

CHAPTER XII

Kat heard the whisper of air again, louder now, like a coming storm. She stepped back toward the abyss where she had almost fallen. Somewhere down there, a pocket of air had to be pushing up toward her.

A thermal vent? No, it's cold.

She felt it again—the presence. As if something else was here with her now, something logic could not contend with. And with it came another feeling.

A feeling she was prey.

The air from the abyss was ice-cold around her. When she exhaled, her breath hung in the lamplight, a ghost of who she was.

Something...

Something is wrong.

Her head was spinning. She could feel her blood swirling in the bone teacup of her skull.

She looked down at the yellow gas sensor dangling on her hip. The screen was blank.

Oh God. It's not working.

Could it be the air? Was the air bad?

The hissing seemed to consume her now. No, not air. Whispers. All around her.

The lamp on her helmet flickered. Or was something blocking it? A shadow, directly in front of her. Her eyes couldn't see it, but she knew it was there.

Something warm rolled off her helmet and dripped onto her cheek. She touched her face and looked at her fingertips. They were blood-red.

She looked up toward the ceiling, but it was too far above in the darkness.

Mud?

Just mud.

She had to be hallucinating. Which meant...

She reached into her pocket, pulled out a lighter, and lit it. The flame flickered, sputtered, tried to rise again as a spark, but fizzled, snuffed out by the darkness.

Oh God. It is *gas.*

She was suffocating.

She shone the lamp around her again. It seemed now that she was in a room full of people. She was at the center of a ring of onlookers, their eyes hollow and black, like fish born in the dark depths of the sea, their flesh coated in mud as if they had emerged from the earth.

She felt pain. Not hers. *Theirs*.

Anger. Rage. They had been abandoned. Left. Lost.

And... loneliness. Incredible, distant loneliness. As if she were billions of miles from Earth, alone in a void, lost to all touch. Having known love, having once been touched by it, but now cast aside, as far from its splendor as one could be and yet with the memory still alive in her heart. She was drenched in sorrow—a sorrow she recognized. A crippling emptiness that carved out her insides and left her a slab of cold, lifeless meat.

Scratching.

It was the sound of sandpaper. Something rubbing like against the rock.

She scanned with the lamp, and there, kneeling before her, their legs twisted like grasshoppers, were a dozen naked people, writhing and jerking, rubbing their foreheads raw on the rocky floor as they crawled face-down toward her, bowing and dragging their flesh across the rock.

She tried to scream, but no sound emerged.

The whispers grew into a symphony of hisses and the chirping of crickets.

She backed into the cave wall and slid down to the floor, her mind broken by the things that could not be, devoured by a dark root that dwelled deep in the core of the universe and sought only to surface.

CHAPTER XIII

On the other side of the narrow shaft, Sunday heard Kat's gas alarm screaming.

"Kat!" he yelled. "Kat!"

The only answer was his own voice bouncing off the rock.

Jesus Christ. He was going to have to go in there and get her.

He clicked his radio. "Surface team. I need O2 tanks and respirators down here. Fast."

There was a crackle of static. No response.

Fuck.

"Danny?"

Another pause, and then, as if surfacing, "Yeah, copy. On its way. You need a medic?"

Sunday peered into the tiny tunnel. God damn it. There would barely be room for him to move.

"Negative. Just lower down a skiff. Get ready on the surface."

"Copy that."

Sunday peered into the hole, unsure if he'd be able to make it through that tight squeeze. He'd have to push the tank through first, ahead of him.

A few minutes later the tanks descended on a line, bound to the skiff like a bundle of metallic yellow bananas. Sunday pushed one tank into the tunnel and tethered another tank to his ankle. Then he dropped down to his belly and pushed the tank in front of him into the opening, dragging the second tank behind.

The space was almost too tight for the tank, let alone him. His ribs were in a vise of rock, slowly squeezing him, and he had to exhale completely to move forward. He slid, inches at a time, unable to take a full breath. His fingernails scratched at granite and his chest scraped painfully across cold, jagged stone. But he kept moving. He had to keep moving.

He pushed the oxygen tank out of the hole, and it clanged onto the rocky floor below. Then he emerged. First a hand, then an arm, then his head. He pushed his right shoulder close to his cheek so he could breach, then finally he freed his chest.

He took a deep, desperate breath. It had taken him a minute and a half, and he was lightheaded from the shallow breathing he'd had to endure.

"Kat!"

No answer.

The light barely penetrated the cavern, like he was flicking a Zippo in space.

There! Against the far wall. She was slumped over in a pile.

He got to his feet, unstrapped the tank at his ankle, flipped it around, re-strapped it to his back, and donned the mask so the gas wouldn't get to him. Carrying the other tank, he moved over to Kat, checking his steps to make sure they were touching solid ground.

Her head had flopped forward, and he lifted it gently to check her neck for a pulse.

There?

Yes. But faint. Maybe thirty beats a minute.

He pulled back her hair and slipped the mask over her mouth, securing it around her ears. He turned it on and heard the rush of oxygen hiss through the line. Then he watched and waited, keeping a finger on her pulse.

Come on, Kat.

After a minute, her head moved. Slowly, like she was waking from a dream. Her eyelids fluttered and opened.

Then she saw him. Suddenly awake, she pulled back in a panic.

"Whoa, whoa," he said. He grabbed her so she wouldn't fall. "Kat, it's me. You're okay."

Her eyes widened, and she looked to her feet as if expecting to see something there.

"You're safe," Sunday said.

She nodded. "I… I found something." Her words were muffled by the plastic. She turned, shone her headlamp on a clay jar.

"Okay. Just take it easy."

She looked around the cave, her eyes darting, paranoid. Afraid.

She tore off the mask. "I have to get out. This place… something isn't right." She picked up the clay jar and moved toward the opening. Her movements were jerky, panicky.

Sunday followed her closely, making sure she didn't fall into some unseen pit. Hopefully she would come back to her senses once her body had cleared the gas from her system. For now, she was moving toward the exit. That was what mattered.

She slid the clay jar into the tunnel and crawled in after it. Sunday kneeled in front of the hole and watched her wriggle away. She was faring better than he had, but still moving very slowly. Suddenly she stopped altogether.

"What is it?" he asked behind her.

"Listen," she said.

He leaned in and heard it—echoes within the rock. Distant *pomp*s, the earth relaying the sound like a stone telegraph.

He knew that sound well. He heard it in his dreams. Gunfire.

Sunday had left the cave-to-surface CB radio on the other side of the hole. He squeezed the smaller radio on his shoulder and flicked to an open channel.

"Surface team. Do you copy? Danny?"

Nothing. This radio was far too feeble to penetrate through all that rock.

"Kat? Can you scoot backwards?"

He could see her trying to back out of the tunnel, but she couldn't. It was a one-way trip. "No." She sounded slightly panicked.

His mind raced. Someone was shooting on the surface. Attacking the team. If Danny and the others couldn't hold them back, they'd most certainly be coming down.

"Kat, scoot through, then turn around and come back. Okay? You'll be safer on this side. We can contain them in the tunnel."

"Okay."

She moved forward again, perhaps slightly faster this time. It was still painfully slow.

She stopped again. "John," she whispered. "Someone's coming down."

* * *

"Turn off your lamp," John said behind her.

Awkwardly, clumsily, Kat ducked her head and pulled her hand back so she could reach the switch on the lamp. Her cheek was pressed hard against the cold rock, and her arms pinned tight against the floor. She moved like a tethered bird to flick off the light.

She was plunged into darkness.

She reached her hands forward once more, toward the clay jar. Her instinct was to pull it toward her, to hold it tight, but it was too wide, the shaft too narrow. And then she heard the sound of a carabiner unclicking, and froze.

Maybe they won't see the hole. No, that's stupid. They'll look. They know we're down here. That's why they came.

A light shone ahead, flashing across the far wall of the smaller cavern like a wandering searchlight in a prison movie. When they turned the light this way, they'd see the jar—it was only about two feet from the opening. They'd grab it. And then they'd grab her.

Boots ground against the floor, coming closer. The light moved with them, scanning back and forth. It stopped. Kat wanted to curl back, to disappear.

She closed her eyes to pray. *Please, God, please…*

Suddenly the light shone clear into the tunnel. She tried to raise her hands up defensively but couldn't move them more than a few inches. The jar slid away from her. Whoever was out there was pulling it out of the hole.

He used the light to examine the clay jar. She still couldn't see his face, but she could tell he was kneeling by the hole. And then he stood, and his boots retreated across the floor. Harnesses were clicked and tightened. He must be strapping in the clay jar to lift it out.

Maybe he's done. Got what he came for. Oh God, what did they do to the others? What about Danny? All the rest? Are they dead?

The boots came back toward the hole.

He was coming for her.

This time his light shone directly into her eyes.

"You can crawl out alive… or I'll drag you out dead." His voice had a slight accent.

He lowered the light a bit so that she could see the rifle he was pointing into the hole. She knew the weapon. A Heckler & Koch PSG1. John had taken her out to the range several times and had given her lessons on how to shoot. She remembered what the PSG1 rounds had done to the liters of Coke he'd set up for her. Five hundred yards out, they sprayed geysers of syrup skyward. She couldn't imagine what it would do to her skull here, up close, in this confined space.

She thought about calling back to John, to tell him that she was going now with this man. That she was surrendering to him, in the full meaning of the word. Would she be tortured because she was an American? Did he know she was CIA?

Would he rape her?

The answers didn't matter. Because it all boiled down to one thing.

She wanted to live.

So she crawled on her belly, reduced to primordial spawn, moving forward to accept a fate crafted by this man—or perhaps his god.

CHAPTER XIV

Sunday waited, crouched in the darkness, as Kat crawled from the hole. With any luck, the man would need a little time to get her harnessed up, which would give Sunday a chance to sneak up on him. He hadn't brought any weapons down with him, just a curved Petzl knife for cutting rope, so he'd have to get close for a kill. It would have to do; the cave was tight anyway.

As soon as she was clear, the man on the other end sent a beam of light down the full shaft. Sunday ducked back to avoid being seen.

The light receded, and the tunnel was again dark.

The worst part would be the crawl. Sunday would be completely defenseless. The shaft gripping him on all sides. Toxic gas to his back. An enemy to his front, probably armed with a gun. A million tons of rock pressing down on his skull.

He took one last deep breath, let it out, removed his oxygen mask… and entered the tunnel.

* * *

The moment Kat was out of the hole, the man yanked her to her feet and pushed her toward the rope. His rifle was a black-barreled dog at her back.

"Get on the line," he said.

She followed his directions and attached herself to the harness.

He radioed to the surface. "Pull her up."

She felt a sudden tug, and then she was off her feet, being pulled back to the surface by a power not her own. She looked below her, but still couldn't see the man's face, just his headlamp, gradually being absorbed into the darkness of the cave as if it had been a part of it all along.

She wondered if he knew about John.

Worse still, she wondered if any of her team would still be alive to greet her on the surface.

* * *

Sunday crawled quietly forward, his rib cage screaming for release. He ignored it, his thoughts occupied with what was to come.

Could he get out of the hole silently enough to take the man by surprise? It seemed unlikely, but it was his only option. If he waited for the man to leave, he would be trapped down here forever. This cavern would be his own personal tomb.

And even assuming he could get past the first man, how many more were on the surface? There would be no taking them by surprise.

But he would find a way. He had to. He wasn't going to die down here. And he wasn't going to let Kat die up there.

As if to mock his bravado, a light shone full into his face, revealing him fully.

A man spoke with a slight accent. "This must be what they mean, between a rock and a hard place, huh, John?"

He knows my name?

"Know that we appreciate your service. Know that your suffering and your sacrifice gives rise to a greater good."

The man raised the rifle and stuffed it into the hole.

"May the burden of your sins be lightened by God."

"Wait!" Sunday said. He wanted to negotiate, as all men do when they hear the sound of the riverboat oars coming for their souls.

But he said nothing. Heard nothing. Because the steel-jacketed, lead-cored round had already entered John Sunday's skull. His neck recoiled like a bone slingshot, and his head collapsed into a blood sponge on the rock bottom of the tunnel.

And he was engulfed by the darkness.

* * *

As Kat rose toward the surface, she was blinded by the brightness of daylight. Hands fumbled at her body and raised her upward like a silt corpse from a grave. She was dragged across the sand, then pulled to her feet.

As her eyes adjusted to the light, she saw what she had dreaded.

Everyone was dead.

Everyone.

She spotted Danny off to one side. His head had been split by a bullet. He would never go home to the little girl who awaited the return of her daddy.

Kat felt a sickness in her gut and the need to vomit, the pit in her stomach deeper than the pit from which she had just emerged. Tears streamed down her cheeks.

As they moved Kat through the campsite, they passed an open tent where several men were gathered around the clay jar. At their center was a gray-haired older man, his fingers thick as tusks, a latticework of scars on his face. Dark eyes peered out from this mask of flesh, making his very skin seem a lie. He was assessing the jar with a clinical eye, admiring its fragile crust, appreciating what he held.

Then he cracked the seal.

Kat heard a voice in her head. The words were from her Catholic school days.

And I saw when the Lamb opened one of the seals, and I heard, as it were the noise of thunder, one of the four beasts saying, Come and see.

Even as she was dragged past the tent, she turned her head to watch. The old man removed the lid and dumped the contents of the jar onto a tarp. At first only sand tumbled out, the grit a mockery of his intentions. It was empty. All that work. All that killing. For what? Sand.

Then something else slid into the man's latex palm, as if now to mock Kat. It looked like a charred potato, not much bigger than the old man's palm. He held it, and the curl of a smile tangled with the scars on his face. A look of satisfaction. Expectation. Confirmation.

This man knew exactly what he held.

But Kat did not. Was it a rock? No. Too pockmarked. Too porous. A sponge?

She was shoved into one of the vehicles.

Come and see. Come and see.

CHAPTER XV

Lanciano, Italy
39 CE

The smell jolted Longinus awake. Putrid. Rotting. Then a flutter. A squawking cry from a gullet.

Where am I?

He opened his eyes, but saw only a haze of daylight, as if his pupils had been smeared with fat. Still he winced from the bright white light. He wiped at his face, peeling away a slime coating from his eyes. He wiped some more and tried to blink it away.

He heard the rustle of wings. Birds were near.

Is this Elysium? Am I dead?

He blinked again until his vision cleared.

Elysium it was not. He was still in his own home, in the atrium. Ravens fluttered throughout, the smell of dander under wing, their augury led by their stomachs.

He rolled onto his side. How was he alive? His neck burned from the blade, but as he explored it with his fingers, all that he felt were tattered scars. His leg, too, was whole once more.

How?

He rose to his feet… and saw her.

She lay like a bloated doll upon a black lake of her own fluids, her head twisted unnaturally.

Ravens feasted upon the sinew of her slit throat.

Longinus limped across the atrium and swatted at the black-winged devils. They roared with hollow laughter.

He dropped next to his bride, but she was no more. Her eyes were wide but could not see, her mouth hung open to form a word that would never come.

"Licinia," he sobbed.

He wiped the maggots from her swollen face so he could look upon her cleanly. He pulled her in and held her to his chest. And then he, Longinus, a soldier of Rome, a slayer of Gauls, wept.

* * *

It was days later when the centurion arrived at his father-in-law's small farm. He walked the narrow dirt path, past the pigs milling about in their filth, toward the old man who had stepped outside to dump his waste bucket.

"Appius!" Longinus shouted.

The old man placed his bucket on the muddy ground and wrapped his soiled fingertips around the handle of his sword. From under thick gray brows he squinted at this man who invaded his land. "What do you want?" he barked.

Longinus approached slowly and stopped in front of the old man. "I bring terrible news," he said. "Your daughter is dead."

Appius stopped and stared. "How?"

"We were attacked. In our home while we slept. I swear to you, I shall find those who did it, and avenge her."

"In your home? You have the wrong woman. My daughter is home with her husband."

"And as her husband I tried to protect her."

"You? What joke is this?"

"There is no humor here."

"And yet you are not her husband."

"Have you gone mad?" Longinus could feel his patience waning. "Your daughter," he repeated slowly, "my wife… Licinia… was murdered. In our home. I tried to save her." A lump stuck in his throat. "I am sorry, Appius."

"Why do you spread these lies?"

"Stop!" Longinus shouted with such ferocity that spittle flew from his lips.

Appius pulled his sword and held the tip toward Longinus. "Now you listen to me. I do not know who you are, or why you speak these ills against my child. But I will slay you where you stand and feed you to my pigs."

With one quick step forward, Longinus wrapped his arm around the outside of the old man's elbow, squeezed the arm upward, and swept the old man's leg. Appius fell into the slop pile made from his own waste bucket.

Longinus grabbed the sword and held it to the old man's throat. "How dare you draw your weapon on me! What is wrong with you? Is your mind sick? I shall say it again, in case there be mud in your ears. I am Longinus, your daughter's husband. And she is dead."

"Longinus is my friend. And you are not he," said Appius.

Longinus stared into Appius's eyes. The old man's mind must have failed him.

"I do not know who has sent you to mock me about my daughter's demise," Appius continued, "but it is truly a cruel and heartless jest."

"I do not mock you, old man." Longinus slowly lowered the blade. "What I speak is true. And I mourn her with everything I am."

Appius rose to his feet and squinted at this man he did not recognize.

"If you are who you say, then Vertumnus has seen fit to change you. For what reason, I know not."

Longinus stared into the old man's eyes. "A glass," he said. "Do you have one?"

The old man nodded. Longinus gestured with the blade for him to fetch it from the house. He returned holding a lead-handled mirror.

Longinus held it to his face. Appius had spoken true: even Longinus himself did not recognize the man who looked back at him. His eyes had changed from brown to blue, and his hair, once a graying black, was now dark brown. His cheekbones were lower and more defined, his nose wide and flat.

His face had been re-formed, like fingers working clay.

"You are not Longinus," Appius repeated.

Longinus traced his fingers along the thick scar that traced his neck. He lowered the mirror. "I do not look as I once did, but I am who I say, and the news I bring is sorrow."

CHAPTER XVI

Amman, Jordan
Present Day

Two hours after the attack in the desert, David Conrad's desk phone rang. Langley was on the line—CTC Director Tom Ferguson. Ferguson was heir apparent to become the new deputy director, and Conrad hoped to take his vacated seat.

But as Conrad's boss told him what had happened to the team in the desert, his career was the last thing on his mind. Someone had betrayed those people. And he had the sinking feeling that someone was Tom Ferguson himself.

"Survivors?" he asked.

"Not that we see," Ferguson replied.

The muscles tightened in Conrad's jaw.

"You've got two, maybe three hours, to get the site cleaned," Ferguson said. "If Jordanian intelligence finds out we were out there, it'll create problems. I want this to look like a civilian operation, with light security personnel. Emphasis on *light*. Clear any guns, comm links, anything that makes this look like more than just Harvard archaeologists. FBI fly team is en route, and they know we're involved."

"What's on satellite?" Conrad asked. He rose from his desk and gazed out the bulletproof window, past the city traffic of Amman, toward a desert too far away for him to actually see.

"Satellite was re-routed overnight to keep tabs on a suspected safe house in the Deir Az Zor province. It wasn't back over the site until a half hour ago. Whoever did this was gone by then."

That definitely triggered Conrad's bullshit detector.

"I want hourly updates. Report only to me," Ferguson said, and hung up.

Conrad was left with a curious itch, like dandruff had worked its way inside his brain. This should never have happened. He had concocted this operation. Had cooked up the idea of setting this trap to snare the Father. The plan had been to leak that American archeologists were digging here after uncovering part of a gospel found beneath a portrait picked up in Syria. That was the bait. And then they were supposed to watch the dig site from overhead, constantly. They were *expecting* company. They'd asked for it. And they needed to know when it was coming, so that they were ready if the Father—or anyone else—attacked. They had hoped to capture a prisoner or two, perhaps even the Father. Interrogate the living, DNA the dead.

Now *Americans* were dead. It was a mess, and it was made up of many consistencies of shit.

First there was the peripheral shit. Like when Jordanian intelligence found out that the CIA had been digging in their desert, they'd know the agency was looking for something more than just prehistoric Tupperware. They'd ask what that something was. And Conrad would have to concoct a lie and feed it to the ambassador. The Jordanians might or might not swallow it.

But the real shit had chunks.

Because David Conrad was being lied to. And those lies were coming from the very top of the agency he so faithfully represented.

From Tom Ferguson.

He knew this, because he had told no one else about this operation because Tom Ferguson was a traitor.

* * *

Fairfax, Virginia
One Month Ago

David Conrad sat at the dinner table with his wife and daughter. They ate in silence, except for the tap-tapping of Gracie's fingers on her cell phone as she texted someone. Eleven years old and addicted to technology, engaged in the new language of symbols, like the pictorial languages of the old and the dead, tied to tongues no longer spoken. Tap, tap, tap, upon the golden calf of the new gods.

He and his wife didn't speak for other reasons.

He looked down at his plate of salad. Salad would be courtesy. It was actually just lettuce from a plastic bag with a handful of shredded carrots thrown in and a dump of dressing. When Conrad was at home, he ate a lot of meals that came from a bag.

"Gracie, put it down," he said. "Let's talk."

His daughter looked up at him as if only just now returning to the planet. "About what?"

"How's school?"

"Uh… fine," she said, returning to her screen.

She didn't want to talk to him. Neither did his wife. He'd lost them somewhere along the way. Along their journey together. They'd fallen out of the wagon while passing along the Oregon Trail.

He tapped on the table to get his daughter's attention. Harder than he meant to. The plates shook like ceramic creatures come to life. It was time to take a stand. Stand up for the reunification of his family. Say something to unite them all in a common cause of Conrad family magnificence. Instead, his own cell phone rang.

He looked at the number.

"I have to take this," he said.

His wife said nothing. She nodded and chewed. He could have told her he was going for a sex change, and she probably would have given the same response.

He stepped into the side room that doubled as his office, closed the door, and accepted the call.

"This is Conrad," he said.

"I need to see you." Ayelet Tal's voice had a raspy edge, like her own dinner had consisted of Marlboros and milk. Conrad felt a prickle on the back of his neck.

"When?"

"Tonight."

He looked at the closed door that separated him from his family. "Give me an hour."

When his wife and daughter settled down to watch Netflix, he told them he had to go back to the office—that there was a situation in Syria. That last part was true—there was always a situation in Syria—but it was still a lie. Lying was easier than facing all that was broken.

He paused, thinking he should kiss them. That's what real fathers and loving husbands do.

Instead he turned and left. Hungry for something more than salad.

* * *

Forty minutes later, he knocked on the door to room 217 in the St. Regis Hotel in DC. It opened, and there she stood, her long black hair cupping her face like the wings of a raven. Her tight white blouse and gray skirt did a weak job of hiding what lay beneath.

They had met a year earlier as part of a joint CIA/Mossad honeypot operation designed to snag a Libyan scientist who was helping the Iranians develop their nuclear program. Ayelet's job was to lure the scientist upstairs to her room in Beirut, seduce him, and then implant a virus onto a drive in his briefcase. But the operation hit a snag. She was picked up outside the lobby by three armed men who threw her into the back of a van and drove off.

Conrad remembered the panic he felt as he raced down the sidewalk toward his car so he could catch up with the van. But the Mossad agent he was working with, a man named Uri, told him to relax.

"She has the Hand of God," he said.

"The what?"

"A chip. Under her skin. Wherever she goes, we can track her."

She had been built to lure and to trap. Even when the flower had been plucked, she could still draw in the bees.

An hour later they stormed the building where she was being held. They killed thirteen men, all with ties to Hezbollah. The honey had worked.

It had also worked on David.

She had a husband. He had a wife. But riding on their remnants of adrenaline, they spent the night together. Months later, he could still taste her skin, like opium on the lips of the addict.

He stepped into the hotel room, her hand—and his loins—drawing him forward.

"We need to talk," she said. She gestured toward a table and two chairs. "Have a seat."

He looked over at the bed. "You sure you don't want to start there?"

She sat and smiled. A polite smile. A working smile. "First I'm going to tell you a story, and then perhaps you can help me with the ending."

"Well, I love a happy ending."

As he took a seat, she pulled out a manila folder. "This story begins with a man you know—Amir Taresh, a black-market smuggler and slave trader for Al Tariqa. What you did not know is that we had an informant inside Taresh's operation. A month ago, looters from Apamea brought him a Fayum mummy portrait of a woman. Taresh emailed a contact about it.

He wanted forty million dollars for it. That's a lot of money for an old picture."

Conrad knew all this—well, except for the bit about Apamea. But he stayed silent. It was always better to receive intel than to share it.

Ayelet pulled out a photo and slid it across the table. It showed a handsome man with a stubbled face and a dark Brioni suit getting out of the back of a black Mercedes. "This is Taresh's contact. Silas Egin. Do you know him?"

"No." That part was true. They'd never been able to figure out whom Taresh had been trying to sell the painting to.

"He's not Al Tariqa. Not technically. He's an attorney who works for the Institute for the Works of Religion. The bank that runs the Vatican. A strange man for a Muslim terrorist to email, wouldn't you say?"

Conrad pursed his lips and raised his eyebrows. The Israelis seemed to know a lot more about this than the CIA.

"Taresh would have made the deal, but instead our guy inside says Taresh starts going crazy. Hallucinating. Seeing things that aren't there. He demands even more money from Egin and threatens to destroy the painting if he's not paid within twenty-four hours. Then suddenly, out of the blue, the CIA raids Taresh's compound. Taresh is killed, and you walk off with the portrait."

"Is this where the story ends?"

"No," she said. "Let's go back even further. We'd been watching Egin for months. He came to our attention when he was in Tel Aviv to avert a labor strike that would have interfered with the building of a new

Catholic hospital. When he was there he dealt directly with the head of the Gerich crime family. He's a negotiator, a problem-solver for the Catholic church. He's also a money launderer for terrorist organizations, the mob, and cartels who push their money through Catholic charities and businesses."

She slid another photo across the table. "A year ago he hopped a flight to DC, and do you know who he met with?"

The grainy photo looked like it was taken by a security camera. It showed Egin sitting in a small chapel with another man.

Tom Ferguson.

"That's your counterterrorism director, if I'm not mistaken," Ayelet said. "This is in a hospital chapel. Ferguson's daughter had just been killed in a car wreck. And this man, Egin, a man who deals with some of the most dangerous people on earth, flies four thousand miles to hold his hand."

"Maybe Ferguson recruited him."

"Maybe. The next day, Ferguson shows up here. A Catholic outpatient clinic." She slides another picture across the table, like they're playing bridge. This photo shows Ferguson leaving the clinic, accompanied by a young woman with black hair. "Do you know her?"

"No."

"She goes to Georgetown. Tom Ferguson pays her tuition. He also deposits sixty-five hundred dollars in her account every month."

"So he's got a college girlfriend. Good for him."

"Not exactly. We went through her garbage, got a container of yogurt. We ran a DNA test. That woman is not his girlfriend." She tapped on the photo. "That's Tom Ferguson's daughter. The one who died."

"What?"

"We pulled the medical records from the hospital where she was taken after the accident. They confirm her death. According to the records, her body was released and buried in Fairfax. But this girl... she *is* Tom Ferguson's daughter."

"That makes no sense. She doesn't even look like Tom's daughter." Conrad had never met the girl, but he'd seen photos in Ferguson's office.

"She's had some kind of work done. Changed her face, her hair. But DNA doesn't lie. It's her."

Conrad shook his head. "Let's say for a moment it is. Why? For what? Protection?"

"We don't know. In fact, David, we don't know a lot of things. Like why the CIA and the Vatican are so interested in a portrait. Why someone would think it's worth so much money. Why your CTC director is meeting with Egin. Why he's hiding his own daughter."

Conrad remained silent, letting the implied questions hang in the air.

She slid the photos back into the folder. "You can go," she said.

He looked at her. "Wait. Are you kidding? Come on, don't be that way. I don't understand this any better than you do. I'm telling you the truth."

Her deep black eyes were now onyx cold. "That's what all liars say."

CHAPTER XVII

Amman, Jordan
Present Day

On the drive to the site, thoughts raced through David's mind like the desert dunes that zipped past.

Yes, he'd lied to Ayelet. He could have told her what they'd found hidden underneath the painting. He could have told her it was possible the body of Jesus Christ was lying in a cave in Jordan. But that would have warranted Israeli intervention. And David didn't want any more people in the desert.

But he'd been honest about the bigger picture: he really *didn't* understand what was going on. Could it be that the raid on Taresh's compound had had nothing to do with getting Taresh, and everything to do with getting the portrait? If so, why? And what was Ferguson's play in all this?

It was just after noon when he pulled up to the site. The bodies were a short distance from the abandoned tents, but it took no effort to find them—their stench was a physical thing in the desert heat. The flies, too, showed him the way—they were buzzing all about, already busy laying their eggs in the blood that curdled like dark jelly on the bodies. Egyptian vultures circled above, their heads orange as flame, their narrow red eyes watching the lone living man who had dared venture into this valley of the dead.

Four of the bodies, all of them Delta, were scattered about as if they'd been caught while running for cover, scurrying rabbits taken out from afar. The others, the archaeological team, had been executed. Fifty-caliber shots to the backs of the victims' heads had blown their faces off like theater masks removed at the final reveal. All were toppled, face-first, in the sand that ringed the cave.

Scattered among the bodies were three dead men Conrad didn't recognize. Middle Eastern, armed with AK-47s. Perhaps the Deltas had given as good as they got. They didn't go down without a fight.

Conrad turned away and gazed toward the horizon. Heat simmered off the dunes, a cauldron of radiation. There had probably been several snipers out there, tucked in like serpents, waiting to take these shots. He wondered if they were all gone, or if like a great mountain judge, they watched him now too.

He searched the rest of the site. The camp itself was still intact. Tents were still erected, equipment still in place. But there were two things missing.

First, the radar system was gone. Why would they take that? Did the attackers want to reuse it? Or they were hiding something?

And second… there was no sign of the bodies of Kat Devier and John Sunday. Were they taken? Were they dropped in that pit?

Conrad crouched next to the hole and looked down into the darkness. Anchor bolts had been hammered into the rock wall, and two severed ropes had been cut and thrown to the side.

So—they had gone down. They had entered the cave. Perhaps they were even down there when the attack came.

Which means maybe they're still *down there.*

He sighed. He was going to have to go down and find out.

* * *

A half hour later, David had re-rigged the lines, grabbed a spare helmet with a lamp, and strapped himself into a harness. As he leaned back, the harness neatly framed his junk, a cupping feeling that reminded him of his days in Marine Recon. He abseiled the shaft, drifting into the dusty darkness as if being swallowed. He tried to look down, to see what was coming from beneath, but saw only black.

Finally he touched down in a baby plume of dust, like Armstrong on the moon.

He was in a small cave. And it was empty.

He was just about to climb back out when he noticed a small opening in one wall. He unhooked from the line, kneeled in front of the hole, and shone his light into the darkness.

There, pinned between the rocks, lay the body of John Sunday.

CHAPTER XVIII

Fifty Miles Outside Pella, Jordan

In the total, absolute darkness of the cave tunnel, John Sunday lay in a cooling pool of his own blood, well aware that his life was slipping away from him. He was unable to move, unable to get his hands and feet to follow his instructions. His head was frozen to the rock, a spongy mass of blood and shattered bone.

Yet he felt a strange alertness here, now, in this time before his death. In a small vestibule within his mind, his entire existence played out in front of his eyes, a movie on fast forward, flicking rapidly from one scene to the next.

He saw his childhood in Florida. He could hear the sway of the Australian pines, their soft needles blowing in the wind. He smelled their pine tart in the field where he played.

He saw himself in school, being teased by the other children, because he grew up poor. Because he lived in a trailer.

He felt the fear of his father's rage as he lumbered down the hallway, shaking that trailer with his weight, as he was bound for Sunday's bedroom to discipline him for some slight.

He watched his mother leave, as he stood in the rain, driving away down the muddy road that would never be paved.

Then he was in the army because he couldn't get away fast enough, get away to another realm of yelling men. Men were always yelling.

He was in Iraq. Entering a house as part of a raid, opening fire as a man reached for his gun. Sunday shot the man down in front of his young son. Then he felt that man's life. His fear, his pain, his love for his family. And Sunday felt a deep sadness for the life he had taken.

The feeling repeated again, for all those he had killed.

And then he came to Kat.

Rolling around in the bed on a weekend. Sipping wine in Egypt, looking out over the pyramids. Asking her to marry him as they stood in their tiny kitchen. He felt her love. The most he'd felt in his life. It blanketed him, bathed him in warm light.

He even saw a scene that he had never seen in real life. He was in the hospital room with her, watching from the corner, as she gave birth. The baby was so small, so tiny, lying on her chest. It was beautiful, because it was theirs. And as she held it, he was gripped by her sorrow, and by her hatred for him that he was not there to comfort her.

That he had *done* this to her.

He felt himself slipping from his cooling body, being peeled from his dead flesh. He saw lights dancing in the darkness, even though he was certain he could no longer physically see. A brief flicker. A circle of rainbows. A light at the end of his tunnel.

But he was also aware of something behind him. Something rancid and rank. Something emerging from the darkness of the cave. He had a childish, primitive fear of letting his toes poke out of the tunnel behind him, lest that unseen creature grab hold of him and drag him into the shadows.

He heard whispers. Whispers about him. He knew this, though they spoke in a language he had never heard. Or languages. The tongues of many, overlapping, talking down to him. Berating him.

Hands gripped his feet, his ankles. Cold, sharp fingers tore into his flesh. In his mind's voice, he cried out in pain as their jagged fingernails pierced skin and latched their hooks into bone.

Whatever was behind him, it was attempting to drag him backward into the cave.

He screamed in pain, but his physical mouth was unable to do more than froth and blow bubbles in a pool of his own cold blood.

He saw more flickering ahead of him. A light. An *actual* light.

Someone's here!

"Please…"

But the sound merely exhaled in a breath.

The light scanned back and forth. The whispers grew louder and then stopped as a face appeared at the end of the narrow tunnel.

A little boy's face. Maybe ten years old. He wore a blue winter jacket and carried a plastic flashlight.

Why is a child down here?

The child reached in and touched Sunday's hand, ever so gently.

Sunday knew this boy. Knew that blue jacket. This was the child from the construction site. The one hit by the car. The child of the dream. The one who had appeared in the fading, who had now returned for the final act.

Am I dead?

"Just stuck," the child answered. He squatted and peered at Sunday like he was an alien lifeform.

Who...

"Your world is ending. Men will devour men in the time of sorrow, and the beasts within shall rise."

The whispers behind Sunday began again in a frenzy at this news.

The child looked deeper into the tunnel, as if he could see past Sunday. He withdrew his hand. "You must pay for your sins."

The whispers grew even louder.

"To serve God, you must be reborn."

Sunday felt the hooks in his flesh tighten, and he was sucked backward, dragged from the tunnel, away from the boy, away from the winter jacket, away from the light... and back into the darkness of the abyss.

CHAPTER XIX

Rome, Italy
41 CE

Longinus looked up at the balcony of the Circus Maximus, where the emperor sat. Gaius Caligula was a tall man with a balding head and protracted appendages, a disproportioned spider with pale-yellow skin. He had a face as long as a goat's, and his eyes stood too far apart on his head. Had he not been emperor, he would likely have been mistaken for a beggar on the street.

Caligula laughed and snorted as he took in the show. An actor had pretended to be murdered, and the stage had been flooded with an absurd amount of animal blood, a gory excess. The comedians on stage slipped and fell in the blood, to the clapping delight of the emperor.

It had taken Longinus much work to get this close. When his face had changed, so had his identity. He still had no idea what had happened to him upon his death, but he had accepted his physical change as a gift from the gods—a gift that would allow him to avenge his wife. He had returned to the Roman army, where his skills with a sword helped him rise quickly through the ranks. All with the goal of getting to this point, this day, this close to the emperor.

Longinus stepped from the theater and took up position in an underground corridor that led from the theater to the palace. He did not fear death. His only concern was that his plot would fail, and he would be unable to get this close to the emperor again.

He turned as three soldiers approached.

"He has decided to stay and watch another show," said one of his co-conspirators, a fellow guard who had lost his father to the emperor's madness. "What do we do?"

"Our plot will be discovered," said Longinus. "We must strike him down now, where he sits."

The others nodded in unison. "We are with you. We shall see this through."

They had just turned back toward the theater when laughter came down the hall. The emperor must have changed his mind once again and decided to leave the theater after all. He was now walking toward them.

Longinus and his co-conspirators stood back respectfully, allowing Caligula and his entourage to pass. The emperor paid Longinus no notice.

As soon as they were past, Longinus drew his sword and stepped quickly toward Caligula from behind.

Caligula turned, a smile still on his face. The smile turned sour as he saw the sword moving toward his gut. "Wait!" he begged weakly. He swatted, ineffectively, at the oncoming sword.

Longinus plunged the blade in deep.

The emperor doubled over, and his entourage—men who had acted as his friends and companions—fled down the hallway. They were no fools; they recognized their path to power had just ended.

As Caligula fell to his knees and then to his side, Longinus and his co-conspirators struck at him with their boots and the butts of their swords. He curled his skinny spider legs into a ball to protect himself.

When the men paused, Caligula looked at them through slits of swollen flesh. His lips were torn, his front teeth knocked out, his nose flat. But he was defiant.

"Is that all you have?" he snorted.

Longinus leaned down and whispered in the emperor's ear.

"I am Longinus Castus," he said as he pulled a coin from his pocket. "You killed my wife. You killed me. But the dead have sent me for you." He held the coin against Caligula's right eye. "This is for Charon." As he pressed the coin through the jelly of Caligula's pupil, the emperor screamed. "Your wife and child will soon join you," Longinus said.

He raised his sword, stuck it through the side of Caligula's neck, and twisted it so quickly that the blade ripped the trachea from the backbone.

The other soldiers echoed the violence, and some sixty strikes later, there was not enough flesh left to hold the emperor together.

Longinus and the other soldiers then stormed the empress's chambers, as promised. He didn't hesitate to hold down Caligula's wife and slice her throat. But when he approached the newborn girl who screamed in her crib, he paused. He lifted her up in his hands, the blood of her mother smearing the child's pale skin like paint, and she stopped crying and stared up at him with wide eyes.

How could this pig have such a beautiful child?

Longinus and his wife had tried for so long, and yet the gods had denied them. Yet here was this beautiful baby, born of such wretched seed.

With all his might he slammed the infant's head against the wall until her skull fell flat beneath his palm.

And behold, a great red dragon having seven heads and ten horns, and on his heads were seven diadems. And his tail swept away a third of the stars of heaven and threw them to the earth. And the dragon stood before the woman who was about to give birth, so that when she gave birth he might devour her child.

Revelation 12:1

CHAPTER XX

Kat's wrists were zip-tied behind her back, and a hood was pulled over her head, but she knew she was in the back of a moving vehicle. She could feel the vibrations, hear the tires on the road.

Fear rose inside her slick as vomit. She'd been taken. Removed. Controlled. She was at the mercy of these men. Faces she could not see. Hands she could not stop. They could do with her as they pleased. Cut her. Rape her. Kill her.

The truck stopped, and a door opened. A man grabbed her, pulled her out, and escorted her into another vehicle. The back of a box truck, perhaps, judging by the darkness. Her ankles were shackled to the floor, using chains already there. Apparently this truck had been used for transporting prisoners before.

They stopped again, and a scattering of light particles drifted like cosmic dust through the fabric of the hood as she was taken into a building, stumbling, guided roughly by two men. She was pressed against a metal wall. The zip ties were cut, and her wrists and ankles were secured by leather restraints built into the wall. They cut away her clothes with scissors, and she felt the points brush her bare skin.

"Please… don't," she cried, but the words fell on deaf ears.

This is it. They're going to rape me.

Her shirt fell away, then her pants. Then her undergarments. She was fully naked except for the hood.

And then her whole body tilted backwards, and she realized she had not been strapped to a wall, but to a metal gurney.

Her hood was removed, and the two men exited.

A bright light blinded her. As her eyes adjusted, she took in her surroundings.

She was in a small white room, underneath a surgical light. Beside her gurney, a tray held sharp metal instruments that glistened like silver snow. She was a butterfly pinned to a board. Waiting to be examined. Or worse. Her breathing was heavy and fast, and her heart pounded.

The door opened, and a man walked in. Asian, balding except for two wild bushy tufts of hair over his ears, in a white lab coat and round glasses. He said nothing as he rolled over a chair and sat between her legs.

"Wait," she said. "Please. I'm an American. I can pay you."

She heard the snap of latex. He pulled an instrument from the tray.

"Please," she begged again. She could feel his breath warming the area between her thighs.

"You move. Hurt." His broken English was as blunt as the probe she felt enter her.

"Please," she sobbed. "Don't."

When he was done, he stood, flicked the gloves into the trash, and left.

She lay there, tears welling, naked and open.

Why are they doing this?

The door again opened, and two guards entered. One pinned her head to the gurney while the other latched some kind of gold circlet around her neck.

"Don't fucking touch me!" she screamed. She was primed now, ready to fight, at least with her words.

The circlet latched, a cold collar tight against her throat.

One of the guards held out a tiny device for her to see. It looked like a key fob for unlocking a car door. With a leer, he pressed one of its buttons.

Kat felt needles emerging from the collar and puncturing her neck. At the same time she was struck by an intense electric charge that felt like a nail gun to the throat. Her entire body spasmed, not under her control, and a stream of urine rolled down the inside of her thigh and pooled beneath her on the gurney.

When the current subsided, her muscles felt like limp rolls of deli meat.

The guards unstrapped her and half-carried her to another room. Here, her head was shaved, strands of long hair falling like petals to her bare feet, and she was hosed clean. The men dressed her in a plain white gown of rough fabric, handed her a set of folded sheets, then led her down a long white hallway of gunmetal-gray doors.

They stopped in front of a door numbered 6718-6719. One of the guards pulled a small tablet from his vest pocket, punched something in, and looked down at the screen. "6719, step back," he barked. For a moment Kat thought he was talking to her. Then she realized he was talking to someone on his tablet.

After a moment, the other guard clicked the radio on his shoulder. "Open 6718."

The door latch clicked, and the guards pushed Kat through. The door slammed behind her and she heard the lock return home.

She was in a cell. Small, concrete, white. The only furnishings were a metal toilet, a tiny washbasin, and two bunks.

And there was a woman in the corner.

She was young, no more than twenty, with light sepia skin and short black hair. She wore a white gown like Kat's and had the same kind of collar around her neck.

"Where am I?" Kat asked.

"The Way Station," the woman said.

CHAPTER XXI

Amman, Jordan

Sasha arrived to work at Queen Alia Military Hospital on a Tuesday morning, and before she could even put her purse down at the nurse's station, the lieutenant colonel called her into his office.

She stood in front of his desk, worried she had somehow made a mistake and her boss was about to begin the barking for which he was known. Instead, Lieutenant Colonel Asnar Mubak spoke calmly, but with a matter-of-fact tone that conveyed this was not up for discussion.

"What I tell you must remain in the strictest confidence," he said in Arabic.

She nodded.

"We are moving the patient in room seven to a bunker in an undisclosed location," Mubak said. "You, and you alone, are going with him. Your personal belongings and all necessary supplies will be awaiting you there. You will have access to everything you need to care for the patient."

As a member of the Royal Medical Services of Jordan, Lieutenant Sasha Bahar was prepared to perform whatever duties were requested of her. But this was an unusual order. Most unusual.

Then again, there had been nothing "usual" about the patient in room seven since the day he had been brought into the ICU.

Sasha's mind was flooded with questions. Why? How was she supposed to care for this patient by herself? What kind of support system would she have if there were problems? But despite her concerns, she simply nodded in agreement, because of what her boss said next.

"You will receive a bonus at the end of each month. Twenty percent your annual salary."

She asked only one question. "Why me?"

"Because, Lieutenant, you are a dedicated nurse, you have no family, no restrictions that should prevent you from performing your duties. You do not go out with the others on weekends, and you seem content in your isolation. So it seems we have a fit."

Sasha couldn't tell if she'd been complimented or insulted. But the lieutenant colonel was right. She didn't have anyone. She did once, but not anymore. Now she fluttered through her daily routine, a leaf falling from a mountaintop tree. She had her flat, and her books, and she'd considered getting a cat. She preferred dogs, but cats could take care of themselves, and she was gone so much...

After being dismissed, she made her way to room seven, to look in on the man who had just upended her life. The patient lay in bed, his eyes closed. Half of his face was gone, hidden behind thick gauze and bandages. His breathing tube had been removed a week earlier, and his mouth hung open like he was gasping for air. And he was white, which was itself unusual—not a lot of white patients found themselves in Queen Alia Hospital. If they were American, they flew on to Germany before heading back to the States.

He had been the talk of the floor when he emerged from a month-long coma, but he had quickly returned to his mental fog. His so-called awakening had certainly been dramatic, however, thanks to his blood-curdling scream. It was an intense, guttural yell, as if he were being burned alive. Even Sasha had heard it from far down the hall.

The duty nurse later told her that the man's right eye had popped wide open while she was dressing the surgical wounds on the left side of his face, and it nearly gave her a heart attack. He then flailed in the bed like he was riding an electric current, and it took several nurses to restrain him.

Sasha looked at him now as he rested. She wondered what he had seen in the depths of his mind—what past trauma he had relived. Was he seeing that moment again now, playing out over and over again? Or had he moved past that, and now stood before the gates of Jannah, begging for them to let him in? Perhaps his scream had come from the scorching winds of Jahannam, where he paid for past sins. She'd see his many scars from old gunshot wounds.

She stepped into the room, came close, and touched his hand. Perhaps if she cared for this man, then someone, or something, would do the same for her lost love. For Yusef. If she was good in this world, Yusef's sins might be forgiven, and he would be there with her in the afterlife. For how could she be expected to spend eternity in paradise without her most beloved?

"Can you hear me?" she asked. Her tongue struggled with some of the tartness of English, especially the letters 'p' and 't'.

He didn't answer.

"Can you squeeze my hand?"

Again, nothing.

"You and I are going to be spending a lot of time together," she whispered.

This ward was full of coma patients. Some of those comas were medically induced, to cut down on the amount of swelling and stress on the brain, while others were the result of stroke or trauma. Almost everyone had someone—family, friends, someone who would come in and talk with them. Show them pictures they could not see. Remind them of memories they could not remember. But this man had no one. No one was here to walk with him down this path. He was like an astronaut, disconnected from the umbilical of his ship, drifting farther and farther into the eternity. Lost in his mind, lost to the world.

She squeezed his hand one last time—and to her shock, his right eye opened.

He stared at her. No, he stared *through* her. At something behind her. And then he jerked and flinched, his mouth wide, and he wheezed out a hoarse scream.

She turned around, half expecting someone to be standing over her shoulder. But there was no one.

No one *she* could see, anyway.

He exhaled one long gasp of air, his frayed vocal cords fluttering in bursts of sound and silence. Finally, his eye closed, and he returned to whatever place now claimed him.

CHAPTER XXII

Near Belevi
54 CE

Even at night, the heat was sweltering.

Longinus sat on a wooden stool in the front room of a dried mud home on the eastern side of the city. The fire burning in the hearth cast long shadows, flickering fingers that danced across the faces of the six men crammed into the space. At their center, a man in his eighties rested on a cot, his long gray beard clumped with dried spit, his eyes crusted with cataracts. The acid of his breath hung thick in the air, like the smell of wet metals in a quarry.

"May Yahweh smite you with a mighty blow in order to destroy you," said the priest who stood over the dying man. "And in his fierce wrath may he send against you a powerful angel to carry out his entire command, an angel who will show you no mercy, who will send you down into the great abyss and to deepest Sheol, and there you shall lie in darkness."

Longinus wondered if any of this theater would bring him closer to answers.

After the murder of Caligula, Longinus had begun life anew. Every death meant new life. He had fled, but the emperor's Germanic bodyguards had hunted him down, along with his co-conspirators, presumed co-conspirators, and uninvolved political enemies, and killed them all. This time Longinus was killed in his sleep as he hid in a grain warehouse. When he woke again, in a trash-filled pit outside Esquiline Hill, his face and body had once again changed, except for the scars that marked his wounds. And once again, he re-membered nothing of what had happened during his death. Only blackness.

In the several years that followed, he struggled to survive. He had no family, no history, and no name, which made things difficult. At one point he even joined the ranks of the crippled outside the gates to beg. And then, in suffering, and drunk on stolen wine, he took his own life. He fell upon a sword, and his limbs grew ice cold as he bled out in the street. He plunged into the darkness.

Three days later he awoke again, abandoned by death.

Will this be my plight forever?

He had heard of the cult that had risen up around the Jewish prisoner he had executed on the crucifix so many years ago. There were rumors that the man had somehow defied death. That he had indeed died, but had then returned from the dead before being grant-ed final entrance into the Elysian Fields. Longinus had seen the man dead with his own eyes, but he won-dered... could that Jew return from the dead, like him?

Now he watched as the head priest and his sons prayed over the old man who seemed all but dead already. The high priest wore white robes tinged in gold, and a large white turban that made his head look absurdly small. He chanted and bobbed like a bird pecking for grain.

"In the name of Yeshua, whom Paul preaches, I command you to come out!"

That particular phrase must have jarred something loose in the old man's head, for he suddenly shot up in bed as if he'd been pulled upright with a cord He lurched to his feet and grabbed the high priest by the front of his golden robes.

Longinus leaned forward. Finally, something interesting.

The old man pulled the priest in and spoke in a coarse whisper. "We know Yeshua and Paul," he said, "but who are you?" His voice sounded like many.

"I am Sceva, the high priest of the Zadokites."

"You are no thing," the old man hissed.

With impossible speed and strength, the old man flung the priest onto the bed and wailed on him with his fists, blow after blow, until the priest's face cracked like mud flakes in a sun-baked puddle.

The priest's sons tried to peel the old man off, but he pushed them back with ease. With his eighty-year-old bones and hanging flesh, he grabbed one man by the jaw and twisted quickly, pulling the bone away from the skull.

Another of the sons tried to flee. The old man jumped onto his back and twisted the man's head backwards with such force that Longinus almost expected it to come off completely in his hands.

Longinus pulled his sword and stood, and the old man turned in his direction. He moved forward slowly, sniffing the air like a dog, smiling a wide toothless grin.

"Longinus?" the old man said. But his voice was that of a woman. A woman Longinus could never forget.

"Licinia?"

"I see you through these eyes," the old man said in her voice, though his eyes were blind and clouded.

"How can this be?" Longinus asked.

The old man began to sob. "They keep me here," he said. "Help me! Find the key to the gates and bring my freedom. Both are kept hidden from us. Seek the followers of Yeshua from Nazareth." Tears rolled down his cheeks. "Please! I suffer so."

One of the surviving sons of the high priest raised a sword and struck from behind. His blade pierced the old man's neck and emerged on the other side.

"No!" Longinus yelled. The old man sputtered blood and fell to his knees, and Longinus caught the man in his arms. "Liciana!"

The old man only choked on a mouthful of blood.

The centurion laid him down and watched as he bled out on the floor. He was no longer Licinia. He was but a man now. Or the remnants of one.

CHAPTER XXIII

Rome, Italy
Present Day

The straight razor traced Silas Egin's face, the shaving cream peeling away in scoops of soapy molt, his face slowly revealing itself in the steamed edges of the mirror. He was grateful for the hot shower, grateful to God, who had chosen to direct his path, to oversee the slaughter of the heretics, and who had placed his followers in search of the one who must come.

Still, there'd been one problem in the desert. A loose end that needed to be found and cut.

In time. In time.

He patted his jaw and cheeks with a soft cotton towel and looked upon his face. His eyes were green like his mother's, a mother he'd never known, one destroyed after his birth, her mission complete. He wondered what would happen to his eyes after he died. Would everything just rot in the ground, the larvae of the earth feeding upon his pupils, or was there something more?

He pressed the straight razor firm against his throat and held it there until it drew blood. If he slit all the way, bone deep, what would he see?

He blotted the blood, then tied the towel around his waist and adjusted it. He stepped out of the bathroom, his skin clean from the desert, and there she was. Naked on the bed, reclined like Venus of Urbino. Ah. Ayelet. She was beautiful, her body crafted for pleasure, for attention.

And yet her allure was not in her flesh; it was in her secret. She was a Jew pretending to be a Catholic. Pretending so she could get close to him. And he *knew*. Which made fucking her so much more pleasurable. She was a whore, and he would make sure that when the One returned, her sins would be exposed and she would suffer.

Until then he would take pleasure from all parts of her. She was a whore. It was her duty.

She smiled up at him longingly, an actress playing her role. He smiled back, an actor reciprocating. In that moment, he felt the urge to ditch their ruse, go to the closet where he kept his toolbox, and take out the flagrum. He would whip her on the silk sheets with the metal-pronged tassels until chunks of her beautiful flesh fell onto the bed like blood petals.

She pursed her lips, indicating she was ready for him. He let the towel drop, then climbed onto her, trying to convince himself that he needed this woman alive, although it was the mental image of her split and splayed, her blood upon the sheets, that had hardened his cock.

* * *

Ayelet watched as Egin stepped back into the bedroom wearing nothing but a towel. He was darkly handsome, his jaw strong, his body chiseled. To any other woman, he would have been a fine catch. Fit. Sophisticated. Educated. Wealthy.

But beneath the fancy suits and refined manners lurked something sinister.

And Ayelet couldn't shake the feeling that he knew. Knew who she really was. That he was toying with her. And that, when the time came, he would kill her. Even with her security team down the hall. She'd be dead long before they got to her.

She had been seeing him now for two months. She had his phones tapped, his computers hacked, his movements followed. Yet he was like a ghost, able to disappear whenever he wanted. He could ditch their tails, as if he knew where they were, and she worried that he did. He was always a step ahead.

For the last week and a half now, he'd been gone, and no one knew where.

He let his towel drop. He was hard. Ready for her.

She prepped the little girl who lived in her heart. She returned that child to the room of her mind, to the place locked away, and lay back on the bed to accept this man.

He climbed on top of her and kissed her neck, his breath hot upon her flesh, and he whispered in her ear.

"I know who you are," he said. He full weight was on her, and his hands curled around her wrists.

She looked up at him, feeling the entirety of their nakedness, his hardness, her vulnerability.

"Who?" she said, acting coy.

He spread her legs with a nudge of his knees. She couldn't be wet, could she? Not as her stomach was doing somersaults. She brought her knees to the outside of him, in preparation to pull guard, to control him if she had to.

He smiled as he slid himself into her. A smile of a man who knew something she did not.

"An angel," he said. "My angel."

CHAPTER XXIV

Somewhere in Jordan

She changed his diaper. Washed him. Shaved him. Applied lotion to his body, carefully massaging around his many scars, cratered reminders of stolen flesh.

On his back was a tattoo. The names of twelve men ran down his spine.

Brothers in arms? Men who died?

His name was John. That was all Sasha had been told.

Together now. The two of us.

She didn't even know exactly where they were. A subterranean bunker, somewhere on the border between Israel and Jordan. The electricity, piped in from the building above, only fed the essential sections, so there were dark corridors, flickering lights, and a chill that had no place in the desert.

You had a rough night. But you're safe now. I'm here.

John was a screamer. His horrible, gut-wrenching cries routinely yanked her from bed in the middle of the night. She would run across the hall, from her room to his, and soothe him as best she could. But John wasn't there. He didn't hear her. Not truly. He was still trapped in some far-off place, his mind locked tight in its bone box. He was in and out, a drowning man who could only surface momentarily before disappearing once more beneath the black deep.

He was alive, but not aware. Agitated. Confused. When she fed him, the food would try to slip back out, and she would have to use her spoon to bring it home again.

The massages helped. A gentle touch, and eventually he would drift back to some distant island, the black waters lapping at the shore.

Such were their days. And their nights.

Occasionally she would venture to the surface to gaze at the pink sky and the setting sun. Then she would return to the darkness, alone with him.

It had been a long time since she had been alone with a man.

Two years. Two years since Yusef.

She still replayed the phone call in her mind. He had been crossing the street. She heard it all. The squeal of brakes. The crunching thud. Then the whisper, his last.

"Lays ladayhim euyun."

They have no eyes.

Not *I love you.* Not her name. Not even a call to Allah. Sasha had had to go to a shrink for three months because he'd said that.

She worked the lotion into John's arms. His muscles were smaller each day, as if being eaten. Her fingers caressed him. Enjoyed the feel of him.

What are you doing?

It was those cursed romance novels. The ones she read in her room alone at night. She was addicted to their words, their pulp that conjured a simmering heat in her mind.

She paused with the lotion. Tried to regain herself, fetch the clinical.

What was she thinking she was going to do, anyway? Massage him until he hardened? Ride him here in the dark?

He's clean. I cleaned him. He'd respond...

It was a terrible thought. He was like a baby. She was like his mother. She was here to care for him. Besides, he wasn't even here.

She resumed massaging. She rubbed the lotion down into his right hand, across his fingertips.

His eyes opened.

His head was turned to the side, and he stared at the wall as if expecting someone to step through the lime-green tiles. He always stared like that. Seeing something, someone, that wasn't there. Just like he himself wasn't there.

He began to stir. Something was drawing him back to the surface. He squeezed her hand, and the lotion slid and slurped between their fingers.

His eyes found her, but didn't see her. His look was distant. Vacant.

"Yusef," he said.

She dropped his hand in shock. "What?"

There was nothing more.

"What did you say?"

She grabbed his hand once more, firmer than she should have. "What did you say?"

His eyes closed. He was gone again.

Did he say "Yusef"? No. He couldn't have. I've never said Yusef's name around him. He doesn't know Yusef. He must have slurred something and I lost it in translation.

But as she uncurled from his grip, she wasn't certain.

She rose from his side. Went back to her room. Sat on the bed.

Do you see me, Yusef? Did you hear my dirty little thoughts? Are you watching me?

And she began to cry.

CHAPTER XXV

Kat woke to the sound of a little girl singing. But she wasn't actually there. The voice came through a speaker in the ceiling of the cell.

"*Abwoon d'bwashmaya,*" sang the child. "*Nethqadash shmakh. Teytey malkuthakh.*"

Kat knew the words. They were Aramaic. The Lord's Prayer.

The lights flickered to life, and even over the song, she could hear the sizzle in the fluorescents.

Her cellmate, Mara, rose to her feet and squatted on the toilet. Kat turned her head to give her some privacy.

"You must wake," Mara said. Her English was accented. "They come."

Wearily, Kat sat on the side of her bed.

Mara pulled her white gown up and over the collar around her neck, exposing her ungroomed body, and swatted talcum on her armpits. She switched the gown for another identical one, both stitched with "6719-M," then quickly brushed her teeth and kneeled beside Kat's bed. "The Grigori," she said. She gestured to the ceiling with her eyes.

Kat had seen the black globe in the ceiling yesterday when she arrived, and she already knew what it was. A camera. But the girl, Mara, had told her little about their captors.

Grigori? That was the name for the eighth order of angels. The Watchers.

"The morning ritual," Mara said. "Please."

Kat took her turn squatting on the toilet. *Fucking morning ritual? Seriously?*

As Mara mouthed a silent prayer, Kat wondered what would happen if she didn't follow the rules. She rubbed the collar on her neck, searching for a latch, but there was only solid metal. At least the prongs that had punctured her neck had retreated into the collar. It seemed they would only appear when she needed to be controlled.

What if I run? What's the distance on this thing?

Even if she were to escape this room, or this entire facility, she had no idea where she was.

When she rose from the toilet, she followed Mara's lead by haphazardly swatting some talcum powder beneath her armpits. She didn't have a second gown to change into, so she just kneeled beside Mara to pray. Or pretend to.

"Your teeth," Mara said, opening her mouth wide to show hers.

Kat rolled her eyes, but she rose and brushed at the small basin, using the toothbrush that she'd found on her bed when she arrived. Then she again kneeled to pray.

A minute later, the door clicked and opened. There was no one there. *It must be controlled by remote.*

Mara gestured for Kat to follow, and the two women stepped out of the cell.

The doors all up and down the hall were open, and at least forty other girls and young women had already emerged. Dark-skinned Africans, Middle-Easterners, Asians, pale Europeans. All had mostly shaved heads. All wore white gowns and gold metal collars. They stood two by two, like they were waiting to board an ark.

Kat stayed at Mara's side as they followed the others through the corridors. Apparently this was part of the "morning ritual," too.

They arrived at an open dining room with cafeteria tables and bench seating. At one end of the hall was a low stage, where a large cross bearing a wooden Jesus was affixed to the wall.

Without a word spoken, the women entered a serving line. Kat expected stale bread and dirty water, but instead there was oatmeal, fresh fruits, and Greek yogurt. She grabbed a bowl of oatmeal and looked around the dining hall for a place to sit. All of the other girls seemed to know their places and went directly to them. At one table, all of the women were pregnant.

"Come," Mara said, guiding Kat to a different table.

As soon as they were seated, Kat picked up her spoon, but Mara quickly clutched her wrist and shook her head.

"Wait," she said. "For Grand Mother."

A few moments later, an elderly nun in a black habit hobbled onto the stage. Six other nuns followed in similar garb, each carrying a crooked rod like a shepherd would use for his flock.

The elderly woman stepped to a microphone and cleared her throat.

"Good morning, children," she said. The mic crackled.

"Good morning, Grand Mother," the girls answered in unison.

The woman looked out across the crowd, her eyes like cold stones. Around her neck dangled a wooden crucifix with a golden Jesus upon it.

"I had hoped to begin the morning with Ecclesiastes. But…" She trailed off as if disappointed. Then she straightened up, rekindling. "There is one among you… who—is—empty!" she shouted, punctuating each word.

The girls seemed to shrink into their seats. The nuns with the twisted staves stepped down from the stage and paced the aisles.

"One who is unable to ripen! As rotten as the fruit on the lips of Eve!"

The six nuns tapped their staves hard on the concrete floor as they passed by each girl.

"Do you think the Grigori do not know? Do you think God does not know? Do you think *I* do not know?"

One of the nuns slowed as she passed Kat. Kat began to turn around, but Mara squeezed her wrist for her to stay still.

Another nun grabbed a young woman sitting at Kat's table and dragged her to the floor. The rest of the nuns gathered, circled the poor girl like hyenas, the tapping of their rods increasing in speed.

"Please!" the girl screamed, curling into a ball. "I'll try again!"

Grand Mother revealed a remote like the one the guard had used on Kat. She raised it skyward as if it were a crucifix to ward off vampires.

"Please!" the young woman screamed over the frantic tapping.

Grand Mother pushed the button.

The girl's collar pulsed and crackled. Blue bolts danced around the ring. The poor girl's eyes rolled back in her head, her fists clenched, and she convulsed like a fish on a spear. Her face and flesh turned bright red, her skin stretched tight, and the room was filled with a sizzling sound, like bacon in the pan. The smell of burning meat filled the air.

"Do you see?" Grand Mother shouted into the microphone. "Do you see what happens when your field is barren? When your temple is broken? *So—is— your—crown!*"

As if on cue, the young woman's hair burst into flames. Her skin sizzled and popped, and the fire engulfed her entire head. Her skin turned black, her blood and brain boiling.

When she was dead, the tapping stopped, and the room fell silent. The nuns left the burnt woman where she was and rejoined Grand Mother on the stage.

"Now she burns in Hell. Now, even God does not want her." Grand Mother scanned the room. "You are the carriers of the way!"

"THE WAY!" shouted the women.

With a nod, Grand Mother turned and walked out of the room.

Immediately, the rest of the girls began to eat, as if unaware of the woman on the floor, her skull black as ash, her putrid smell clogging the air.

Kat couldn't do the same.

* * *

After the meal, as they lined up to leave, one of the nuns approached Kat. She was a large woman, with a solid fifty pounds and six inches on Kat.

"6718," she barked in a heavy Eastern European accent.

"Me?" Kat answered as she checked the number again on her gown.

"Come," the woman said.

Mara nodded for Kat to go.

Shit.

The nun escorted Kat down a long white corridor. Her heart pounded in her throat. They stopped at a metal door, the latch clicked, and it opened automatically. Kat stepped inside.

It was a small room, furnished only with a worn, red-upholstered swivel chair and a flat-screen television. The nun gestured with her staff for Kat to sit, then navigated through a language guide on the TV. She clicked on "English (American)."

The lights dimmed, and a man with closely cropped gray hair appeared on screen. He had large shoulders and hands, like he'd spent a lifetime fishing or farming. His face was caked in makeup, as if covering the wrinkled scratches of time. She had seen him before. This was the scarred man from the dig site—the one she'd seen opening the clay jar.

"Welcome," he said, his voice heavy and deep. "You are no doubt wondering why you are here. What is your purpose."

A woman in a white linen gown stepped onto the screen and handed the man a bundled, sleeping baby. He took the child in his hands and held it up to the screen like he was about to sell it.

"Life. If your womb is fertile, you will become a host—a provider. You will help grow the seeds that I give you. With my seed, you shall have a piece of Jesus Christ inside of you. You shall birth the way."

What?

The woman on screen whispered beneath her breath. "The way." The nun standing behind Kat echoed the same.

Is this guy for real? What is this? Some kind of cult?

The man handed the infant back to the woman, and she disappeared off screen. The man turned to a different camera, and this time his face filled the screen. The whole video played like a bad late-night infomercial from 1986.

"And who am I to make such a boast?" He smiled, like he knew something the viewer did not. "I am many. I am one."

The screen switched to an overhead view of a different man, a very old man, bound to a gurney in a hospital suite. It was an old, grainy video. A doctor pressed a bone saw against the man's throat and began to tear through the flesh. Kat had to avert her eyes as the saw's whirring filled the room and blood splattered across the doctor's gown. The doctor didn't stop until he had sawed most of the way through the man's neck, leaving only a flap of hanging skin to keep the head attached.

The first man spoke, a voiceover. "I have lived a thousand lives. Died a thousand ways. But the blood of the Christ is my blood."

The video proceeded rapidly, in time-lapse. The dead man lay on the gurney, and a web of white gelatin formed on his face and neck. It encapsulated him in a milky-white cocoon, forming a netting between the decapitated head and neck. The web pulled the head back toward the rest of the body and reattached it. Beneath the mask of fibrous white spindles, the dead man's face twitched ever so slightly. And then he sat up on the gurney, his face still covered in the white gelatin.

"When I die, I too shall wake after three days."

The man on screen wiped the gunk from his face, revealing that he had become the man from the start of the video, except younger.

Am I supposed to believe this?

The camera returned to the tight shot of the first man's face.

"I am the carrier of the way. Within me is the seed of the Christ. And soon it shall be within you."

The screen froze on his smiling face. The TV went black, and the lights in the room returned.

Kat didn't know how to react to what she'd just seen. Was that it? Some entire cult was based on a grainy video of cheap special effects? Were these people serious?

"Come," the nun said.

"Where?" Kat asked.

The woman smiled. "You are M-class." As if that was an answer.

"What does that mean?"

The woman smiled again, proudly.

"Mother."

* * *

It was hours later when Kat was finally, mercifully escorted back to her cell. She immediately collapsed in front of the toilet and vomited.

Mara rose from her bunk, where she had been reading a Bible, and wet a washcloth in the washbasin. "You'll get used to the shots," she said, dabbing Kat's forehead with the cool cloth.

Kat turned to her. "Are you pregnant?"

"They started me on the shots last week. I pray for it."

Kat took a breath. This girl bought into all this?

"Why?" Kat asked.

"With life, you live. Without it, you don't."

That was a fair assessment of the situation.

"How long have you been here?" Kat asked.

"About four months, I think."

"Where are you from? How did you end up here?"

"I lived near the Khabur River. Al Tariqa traded me, and I was brought here. Top dollar because I am a virgin. Some girls were raped many times. Not me. I come here."

This girl was smart, and her English was impressive. Kat wondered if she could be an ally—if they could do this together.

"We have to get out of here," Kat whispered.

Mara pulled away, her face turning as white as her gown. She looked up at the black orb in the ceiling and slowly shook her head.

Kat felt the prongs in her collar jab into her neck. "No!" she shouted, scratching frantically at the collar.

Mara quickly grabbed her Bible. "Bite!" she instructed, jamming the book's pages into Kat's mouth.

The powerful current coursed through Kat's body, and she seized, her teeth clenching around the holy pages. She could almost taste the ink of the word on her tongue.

CHAPTER XXVI

Washington, DC
Thirteen Months Earlier

Tom Ferguson stepped into a sleek, spacious lobby with a white-marbled floor. At the front desk, an attractive young woman with black hair worked at a computer.

"My name is Ferguson," he said. "Tom Ferguson. I was told to ask for a Mr. Belac."

The woman, who was just as sleek as the marbled lobby, stopped typing and looked up, smiling like a plastic doll. "Of course." She picked up the phone. "Mr. Ferguson is here."

With a nod, she hung up, then gestured toward a white leather couch. "Please," she said.

Tom sat and waited.

This morning, he'd dialed the number on the business card the man had left for him in the hospital chapel. He didn't for a second believe what the man was saying, but he had to know more. An unidentified voice on the other end of the line told him to come to this address. Alone. The voice assured him that if the CIA or FBI were told anything, anything at all, his daughter would be lost forever.

Yes, these people were definitely full of shit. This was probably some Russian plot designed to get him to give up state secrets, turn traitor. Perhaps these people were even the ones driving the tow truck that had killed his daughter. All the more reason to play along. See where this thing led. See who these people really were. He had everything to gain, and nothing to lose.

He'd already lost everything.

The elevator doors opened, and a middle-aged woman stepped out. She wore a sharp black business suit, and her blond hair was up in a tight bun. As she approached Tom, her heels tapped against the stone floor like Morse code in a marbled tomb.

"Mr. Ferguson," she said. "Thank you for coming."

He stood to shake her hand. "My daughter is here?"

"She is. Please…" She gestured to the elevator.

Bullshit, he thought. He knew where his daughter was. In the hospital morgue. He hadn't even picked a funeral home yet.

They took the elevator to the twelfth floor, and the woman led Tom down a corridor. Along the way, they passed a large window looking into a laboratory where men and women in white lab coats were working.

"What do you do here?" Tom asked.

"A little bit of everything. Mr. Belac has many interests."

A non-answer if ever there was one.

"Here we are," she said, stopping at a pair of wide double doors, like the ones in an emergency room. "Mr. Belac will be with you in a moment. Go in and have a seat."

She pushed one of the doors open, and Tom stepped through. The door closed behind him, and he heard the woman's heels clicking away, back down the corridor.

He was in a dim medical lab full of tables, tools, and equipment. But he noticed none of it. He had eyes only for the figure lying on an examination table at the center of the room.

Sara.

Her body was draped in a white sheet. Her curly brown hair framed her bloated, pale face. She smelled of slight rot, even over the sterile smells of the room. He couldn't believe they had brought her here without his permission. He couldn't believe he was looking at her in this state. He couldn't yet believe that his daughter was dead.

He touched her fingers. They were cold. Her little fingernails, bitten to the quick—a bad habit she had picked up after her mother's death—were pooled with dead black blood.

Tears choked his throat and welled up in his eyes. He wept for the baby that was, and the woman that would never be.

"It is temporary," said a voice from the shadows.

Tom wiped his eyes and looked in the direction of the voice. A man in a black suit was sitting in a chair in the corner. The light was too dim for Tom to make out his features.

"Who are you?"

"My name, for now, is Belac. I know what you're thinking, Tom. That these people are lying. That it is wrong for us to bring your daughter into this. But what

I offer you is real. Look at her, Tom. I promise you. She will rise again from that table."

He realized then he was still holding her hand. He looked down at her, and the fantasy of the man's offer carried him.

"How?" he asked through the lump in his throat.

The man in the suit leaned forward.

"There is a way. But you must have the key."

The man rose from his seat and stepped into the light.

Tom had to withhold a gasp. Belac's face was stitched together with a multitude of scars, like the thread on a dead man's lips. Not just his face, but his entire scalp. Bare wisps of gray hair struggled to grow in between the collagen rows.

"I shall awaken her, bring her back to you," Belac said, exhaling deeply. "And then you shall witness the power of the Lord. I will show you the way, and you shall become a man humbled to do what is asked of you."

"Asked of me?"

"We will get to that. First, let me show you that I am a man of my word."

Tom looked down at his daughter. Her skin was as white as the surface of the moon. Slowly, he nodded.

"Good, then let us begin."

A doctor in a white medical coat stepped into the room, and fluorescent lights flickered to life overhead. Belac took off his jacket, rolled up one sleeve, and lay down on a second gurney. The doctor inserted a needle into Belac's arm, and his blood coursed and curled like a thick crimson river through the plastic tubing and into an IV bag.

When the doctor was done, Belac rolled down his sleeve and stood over Sara. "This is my body," he said as he touched her cold forehead. "Take this in remembrance of me."

He turned back toward Tom with a slight smile and a nod, as if the chore was done. "We'll be in touch." And then he walked out the door, leaving Tom alone with the doctor.

The doctor hung up the IV with Belac's blood, attached a fresh tube, then inserted a needle into Sara's arm. Rigor had already set in, and he had to push the needle to get it to break the skin. Seconds later, the blood from Belac flowed into her dead veins.

Nothing happened.

"Did it work?" Tom asked.

"Three days," the doctor said.

"What?"

"The process takes three days," answered the doctor as he continued to work.

"Why?"

"That's just how long it takes for the body to regenerate. And when she wakes, she won't look like your daughter."

"She won't—what do you mean?" So this was a scam after all. They'd simply bring in another girl and claim they had revived his Sara.

The doctor read the suspicion on his face. "She *will* be your daughter. The neurons can be woken, and she will have all her memories, every bit of her personality. But the other cells in her body have to start over.

Mitosis, cellular division, all over again. That leads to genetic fluctuations. Maybe she'll be a redhead. Or three inches taller. Whatever genetic dice she rolls."

He checked the IV again and watched the blood flowing. "A bed has been made for you here." He nodded to a cot in the corner. "We encourage you to stay and watch. I promise, what you see will be a miracle."

CHAPTER XXVII

John Sunday's mind slowly surfaced as if from a marshy bog. His eyes were still closed, but he felt them. Felt them pulling at his skin.

In his mind's eye, he saw his torso ripped open, a split melon of organs and entrails. Human-like creatures kneeled like repentant monks over his open gut, chewing on the flaps of flesh, feasting on the juicier bits within. Their eyes were black holes and their skin was pale and flayed. They slurped at his open abdomen like horses at a trough.

And then his eyes opened, and he found himself in a darkened room.

"Hello?" he tried to call out, but couldn't speak. He tried to move, but found that his hands were bound to whatever surface he lay on.

He pulled, tried to break free. His arms felt heavy, like he was underwater. But after some minutes of exhausted yanking, he managed to wriggle one hand free. He put a hand to his face. His skull was wrapped in bandages.

"Hello?" he called. He formed the word this time, but it was no more than a whisper, his throat raw and hoarse.

A door opened, and shoes shuffled across the floor. He was not alone.

"Who's there?" Sunday asked. Again, his voice was faint.

"You're safe." A woman, with a slight Arabic accent.

"Where are we?"

"A safe place. Here, drink this." He felt a straw on his lips. "Slowly."

He drank. The water soothed his throat.

"Do you remember my name?" she asked.

"No."

"Sasha. I'm a nurse."

"Why were my hands tied?"

"To prevent you from hurting yourself. I'm going to touch you now, okay?"

She unfurled the bandages from around his head like unwrapping a gauze present. As the last of the bandages came off his eyes, he blinked in the sudden brightness. But only one eye could see—his right. The left eye, even now uncovered, remained blind.

A hospital bed. Medical equipment. Darker than a hospital. No windows.

It's cold...

He looked to the woman who had given him the drink. She looked to be in her thirties, olive skin, dark black hair. Squat and strong, in dark-blue nurse scrubs.

"Do you remember what happened?" she asked.

"I… I was shot."

"That's right. Good. Very good."

"What's wrong with my eye?"

"Do you know your name?"

"John. Sunday."

"Yes. John, we need to move slowly. There's a lot to take in."

"What's wrong with my eye?" he repeated. "Why can't I see?"

"You've lost your left eye," she said gently.

He reached his free hand to the left side of his face and explored with his fingertips. A tattered line of suture scars crossed his cheek just beneath a concave, sealed eyehole.

"The bullet hit your cheek," she said, gesturing to her own face as a reference map. "The impact shattered the orbital bone, rupturing the eye. The bullet traveled below the brain and exited the back of your neck, causing swelling near the base of your brain stem. You were lucky: a millimeter to the left, and your spinal cord would have been severed. The left side of your face is pretty much one big titanium plate."

My eye is gone.

Sunday's brain was slow to process the information, like she was speaking another language and he was losing details in translation.

"Where are we?" he asked again.

"A bunker. Near the border."

"Why aren't I at Landstuhl? Or the States?"

"I don't know. I was just told to take care of you."

"How long have I been here?"

"You were in a coma for a month, then in and out of partial consciousness for seventeen weeks."

He tried to do the math. His brain felt full of stuffing.

Seventeen, four. Twenty-one weeks. How many months is that?

Five.

Five months!

"Kat!" he said in a rasp, suddenly remembering the tunnel. "Where's Kat?"

"I don't know who that is. I'm sorry."

Sunday sank back into the hospital bed. Five months. He'd been gone five months.

He felt himself fading again, like the bed was leeching vitamins from his bones.

With a burst of effort, he sat back up. "I have to go," he said. With his free hand he fumbled to release the strap binding his other wrist. "I have to—"

"You have to take it easy," the nurse said, in almost a whisper. "Even if you get out of bed, you don't have the muscle strength to walk to the door."

But she helped him release the strap, and even assisted when he tried to pull back the covers. The blanket felt as heavy as an elephant's ear.

Then he saw his legs.

No. Those can't be mine.

These legs were weak, emaciated, as if belonging to a ninety-year-old man. He tried to move them, but they felt like two dead fish attached to his hips.

"Please don't try to stand. The muscles that remain won't support your weight. You'll fall, and your bones are fragile. You'll end up stuck here with me for even longer."

He sank back into the bed, already feeling broken. Defeated.

"I have to…" he said, his voice cracking. He was so sleepy.

He looked to the wall, with its cracked tiles. And he saw them in the web of black darkness. They were there. Waiting all along.

They stepped from the shadows, these sickly pale lepers, their legs bent forward at the knee, their feet twisted into calcified bone hooves, their toes bound like the petals of a Chinese lotus. Their flesh dangled in flaps, like drowning victims who had just washed ashore, and their eyes had been gouged out. But somehow they could still see, their vision beyond sight. They had been observing him, like hungry children with faces pressed against the glass of a restaurant window, and now they came.

He kicked and flailed in the bed, trying to retreat, but they locked down upon his ankles, their yellow nails curved like sickles and slicing like razors.

The nurse tried to console him, to comfort him. But she couldn't see them. She didn't know. Her soothing voice meant nothing.

And the creatures weren't the worst of it.

Beyond these things that scratched at his skin, deep in the dark corridor that had opened in the green-tiled wall, there was something… else. A whisper, the sound of the beast, the creature that had called to him in wake or dream.

It demanded his return.

They pulled him off the bed and dragged him into the wall, and the lime-green tiles closed behind him.

He screamed.

He was theirs once again.

CHAPTER XXVIII

Ephesus
54 CE

The city was grand, a bustling metropolis rising from the harbor, weighed down only by the oppressive heat. Longinus wiped his brow with a cloth as he made his way through the commercial agora section, navigating a narrow street where vendors barked as they sold their wares. Smoke from fried locusts and steaming fish veiled the air. To the east of a large water clock were the stone storefronts where Longinus was headed.

Longinus had sought out the wrong Jewish priests. The Zadokite had promised to prove his footing with his god, but given the head priest's manner of death, his partnership with the supreme seemed doubtful. Their prayers, though, spoke of a Paul, and so Longinus had set out to find him in hopes it would lead him to Yeshua—and Licinia.

Now he stopped outside a shop from which hung various leathers, pouches, aprons, and sandals. He stepped inside and passed three large men working leather hides with sharp tools. They eyeballed the Roman sword that hung from his hip.

At the back of the shop, he approached a Jewish woman who worked a needle and thread over a hide.

"I seek Paul, the tentmaker," Longinus said in Hebrew.

"Paul has other dealings, sir. May I help you?" She continued her stitching.

"Is he here?"

"He is busy, sir, with other affairs," she repeated curtly.

Longinus leaned in and whispered. "Tell him I am the centurion who killed his Christ."

The woman's lower lip dropped and her face indicated fear.

The three men at the front of the shop put down their leather pelts but kept their blades in hand. The woman raised her hand, directing them to stay where they were.

"A moment, sir," she said as she stood and moved toward a door at the back.

The three men didn't approach, but they took up positions clearly meant to block Longinus from leaving. He cared not.

After a few moments, the woman came back, followed by a man with a dingy gray beard. He was an older man, but strong enough to catch a calf, slit its throat, and skin it with little sweat.

"You are Roman?" he asked, his voice deep and calm.

"I call no land home," Longinus answered. "Are you Paul?"

"What do you seek here?"

"I was told you are a teacher of the way, and you can grant forgiveness to thieves and murderers." Longinus watched the old man's eyes for a reaction. "I seek such redemption."

The old man looked at Longinus with skepticism. After a moment, he nodded. "I am who you seek. Place your sword on the counter and follow me."

Longinus did as he was directed.

Paul led Longinus into a back room piled with animal hides. The old man sat and gestured for Longinus to pull up a stool across from him. The woman hovered just outside the doorway.

"You were there the day of our Lord's death?" Paul asked.

"I was," Longinus said.

"Why do you seek forgiveness from me?"

"I have been told it is the way to Yeshua of Nazareth, and He is the key to open the gate between this world and the next."

"That is true."

"Then I must find him."

"He preaches from heaven but has shown us the way."

"How do I find this way?"

"You must become one with the spirit."

"How?"

Paul leaned back. "What you say you have done, must be of great burden. A Roman coming to a Jew for forgiveness?"

Longinus nodded.

"You have reason to be here," Paul said, assessing Longinus. "Something compels you. Something you have seen?"

"Yes," the centurion answered.

Paul nodded. "I too have seen a world beyond this. When the Lord grants you such sight, it humbles you. To find the way, though, you must be pure in spirit. The forgiveness you seek is not something I can grant."

"But I have been told you are a great teacher."

Paul leaned in. "A teacher, yes. But the debt you owe is not to me." He paused again. "But perhaps, there is someone."

The woman stepped into the doorway. "No!"

Paul paid her no attention. "Come back," he said to Longinus, rising from his seat. "Tonight."

"Why?" Longinus asked.

"Because you come to us, a Roman with a sword, who has killed the one most sacred to us. I must speak with the others. Tonight, we will give you our decision."

* * *

They were waiting for Longinus when he returned that evening. Two dozen men in the dark alley that led to the shop. Given his curse, he was without fear, but he needed these men to accept him so that he could learn more of this Yeshua.

Paul stepped from the crowd. "Come," he said.

The men moved around Longinus like wolves as they escorted him to the far side of the city, where a small stone house sat nestled in a row of similar homes.

Paul knocked, and a middle-aged woman answered. She had long black hair and wide, soft eyes. The two whispered for a moment, then she stepped back to let him inside.

Paul gestured for Longinus to join him. The rest of the men apparently planned to wait outside.

Longinus stepped into a small front room, where a single candle cast flickering shadows across the walls. The woman with long black hair went about cleaning plates, but her eyes drifted back toward him.

A much older woman slowly rose from a chair and stepped toward Longinus. Her cheeks were heavy, and a few strands of her gray hair snuck out of her black tichel. She approached as if vapor from a dream.

"They say you were the centurion there the day my son died?"

"I am."

"I remember his face. You are not that man."

"I have been cursed to die, again and again. And when I return, my face has no memory."

The woman's eyes widened. But she slowly nodded. "Leave us," she said.

"But Mother," said Paul.

The older woman raised her hand to indicate she would not argue.

Paul and the other woman stepped outside. "We are here if you need us," the woman said as she closed the door behind her.

The old woman returned to her chair, groaning as she sat. She gestured for Longinus to sit as well.

"When my son returned from the tomb," she began, "his face was also different. We did not know Him until He spoke and showed his scars. He told me there would be another who would share his plight. I did not think it would be his executioner." She leaned in. The candlelight flickered across her face. "What do you seek?"

"My wife suffers in Tartarus," Longinus said. It had been so long since he had spoken of her. But there was something about this woman—a gentleness, an inner peace, something that made him want to seek her counsel. "No matter how I try, I cannot reach her. When I die, there is only darkness. I just wish to end her pain."

She nodded, as if the words filled in a missing piece. "My son said you would seek the key to open the gate between this world and the next."

"Yes," he said, too loudly. "Where is this key?"

"I do not know."

Longinus sank back in his chair, disappointed.

"He knew much, my son," the old woman continued, "as if the world had already been written for him. Because of that, He chose His words carefully, so the order here would not be disrupted. He said when the time was right, His body would be revealed again. This would pave the way for His return, and the souls of the damned would be freed. But know this: when this occurs, it means the final judgment, the end of days."

"When will this happen?"

"God has a plan. And sometimes, good is born from the evil of men. That is why my son knew He would die. And that is why you must walk the earth to do what you must."

She was speaking in riddles. "Please. What must I do?" he asked.

She called out to the others. As Paul and some of his men stepped through the front door, she slowly rose to her feet.

The old woman pointed to Longinus. "If this man so chooses, he may join you as a follower of the way, and you shall treat him as a brother." She looked Longinus in the eye. "We shall fill him with the word, and if he preaches it day and night, then perhaps he shall find what he seeks."

CHAPTER XXIX

There was a routine. And it was not to be broken.

Prayer. Breakfast. Prayer. Bible study. Lunch. Injections. Bible study. Prayer. Dinner. Bible study. Prayer. Bible study. Lights out.

And do what you are told, lest the collar be woken.

Day in and day out. Twelve hours a day. They studied the Bible so much that Kat's brain began speaking in parables and putting "th" on the ends of her words liketh she was a Puritan. Day after day she would stare at the verses until they ran together like rain.

For Christ also hath once suffered for sins, the just for the unjust, that he might bring us to God, being put to death in the flesh, but quickened by the Spirit: By which also he went and preached unto the spirits in prison; Which sometime were disobedient, when once the long suffering of God waited in the days of Noah, while the ark was preparing, wherein few, that is, eight souls were saved by water...

The scriptures held more meaning to her when she was a child in Catholic school. The difference was, she had the desire then to please a fatherly God, particularly after her own father died from cancer when she was six. She sought validation then from the two patriarchs of the sky, the Father on the right, Daddy on the left, both looking down upon her, judging her. She tried to be a good girl, to please the priests, and the celestial judges, because she feared hell and the promise of eternal punishment. God and Daddy would weep for her, but she would nonetheless be cast into the dark abyss all the same.

Then Kat grew up. She had sex without being married. She smoked marijuana at college. She wasn't good about calling her mother. Seemed pretty tame for the halls of hell. But really, who knew?

The next time she studied the Bible was at Harvard, in a Bible archaeology class. This time she saw the words through the eyes of an emerging adult, as a student scholar. She studied it not as a sacred text but as the book of an ancient religion, one that had survived even as other, larger faiths of the time had faded into oblivion. Gone were the gods of the Sumerians, the Egyptians, the Greeks and the Romans. In their place survived the God of the desert nomad Abraham.

And Jesus. A noble figure, the Son of God, like an ancient Superman who could solve problems with miracles. When Mohammed's people were hungry centuries later, he had to organize raiding parties to steal food, but when the followers of Christ were hungry, He needed only five loaves and two fish.

Now she was studying the Bible once more. And the circumstances had changed yet again.

As she read His words, even though it was done by force and fear, she couldn't help but find hope in them like an inmate on death row. The ways of this wandering Jew, this self-proclaimed priest who so troubled the elders, spoke to her. He used no violence to spread his message, only his feet. He preached acceptance and compassion. He even included a woman in his journeys, one who very well might have had more sway than the twelve men.

Yet the sins of men proved too resourceful, a spring of black that bubbles always. Violence claimed Him. And violence then spread His word.

Am I finding religion again? she wondered. *Or is God non-existent, and this is just a book?*

Kat had certainly never imagined she'd one day be revisiting her beliefs on the hereafter in an isolated cell with an Assyrian Christian girl. But there was little else to do. There was no going outside. No feeling the sun. No windows, no view. For all she knew they were underground, or at the bottom of the ocean. No conversations were allowed about anything other than Scripture. No books except for the Bible. No whispers except for prayer.

At least her internal philosophical debate took her mind off her helplessness. She realized no one knew where she was or that she was even alive. Her Arabian knight wasn't going to barge through the door with a Special Forces unit to save her.

The truth was, John was probably dead. Although in her heart, she couldn't face that thought.

It was at night when she felt the most alone. As Mara lightly snored in the bed next to her, Kat's mind always drifted back to John. She had thought she was done with him. That she would just be angry with him forever. Hate him for leaving. But deep down, she understood why he left. Because he didn't know how to love. Because no one had ever taught him. The love he managed was broken and jagged, like the pieces of his heart. It hurt. But wasn't it still love all the same?

Knowing he was almost certainly dead made it easier to forgive him. There was no point in hanging on to old resentments now. She could feel pity and compassion for a man who had been so broken down by others.

She could even admit that perhaps she, too, had played a part in that breaking.

After the baby died, she initiated the divorce. She had the papers delivered via courier and refused to answer his calls. She knew he'd been in the hospital, knew he'd tried to commit suicide. Which meant he'd tried to quit her first, in the coldest way possible. So she didn't feel guilty about just up and quitting him with the same disregard.

Suicide and divorce are similar, because both end with a kill.

Yet now, at night, with only Mara's snores and the small red light of the overhead camera for company, she found herself holding out hope that he'd somehow made it out of the cave. She liked to believe her Arabian knight wandered the Earth now searching for his love. She knew that if he was alive, he'd never stop. Never stop searching.

Because he still loved her.

And the truth was, she still loved him. She regretted not just how things ended between them, but that they had ended at all. She wanted to try again. She wished they could be together. And she wondered if it was innately human to miss what we have when it is gone.

It had taken a prison cell for these two men to come back into her heart: Jesus and John.

Despite her resolve, despite the camera's silent judging, she wept. The warm tears ran down her cheeks and landed cold on the pillow. She wept because she could not be with him, because death had come into them both, making an early grave of their hearts. She wept for the love that had been snuffed by the winds of the abyss long before they even set foot in that cave.

Most of all, though, she wept because she was alone.

And she didn't know how much time she had left.

CHAPTER XXX

Sunday knew someone was at the dark end of the corridor, but he didn't know who. He just knew they were watching him. He knew it.

It had been twenty-six weeks since the cave and five weeks since he'd first opened his eyes in an underground bunker near the border between Jordan and Israel. Or so Sasha had told him. She said this bunker had once been part of a vast network of bunkers constructed during the rising tensions that eventually led to the Six-Day War. It certainly seemed old enough for that. The lights were dim and pulsed when the electricity fluctuated. The air was stale, like someone was keeping moldy cardboard boxes of cheese in a closet somewhere. The lime paint peeled from the ceiling as if molting.

The food was bad too, like pre-packaged airline food, but he was too hungry to care. It seemed no matter how much he ate, he was still hungry. Still, even now, when he was finally strong enough to hobble to the bathroom in his room instead of using the bedpan, he looked like an escapee from Krakow. There was still no sign of his once-toned physique. His muscle had been peeled from the bone in strips.

The good news was, the other hunger had subsided.

"The drugs are entirely gone from your blood-stream now," Sasha told him one day as she stretched his legs. "Fresh start."

Sunday hadn't had any withdrawals. He'd simply told her he didn't want anything else for the pain. No morphine. No pills. Nothing. Just Jell-O.

Fresh start.

The scar over his left eye wept pus, and his depth perception was off. He was also more vulnerable—he required more pivoting of his neck to be able to assess his surroundings, as his world now was half shadow. Sasha had given him an eye patch—she told him it was temporary, and eventually he'd be able to get a glass eye. He wasn't eager to wear it, but she said it would also help stave off infection in the swollen cav-ity where his eye used to be, so he begrudgingly took her up on it.

The hardest part of his routine was the physi-cal therapy. It was grueling. It took a day to get the strength to grab hold of the silver bar hanging over his bed so he could pull himself into a sitting position. A day just to sit up. A week to stand again. And more weeks to re-learn how to walk. He felt like he was on stilts, his brain unable or unwilling to talk to his feet. When the frustration festered, the rage burned, or the pity threatened to surface, he simply lay down on the floor. It was such a struggle to get back to a standing position that by the time he got back on his feet, he was too exhausted for any more emotions.

He'd had no contact with the outside world, or with anyone other than Sasha. He hadn't felt the warmth of the sun in months, and she gave him Vitamin D shots to compensate. He was a broken mole, blind in one eye, scurrying through dark desert tunnels.

Sasha, too, was a prisoner of sorts here. He didn't know exactly why she was taking care of him, and he believed her when she said she didn't know either. She explained only that she was with the Jordanian armed forces, and she was following orders. She'd been widowed, had no children, apparently had no one on the outside that she missed. She was as alone as he was. But in their dank cell, somehow her candle of hope burned ever bright. He wondered how it was that some exude the flame while others never find the spark.

She encouraged him through his physical therapy, cheering every tiny victory. She wiped his ass when he was too weak to do it himself. She fed him when he couldn't do it himself, changed his sheets, dressed his bedsores. He'd never felt this vulnerable around anyone before. Even when he'd been shot in Iraq, he'd had a fleet of ever-changing doctors and nurses, which made it all feel more clinical, impersonal. Here he had only one, and he relied on her for everything.

It was six weeks after regaining full consciousness before he finally had the strength to hobble, without help, down the hallway outside his room. He was desperate to escape the lime-green tiles, the shadowed corners which still held those dark things either real or imagined. Even in the day, fully awake, he could see them.

Now he leaned against the doorway, preparing to make that trek once more. Across the hall, Sasha had retired to her room for the night, the door closed. To his right, the bunker led down a narrow corridor to a stairwell. To his left, thirty feet down, the corridor turned a corner. He hadn't yet made it quite that far. But tonight, he would. He'd make it to that corner, then turn back.

His gait was awkward, and he walked with all the grace of a nub sailor on a ship. But he made it. He made it to the corner and looked around it to the corridor that lay beyond. Several doors lined its length, and another thirty feet down, the hall ended in a wall of darkness.

I can do more. I got this.

He pushed off again and hobbled to the first door. He turned the knob and flicked on the lights. The overhead fluorescents flickered and hummed, revealing a kitchen filled with boxes and crates. Jordanian military MREs, adult diapers, toilet paper, latex gloves and catheters.

He stepped back into the hall and moved to the next door. There was no switch on the wall, but he felt around and made contact with the dangling chain of a light bulb. He pulled, but the bulb stayed cold and dormant. He reached into the darkness and felt the back wall. Nothing but an empty closet. He closed the door and continued on.

At the third door, he was getting tired. Perhaps he had come too far. He leaned against the door with his shoulder, half to rest, half to nudge it open. The lights didn't work in here, either, but a hallway light was just outside the door, illuminating crates coated in years of dust.

He slid off one of the lids. Inside were a bunch of old M-1s. Next to that were smaller crates containing clips, flares, grenades. Weapons from a long-ago war, their deadly purpose never fulfilled.

Sunday stepped back out into the hall and looked down the corridor toward the wall of darkness, the cutoff point where the breakers had not been turned back on. Beyond it, he imagined, were miles of snake-like halls and corridors coiling deep beneath the desert sand.

And then, from the darkness, he felt it. Something there, something watching. He felt like he was back in the cave. Surrounded by its pitch, drowning in its ink. Or still in the coma.

Perhaps you never left?

No. I'm awake. Alive. I know it.

He heard the whispers. The scratches. They were coming from behind him.

He turned and looked back toward the closet. A light now peeked out from beneath the door frame, revealing the shadows of feet moving back and forth in the cramped space. He debated whether to open the door and see what was there—to confront that which could not be—or whether it would be wiser to turn and run from it.

He spun around again as something clicked in the shadows down the darkened hall, like the steps of a hoofed creature. He was possessed again by the reminder of the coma dreams, of the things he had seen there. For the first few nights after he woke he had been unable to close his eyes again for fear the creatures would return and drag him back through the lime walls.

Because it felt so real.

Tap. Tap.

It paced in the darkness, on the prowl beyond the edge of the light.

It's just an animal.

A stray dog, or a jackal. A wolf. A predator that had gotten down here somehow, into these tunnels that hadn't been used in many years. He tried to tell himself that.

But it didn't sound like a dog or a jackal.

He moved toward it, determined to face this thing that would not break him. If only to prove he wasn't crazy.

Come on.

He scratched the surface of the darkness. The light didn't fade out gradually, but ended suddenly, as if whatever was supposed to lie beyond that dividing line had simply failed to be created. He walked right up to the edge, the linoleum shore between light and dark, and stared into the total blackness.

He heard something.

Breathing.

Not a dog, a jackal, or a wolf. This was bigger. It stank of rot, triggering memories of the decaying bodies that littered the battlefields of his mind.

Had the bullet and the coma scrambled him forever?

He reached for a branch of logic.

There were no boogeymen. No creepy clowns in the closet. No ghosts that crossed between the living and the dead just to play "rearrange the furniture" games with rich white couples in the suburbs.

Then he felt its hot breath and saw a cloud of it hanging like ether in the light.

A primitive knowledge emerged from the base of his brain, as if handed down by ancient ancestors sending him a message. This thing was a sojourner, a tentacle, a thing that had been present long before them. And it was here again. *I am coming.*

The door of the closet behind him rattled, as if whatever grasped at it could not get a grip. Then, slowly, the knob began to turn.

Something was coming out. It would be with him in the hallway, trapping him, blocking the way back.

And still he faced the shadows. Faced the real beast. To confront it.

Fuck you, whatever you are.

A voice responded from the darkness. A voice of many, a voice of one. Deep and animal-like.

"No. Fuck *you.*"

* * *

Sasha woke to the sound of Sunday's screams. There had been a time when his screams in the night were normal, but she had thought they were past them.

She ran to his room to soothe him, only to discover that he was gone. It took her another few seconds to realize the screaming was coming from down the hall.

She found him curled against the wall in a fetal position, right at the edge of the light. He was sobbing, snot and drool all over his face. He had scratched up his arms and legs, and bloody streaks blotted his hospital gown. She cursed herself for forgetting to clip his fingernails as she lifted him in her arms. She was a small woman, but strong. And he was remarkably light—there was still so little of him left.

As she carried him back to his bed, she wondered, not for the first time, what he had seen that had made him so afraid.

CHAPTER XXXI

Crete, Greece
62 CE

The children of the village suffered. Leprosy had come upon them, twisting their arms and legs as one would bend river reeds to make a basket.

Longinus sat on the dirt floor of a room that had been built to contain the afflicted, little more than a mud hut with straw for them to sleep. His condition allowed him to be here with these children, to preach the word, for he feared not the repercussions. If he became afflicted, it was not the sort of scar that would resurface in his new form. His ability, his curse, made him the only follower of the way who was able to preach in the places where the word was needed most. In the places where hope did not live.

One child in particular had taken an interest in his teachings. Her name was Lulit. She was seven. Small, sweet, and abandoned because the affliction twisted her into something she was not: a monster. Her face was barely visible behind a mask of sores, and her eyes had rotted out long ago, as had the tips of her fingers.

Her wrists were twisted into bent stubs, and to eat, she was forced to slurp the bowl on her knees like a dog.

Longinus had told her the stories of how Yeshua had once cured those with similar ailments. How lepers had been healed, and the dead had risen again. He hoped these stories eased her spirit as she lay dying. He sat with her in her straw bed, watching her shrivel, a little person becoming smaller.

"Why does He not come?" she wheezed through broken breath. "And heal me?"

Longinus felt the gnawing in his gut. The fear that the words were only that. Words.

"He clears a place for you in His kingdom. He cares not that the people of this village call you unclean." He placed his hand on her twisted body. "He asks only that your soul be clean."

She looked up at him, her mouth filled with sputum. She said nothing more, and Longinus wondered if the words held truth in her heart.

He lay with her the entire time, her twisted nub of a hand resting in his palm. When she died, he gently wrapped her small body in cloth. If not for him, there would be no one to move her, and the other afflicted children of the hut would have to endure her stench until the maggots split her wide and consumed her bit by crawling bit.

As he wrapped her face, the dead child slowly turned her twisted head and stared full upon him with eyes that were not her own.

"Longinus," she said, "have you forgotten those who suffer?" The child sat up. "Those abandoned by the rabini?"

Longinus stumbled back, then regained his footing.

"He has not abandoned you," the centurion said. "*You* have abandoned *Him*."

The child turned and sniffed, then crawled on all fours toward another sick child. Lulit hovered over the little boy and caressed his tangled leper's hide.

"Do you deny us our salvation then?" she—*it*—hissed. "Are we not lepers in death?"

"The message is for all," Longinus replied. "But you seek to twist the word for your own profit."

The child laughed. "As shall many who will bear the sign of your prophet!" She caressed the boy's shriveled limbs. "Twisting the minds of men for their own gain."

"You taunt me. Why?"

"We come only seeking your divine knowledge. Why does your God not save you? Could He not end your pain? Free your wife with a simple nod? You suffer because it *pleases* Him. And through your curse you shall know the rot of these humans, and it will fill you with such rage, you will become one of us."

"I shall not," Longinus said.

The child turned away from the boy and crawled toward Longinus on her four broken nubs. She came close enough to nip at his feet. "Ten years you have preached His lies. For what? You are no closer to the one you seek." The child hatched a crooked smile.

Then the voice changed. It was Licinia's voice. "Longinus?" she asked plaintively.

"Licinia?" Longinus sobbed.

"Why do you leave me here? I suffer so."

"I'm sorry," he cried out.

"All around me there is only darkness."

"You must find the light, Licinia! The word of Yeshua will set you free!"

"*NO!*" screamed a thousand voices from within the child. It rose to its crooked, broken feet and leapt at Longinus's head with inhuman strength.

Longinus caught the child inches from his face. "Get back!" he shouted. "Leave this child!"

He fought the crippled girl to the floor, then grabbed a jug of water and poured it onto her. "I baptize you in the name of the Father, the Son, and the Holy Spirit!" he cried.

The child smiled, a twisted grin. "Your rituals have no power over us. We are beyond all that you know, and your words and wisdom will not save you from that which God has made. We are part of Him, as He is us, and we exist to claim our stake upon the day of reckoning. We are the maggots who devour the damned."

The child gasped, a final exhale of tainted air, and her eyes went wide with fear. Then she was no more.

As the sun set, he carried her wrapped body to the common grave at the edge of the village. The setting sun created a divine painting of pink and red and blue, of rolling hills and baobab trees twisting in the distance.

Is God's word not written within this picture? Hidden in the birds and the flowers and the trees? Is there not beauty even in the ugliest of places?

He rolled the girl's wrapped body into the pit and pushed earth upon her, burying her out here beneath the sky, the dome of the king, for all in heaven to see. But he wondered if any bothered to look.

He had just turned away when a rider on horseback approached the village. Longinus knew this man, one of the apprentices of Paul.

The rider dismounted and approached. He kept a scarf around his mouth, to keep back the stench of the lepers.

"Longinus, I send word. Paul has written. You are to go to Capernaum."

CHAPTER XXXII

Kat was brought in for her daily shot regimen, led by the big nun—"Ulga," as Kat had named her in her mind. Strangely, Kat now desired the injections, because as Mara had pointed out, the alternative was far worse. The girl electrocuted on the floor in the cafeteria had been killed because she couldn't have a baby—because she was barren and therefore had no worth. And given Kat's track record with pregnancy, she was worried she might face the same fate. She needed these shots, so she could stay alive.

She waited on the papered exam table. A moment later, Nurse Mother—that was the actual name stitched into her white gown—stepped in. She was a small, round woman with dark gray hair, as sterile as the tips of the syringes she carried on a tray.

"Problems?" Nurse Mother asked.

"No."

"The vomiting?"

"It stopped," Kat said.

"Are you icing?"

Kat nodded.

"Fever? Cramping?"

"No."

Nurse Mother wrote it all down, then selected a syringe from the tray. "Ready?"

Kat lifted her gown, revealing her buttocks. The nurse moved behind her and slid the needle through the skin. Within seconds Kat felt like she was going to fall over. The nurse guided her back onto the papered table.

"What did..." Kat slurred, her eyes starting to close.

Seconds later, she was out.

* * *

When she woke, her arms were strapped to the table and her feet were locked into stirrups. Someone was working between her legs.

"What... what's going on?" She awoke more fully. "What are you doing?"

The doctor poked his head up. It was the same small Asian man who had examined her upon her arrival.

"You be still," he said. "Be still."

A monitor stood near the exam table. The screen showed a long tube snaking toward an egg.

Oh God. That's me. That tube is in me. Those eggs are mine.

"You move," the man said, still working between her legs, "very painful. Tear uterus. Much bleeding."

This is it. Please. God. Please. Help me.

Kat closed her eyes and tried to mentally push away the touching between her legs. Tears pooled on her eyelashes and rolled down her cheeks like salty escape pods. She was being violated, by man and machine, inseminated like a farm animal.

After several minutes the doctor stood and threw his latex glove into the trash. He lowered his mask, winked, and patted her belly.

"You good girl," he said before leaving.

Kat sobbed.

Eventually Ulga returned to take her back to her cell, where she found Mara on her knees, praying.

"Did they?" Kat asked, making a round gesture over her own belly.

Mara nodded.

Kat kneeled next to her, and contrary to every fiber of her being, she found herself praying that the foreign seed inside her would take root.

CHAPTER XXXIII

Jordan

David Conrad wasn't followed. At least he was pretty sure he wasn't. He was so far off the beaten path, off the Jordan Valley Highway that laced along the Jordan/Israel border, he would have seen the headlights in his rearview mirror tailing him.

But cars rarely tailed people anymore. If anyone was watching, they were doing so from far above his head, hidden by the darkness and distance. He had no way of knowing if a drone was overhead right now, watching as he turned his car down yet another dirt road. Just as he had no idea if the briefcase full of money on the passenger seat next to him had been spotted missing from accounting.

But what else was he going to do? He'd started something. Now he had to finish it.

Things had changed when he shone his flashlight into the tunnel of the cave that day and saw John Sunday's bloody head. He'd initially assumed Sunday was dead, but then he heard a labored breath, an exhale that sounded faintly like the word "please."

He'd pulled Sunday out of the cave. Dragged him limply to the surface. Put him into the back of the van and drove him to Amman. Not to the base. Not to a hospital where ordinary US citizens would go, but to a military hospital used by Jordan's general intelligence directorate and armed forces.

John Sunday represented the only chance he had at finding out if there was a mole at the top of the agency. But only if the man was alive and could form complete sentences.

His headlights shone on a chain-link gate with a sign in Arabic: "Keep Out: Private Property." He climbed out of the car and unlocked the chain with the key he had been given by his colonel friend at GID.

A minute later he pulled up to an abandoned warehouse half-buried by sand. He stepped inside and used another key to unlock a metal door. He hit a switch, a few tungsten bulbs sizzled to life, and he descended the narrow steps into the bunker below.

* * *

It was six months after John Sunday had been pulled from the cave, and Sasha had told him he was going to have a visitor. She couldn't tell him who it was, because she hadn't been told herself.

He'd hoped it was Kat coming to visit. That she would stroll through that door, happy to see him, maybe even embrace him. And the anger and regret would shed just like the muscle on his body. Perhaps she'd forgive him for his sins and they could build something... new.

He had, however, prepared himself for the likelihood she was dead. Killed while he was underground. Their time and memories together lost in the decaying cells of her corpse. Because he hadn't saved her.

A knock sounded on his door, and Sasha stepped in, followed by David Conrad. About as far from Kat as one could get. He carried a brown briefcase like he'd just come from an insurance seminar.

"Will you give us some time alone?" Conrad said to Sasha.

She nodded politely, as if she were the hired help, and stepped out. But not before flashing John a little smile as if to say, "I'm here if you need me." But he already knew that.

Conrad sat in the room's only chair and studied Sunday. To his credit, the visitor didn't flinch, despite Sunday's appearance. John had a mirror—he knew he didn't look good. His left eye gone, replaced by sealed, swollen flesh. A tattered T-shaped scar that crossed his face like a zipper. Rail thin like a POW, or some guy on a lost desert island who spent his time talking to a volleyball.

"You look good," Conrad said.

"Why the fuck am I here?"

"For your safety. Give you time to get better without… trouble."

"What trouble? What happened?"

"You know what happened. You were the bait. Someone bit."

"Who?"

"On the record, Al Tariqa." He paused, as if deciding whether to move forward. "Off the record, I have no idea."

"What does that mean?"

"Somehow the radar on site failed to alert your unit there were snipers surrounding you. That a ground team was approaching. And whoever hit you did so right at the moment when the satellite had coincidentally been rerouted, giving us no overhead surveillance. What are the odds of that?"

"Zero."

"That's about right." Conrad looked down. "And here's the thing: it can't have been Al Tariqa. Because I never leaked it."

"I don't understand."

"You knew what the plan was. We send you on that dig as bait, leak what you're doing so the Father hears, get him to show up. I was prepared to put it out, just like we'd planned. Your team was in place in Jordan. We were ready. But then I had a meeting with Mossad and they tell me that Tom Ferguson is a traitor."

"Bullshit," Sunday said. He knew as well as anyone that the agency had a way of making people paranoid.

But Conrad was convincing. He explained what he'd learned about the Vatican connection to Tom Ferguson. About Ferguson's daughter. About how Taresh had threatened to destroy the painting if he wasn't paid. That the raid of Taresh's compound was really engineered to retrieve the portrait. And that the attack on Sunday's team was about getting to what they found in the desert.

"It was too late for me to pull you back in without raising suspicion. I thought the satellite and radar would be there to give you warning if anyone was closing in. But somebody rerouted the satellite. And the radar was removed from the site, meaning someone didn't want us looking around inside. I even secretly had a Special Ops team in place to protect you. But the day of the attack, they were rerouted to a skirmish outside Qamishli. Someone very high up was pulling strings. Funny thing is, if I'd never come up with the plan to search for the body, they would have gotten to it another way. The portrait would have just disappeared from some CIA back room, and they'd have gone out there looking without us ever knowing. But instead, they had to wait and watch where *we* were digging. And then take whatever it was you found. Which was what?"

"Nothing. A clay container." Sunday waved the question off. There was only one piece of information that interested him. "Where's Kat?"

Conrad shrugged. "She wasn't there. Her body wasn't on site, and she hasn't been heard from since. We tried to find her, but the trail went cold pretty quick."

"They took her."

"I agree," Conrad said. "And if she's alive, you're the best person to find her. You have an advantage."

"What's that?"

"You're dead. No one's expecting you. I'm the only person who knows you're here—knows you're alive. I found you, John. Barely alive. Miraculously alive. And I brought you here. No one else knows, except Sasha, and she doesn't even know who you really are. We even found a corpse to play the part of dead John Sunday. I called in a favor from a buddy at GID, and we used the body of a soldier who'd died from a heroin overdose, matched your body size. Shot him point blank so no one recognized his face. That's the body we pulled out of the cave. Your body. Officially. We flew him back in a casket with a flag on it. Congratulations. You're buried at Arlington. Your name is on the wall at Langley."

"Why? Why did you do any of that?"

"Because if I start to dig around, ask questions I shouldn't, and the CIA is in on this, I'm dead. My family is dead. But you..." He put the briefcase on the bed and opened it. "There's passports, ten grand in cash, all the reports to bring you up to speed. Do *not* use agency people or resources."

Sunday digested the implications of it all. It added up. Because there was another fact—one he'd been thinking about on and off for weeks. The man who'd shot him in the face in the tunnel was no Arab insurgent. His accent wasn't Arabic. It was Italian.

But before he could say another word, the lights went out. A second later, an explosion rocked the earth somewhere above. Then boots sounded on metal stairs, pounding in sync.

Their bunker had just been found.

"I've only got one gun," Conrad said in the darkness.

"There's a stash of weapons down the hall," Sunday said.

"Can you move?"

"We'll find out."

* * *

Conrad fumbled forward, groping blindly in front of him. He found the door and slowly opened it. Tucking his body behind the threshold, he peered out, but saw nothing but absolute black. He ducked back, listened, waited for his eyes to adjust. But they didn't, and he heard only his heart in his throat, the blood pumping so fast it felt like it was going to burst out his ears.

How many?

He closed his eyes, because in this darkness he couldn't see anyway. In his mind, however, there was light. And in that light, he could see his wife and daughter. He could feel Gracie's hand in his. The moments when they all snuggled together on the couch. He could feel his wife's cheeks, her warmth next to him in the bed. He could smell her hair, her skin. In this moment, they were together. They were happy again.

How had he ever let that light fade?

Down the hall, a door creaked on a metal hinge.

"Now," he whispered.

He extended the gun out into the hall and fired four shots. He felt Sunday move past like a black ghost.

A second later, the hallway erupted in gunfire.

Did he make it?

* * *

Sunday ran blind into the darkness of the hallway, his brain showing him rainbow circles, residual phantoms of images that had since disappeared. He raced forward on weak bones, like running on ice skates, and turned the corner.

Rounds ripped into the wall just behind him.

Two single shots rang out in response. Conrad was trying to hold back the attackers. But this fight was decidedly one-sided, and would be settled in less than thirty seconds.

He had to get to the guns.

Tracing the cold concrete wall with his right hand, he felt the first door, then the second—the closet he most certainly wanted to avoid—and on to the third. Stepping inside, he tried to remember the order and placement of the weapons and crates. His hands immediately found an M-1, but where were the cartridges?

The gunfire suddenly stopped, replaced by the ominous echo of silence.

* * *

Sasha had nowhere to go as the gunshots reverberated in the hallway outside her room. So she did the only thing she could: she ran into her tiny bathroom and retreated as far back into the corner of the shower stall as she could.

Her mind raced, thinking whether there was anything in here she could use as a weapon. The best she could come up with was a toothbrush. That wasn't going to save her life.

The gunfire stopped.

Which meant they were coming.

She stared into the darkness. Waiting. Blood rushed between her ears and she pressed her back against the wall. Her legs and arms felt numb, as if despite her pounding heart, the blood wasn't getting where it was supposed to go.

Allahu Akbar. Please. Please.

Is this how I'm going to die? In a bathroom, beneath the desert?

I'm not going to meet someone? Re-marry? Have children? Watch them grow?

Subhanakal-lahumma.

Wabihamdika watabarakas-muka wataaaala.

I helped save lives. I was a good wife. A good daughter.

A good person...

She heard footsteps. Someone was in her bedroom now, just beyond the thin door. She listened for the sound of the door handle turning. The signal that someone was coming for her.

Allaahumma-ghfir lee warhamnee wajburnee.

Then what? Just close your eyes.

Oh, God, please.

The door handle turned.

She was alone now with this other man, a killer whose name she would not know.

Warfa'nee, wa 'aafinee war'zuqnee.

Allahuma-ghfirlee. Allahuma-ghfirlee.

She turned her prayer position into a crouch, covering her head as if to shield herself from what was coming.

She heard the pulling back of the shower curtain rings on the small metal pole.

Then she heard nothing more. Only silence.

Can he see me in the darkness? Is he looking at me now? Staring at me here on my hands and knees?

Suddenly the darkness was replaced by a blinding light that shrank her pupils. She felt a hand. A calm, gentle touch on the small of her back. And a voice.

"Sasha."

She looked up, squinting, her eyes still adjusting to the rapid switch from dark to light.

There, at the edge of the shower stall, stood a man with a dark beard and gentle brown eyes.

She knew this man.

He gathered her into his arms, and she allowed it. Welcomed it. She knew this man. She knew him.

She smiled. And Yusef smiled back.

And the light was bright.

* * *

Conrad was overwhelmed. Rounds tore into the wall outside the door with such heat and intensity, it was like staring wide-eyed into the core of the sun. Another second, and the rounds burrowed into the door.

And then the men were in front of him, and the bullets struck his body like angry hornets.

They shattered his ribs and tore into his lungs, shredding the sacs and sinew that held his heart in place. Their paths, bound by laws man could not see, opened gaping holes upon exit that poured him onto the floor.

He fell, his breathing labored. He was getting no air. He was going to die here, in this strange, dark place. Alone.

He thought of his daughter again. Had he been a good father? Had he done that right?

And he thought of his wife. And his sins. He asked for her forgiveness. For betraying the promise that they would grow old together, sitting in rocking chairs, their hands clasped, wrinkled and raw from the seasons of time.

The cold of the floor beckoned him. And the pain of the life that was not to be was somehow greater than the pain that now killed him.

* * *

Sunday's fingers found a package of long, slender tubes. Flares. Judging by their size and the pull tabs on the side, they had to be ancient. And then he found what he was looking for: the box with the clips for the M-1. He grabbed a clip, slid it into place, and tucked the flares and three more clips into the elastic waistband of his sweatpants.

He wondered if the gun would even fire.

As he stepped from the room into the hall, the gunfire resumed. Quick, succinct bursts. The sound of an execution.

Conrad. Did they find Sasha too?

Sunday traced back along the wall. He could be walking straight toward someone and wouldn't know it until the bullet tore through his skull. When his fingers felt the corner, he pulled a flare, ripped the tab with his teeth, and tossed it down the hall.

It burst into red fire.

There were three men in the hall, all wearing night-vision goggles, and they recoiled from the sudden light of the flare. That gave Sunday the split-second he needed. From the cover of the corner, he fired three shots. The M-1 kicked like a broken mule, but his aim was true, and all three men fell.

They weren't alone. More men, who had been tucked into the rooms on either side of the hall, returned fire.

Before the flare spiraled and spit and sputtered, Sunday fired another round, this one into the darkened fluorescent lights overhead, sending glass raining down on the floor.

Sunday leaned against the inside wall and tried to catch his breath.

A second later he heard what he'd been waiting for: a boot crunching on glass. He pulled the tab on another flare and tossed it into the hallway. Two men, aware the crunching glass had given them away, were racing down the corridor toward him. He fired twice, slamming both rounds through the eyepieces of their night-vision goggles. They toppled backward with such force it looked like their heads had detached from their necks.

Sunday contemplated heading back down the corridor, past the weapons room, to escape in the opposite direction. Perhaps he could find a place to hide, or, with luck, he might even find another route to the surface.

But the briefcase was still in the room. Passports. Money. He wasn't even wearing shoes.

And then there was Sasha.

I have to see. See if she's alive.

Sunday pulled the spent clip from the M-1, snapped in another, and took a breath. He turned the corner, searching for an assassin he couldn't see.

* * *

He laid down cover fire as he ran and took a diving leap back into his room as bullets whizzed through the air around him. He leapt to his feet and scrambled into his bathroom. He tucked behind the wall beside the door, and in the glowing remnants of the red flare still burning in the outside hall, he saw a gunman step into his room and open fire. If the wall Sunday cowered behind had been made of drywall, he would have been dead, and for the first time since he'd been here he was grateful to be in a concrete bunker.

He brought up the M-1 and stuck it through the doorway to fire. But as he pulled the trigger, the rifle did nothing. It hung there in silence, and then a second later it blew up in his hands, sending the splintered stock blasting across his face.

The gunman took advantage of the hang fire to step into the bathroom, his weapon brought around to fire.

Sunday grabbed the end of the man's rifle and used his weight to press the barrel toward the ground and onto the floor. He swung his own splintered rifle like a club into the man's face, dazing him enough for Sunday to knock the rifle out of his hands. The weapon spun to the floor.

But his attacker regrouped quickly. He was big and strong and slammed Sunday against the wall, shattering the tile over the toilet. Sunday felt the impact from his shoulder to his rib cage. The man then slammed him into the opposite wall, and Sunday felt his back snap the towel rod. He landed on the floor, and the man's knee pressed into his belly.

The man pulled a blade from his vest. Sunday caught the knife wrist with one hand as the blade plunged downward toward his chest, then with his other hand he pulled a flare from his waistband, ripped the tab off with his teeth, and slid it quickly into the space between the man's body and vest. The flare began spraying red sparks like a Chinese parade.

As the man fumbled to get the burning flare away from him, Sunday picked up the AR-15 from the floor and fired into the man's skull. Blood, bone, and brain were sprayed in clumps on the lime-green walls.

Sunday then grabbed the man's night-vision goggles and, as the flare in the hall burned out, he slid them on.

As he crossed out of the room, rifle at the ready, he saw David Conrad slumped next to the door. Sunday first checked the corridor to be sure no one else was coming for him, then kneeled next to David. The man's mouth hung open and his eyes stared blankly into the darkness. Sunday felt for a pulse. Nothing.

He crossed the hall into Sasha's room and found her in the bathroom, in the corner of the shower stall. A puddle of blood had formed beneath her and rolled down the drain, the last of her escape.

He turned her over. A bullet had bored true through the center of her forehead. The wound had already started to swell, but the white blood cells that collected around the wound would lose. Her pulse was gone, the beats swallowed by the silent drum of death.

"Sasha…"

He had wanted to thank her. To tell her he could never repay her for what she had done. She had brought him back to life, and he could not do the same for her.

He would have stayed with her for a moment longer, but he couldn't be certain that more men wouldn't soon come down the stairs. So he let her go, to the boatman, to the river that percolates beneath all feet.

A minute later he'd put on a pair of boots off one of the dead men and was moving once more past the weapons closet, toward the unknown darkness beyond. He dared not leave the way from which the attackers came. He would have to find another way out.

As he walked, her name was illuminated in his mind like a sizzling neon sign. *Kat.* His purpose was clear. He disappeared into that green-tinted corridor, determined to find his way back into the light.

CHAPTER XXXIV

Capernaum, Israel
63 CE

Longinus crossed through the small fishing village on the edge of the black hills, past its lava rock houses with straw roofs, and continued to the docks, the vast lake speckled with white sails and wooden fishing boats.

He walked toward some fishermen casting from the shore. "I seek a man named Simon Peter," he said.

"He's been out since before the sun," said a squat old fisherman with skin dark as hide. "Won't be back until late day."

Longinus nodded. It was hot, and the sun already cast a short shadow beneath his feet. He would wait.

He sat on the dock, watching the fisherman thread their nets, watching the crabs and birds dancing along the stick branches on the shore. Finally, when the sun had sunk low in the sky, the boats slowly began to drift back. On one of those boats, he saw the man he was looking for.

"Simon Peter?" he shouted in Hebrew as the boat drifted closer.

"Who's asking?" the older man barked as he docked.

"I am Longinus. Saul sent word I was coming."

The fisherman nodded as he tied up the boat. He had a thick gray beard and a sun-scorched face. His hands were dry and calloused from a lifetime on the nets. He looked at Longinus with curious eyes. "You are the one who cannot die?"

"I am."

"Shalom Aleichem, I am the one you seek," he said. "I know you have questions, but God has been gracious, and my baskets are full. I must work with haste to salt the fish."

"Allow me to help you, brother, and we shall both accomplish what we need."

They dumped the baskets of fish onto a table set up for cleaning.

"Do you know why I have come?" Longinus asked as he slit a fish.

"Aye. You seek to step through the gates between this world and the next. My question is why?"

"Are you married?"

"Yes."

"And what would you do if she suffered?"

"I would do anything to ease her pain."

"So it is with me. I shall journey from this world to the next and bring her into the light. I shall preach the word of God in the depths of hell."

Peter stopped filleting and looked over at him. "Christ Himself already did this."

"When?"

"After his death, he preached to those within the earth. Despite his sermon, few returned with Him."

"Why would so many remain in such a place?"

"We could ask the same of here," Peter said, gesturing toward the village with his knife. "Many refuse to see the way."

"My wife, she has never heard the word. So how can she even find the light?"

"Brother, I know you must do what you need to save her. But the gates can be breached only by the Son of God. And if somehow you could, you would create a way that could not be closed."

"Are you saying that I should turn from my wife and her suffering?"

Peter pursed his lips. "I think you must take time to consider what you seek. And the tax you ask the rest of us to pay."

"This gate. You know its location?"

"Aye."

Longinus tossed a sliced fish aside, grabbed another, and slid the blade top to bottom. He turned to Peter, the knife in hand as a tool, not as a weapon. But still there.

"Brother," he said.

Peter nodded. "Alas. I can see you have already made your choice."

"I am tormented by devils. They gnaw with words I cannot argue against. What kind of God allows for such suffering?"

"The way is only a candle in the wilderness. If you extinguish that light, there will be only darkness."

"I fear the way is not strong enough to overcome the animals that lurk there."

Peter nodded. "Paul had a vision in Rome. He was told the time had come. That the tide would work against our boats and many of us would be lost at sea. I begged him not to send for you. But here you are. And so it has begun. And who am I to argue with the will of God?" He shook his head. "The place you seek is Caesarea Philippi, near Mount Hermon. It is there I saw Yeshua descend the depths, and not even He could sway their suffering."

"I seek to redeem only one," Longinus said.

"Yes. But at what price?" Peter asked.

* * *

It was late that night when Peter returned home. The house was without a candle, and he was careful not to disturb his wife. But it mattered not. She stirred in the next room and approached from the shadows, her eyes carrying light even in the darkness.

"Are you hungry?" Miriam said with a yawn.

"No. I ate on the journey. Go back to sleep."

He went to the desk where he did his writings, shuffled through the parchments littered there, and pulled out a scroll.

"What are you doing?" Miriam asked, watching.

"I had a visitor on the shore today. He wanted to know where the gate was."

She sat. "And did you tell him?"

"What choice did I have? It won't be long before he seeks her out."

"So you must go?"

He crossed the room, kneeled in front of her, and collected her hands in his to soothe her heart. "I must."

She stroked his hair. "Why Rome?"

They'd had this conversation many times before. "You know why. My time is coming to an end. And I must put the word into the mouth of the lion."

"Then I shall pack our things," she said as she stood.

"*Our* things?"

"It is my duty as your wife to follow my husband, yes?"

"Yes, but not in that way."

"I fulfill my duty. As I follow my husband in the way."

Peter nodded at her interpretation. There was obviously no use fighting. She was going with him.

CHAPTER XXXV

Kat crouched on the toilet in the corner of the cell. As always, she hiked the end of her gown over her knees to hide what she could and tried not to look at the black orb in the ceiling that watched her every move.

The Grigori. The Watchers. The eyes of old that so coveted the daughters of man.

If they could hear her heart, the pounding would most certainly give her away.

Just act normal, she told herself.

She reached for another sheet of toilet paper and blotted herself. Keeping the paper in the toilet where the camera couldn't see, she checked it again. A crimson crime. Heavier this time.

If she miscarried, she knew what would happen. She would no longer have value. Without the ability to give birth, she'd be killed, electrocuted at breakfast.

She was sixteen weeks now and starting to show. The bleeding had started at thirteen weeks, but had quickly subsided. She had thought, until now, that she'd made it past the worst of it.

She still remembered her baby with John. It had been so small upon her, warm and still, the only heartbeat echoing within its chest belonging to Kat. She missed John. She wished he was here with her now, standing upon a ridge that overlooked some horizon, searching for some unseen thing that might do her harm. He would be there to protect her and keep her safe at night from the things that sought her undoing. The cell door would open and he would be standing there to sweep her away...

But she knew that was only a fantasy. She was alone. Alone except for Mara, who was busy reading the Bible, per the daily ritual.

She wouldn't be able to hide the blood for long. Nurse Mother did a checkup on each girl three times a week. She was sure to see.

Kat flushed and stood. She picked up her own Bible and thumbed through the pages. Tracing down with her finger, she stopped on a passage, slid the Bible over to Mara, and gently tapped with her finger.

Mara glanced up at her, then read the passage to herself.

Give them, O Lord, what will you give? Give them a miscarrying womb and dry breasts.

Mara's eyes widened in fear, but she nodded.

Good girl, Kat thought. *Don't speak.*

Mara thumbed through to a different passage, which she pointed at, handing the book back to Kat.

Samaria shall bear her guilt, because she has rebelled against her God; they shall fall by the sword; their little ones shall be dashed in pieces, and their pregnant women ripped open.

Kat raised her shoulders. *What do I do?*

Mara clasped Kat's hands and closed her eyes. She started to pray.

Kat joined in. And she meant every word.

* * *

The following day, after a lunch Kat was too nervous to eat, Ulga escorted her to her checkup with Nurse Mother. Kat assumed the position, feet in stirrups, and waited. She had blotted herself as much as she could, but she feared the signs of bleeding were still there. As her legs hung in the air, she felt cold and numb with fear.

Nurse Mother stepped into the room. She was a small woman, yet always managed to look down at everyone over the rim of her glasses.

"How do you feel, 6718?" Her voice was as warm as an answering machine.

"Tired," Kat responded.

"Are you taking the supplements?"

"Yes."

"Good." Nurse Mother pulled over a swivel chair and sat to look between Kat's legs. She gloved up, the sound like a latex drum prior to an execution. "Hmm," she said. The hum of judgment hung in the air.

"What is it?" Kat asked. Her heart pulsed so hard in her throat it rattled her voice box.

Nurse Mother held up a gloved finger. A streak of blood starkly contrasted with the pale dead white of the latex. Without another word, she stepped out of the room.

Kat looked up at the Grigori, ever-present, always watching. There was no escape. Not with the collar.

A few minutes later, Nurse Mother returned with the Asian doctor. He gloved up, applied a lubricant, and felt between her legs with his fingers, fishing around as if searching a pocket.

Nurse Mother wheeled over an ultrasound machine and slathered her belly with cold jelly like a Christmas ham. She turned on the monitor and began the ultrasound.

Kat turned her head to look at the screen. And for the first time, she saw the baby.

It emerged as from a black hole, the little fingers and toes pale and clear against the darkness of her womb. The little head bobbed and nodded, the fingers grasping at something unseen.

It was there. Her child. Her baby.

The doctor leaned back and pulled off his gloves.

"Placenta previa," he said, adjusting his black-framed glasses.

Kat went cold with fear. "What's that?"

"Placenta cover cervix," he said, his words as smooth as nub fingers on a keyboard.

Nurse Mother explained it better. "Your placenta is a sac covering the opening. It may move as you progress, and get out of the way." This was the first time her tone indicated a desire to actually serve her patient, rather than the other way around. "If so, there's no problem."

"And if not?"

"Then you'll have more bleeding. And you'll need a C-section."

"Is the baby okay?"

"Baby fine," the doctor said, flicking his gloves in the garbage.

Nurse Mother spoke in a matter-of-fact tone. "You must trust us to care for you."

"Nurse Mother… what happens to me after the baby?"

Nurse Mother almost smiled. Almost. "You will help us care for the child," she said. "It is yours as much as ours. You are the chosen now. You are carrying the Child of God."

CHAPTER XXXVI

The security agent at Queen Alia International was uncertain about Sunday's passport, because that picture showed a man with two eyes, and not the scarred man standing before him with an eye patch and a ragged beard. The man in the photo was also forty pounds heavier. The agent tapped his pen several times against his wooden podium, a judge of the journey, looked at the photo, back at Sunday, repeated the process several more times as if downloading a decision, and then finally stamped it.

John Sunday was flying to Richmond International using the passport name of Matthew Levy. After surfacing from the desert, he'd hitched a ride with a Bedouin tour guide back to Amman. Now, as he boarded the fourteen-hour flight, the first thing he did was take off the stolen boots, which were much too small. The dead guy was six feet tall, like Sunday, but apparently he had the feet of a four-year-old.

The woman seated next to him wrinkled her nose in disgust, but said nothing. Probably figured it was best not to complain to a guy with a scarred face and an eye patch.

Sunday had chosen Richmond because it was easy to get out of quickly. He had to assume that whoever had followed Conrad to the bunker knew why Conrad was going there—because Sunday was there, alive. Sunday could no longer trust that he was a dead man in the eyes of his enemies.

In Richmond, he rented a Toyota Corolla, paying in cash. As he waited for the clerk to hand over the keys, he glanced out the window at a homeless man on the curb. He held a sign that read, in scrawled black marker: "Rock Bottom. Please Help."

And he was staring at Sunday as if he recognized him.

The agency had a way of making everyone paranoid.

Sunday watched his rearview mirror as he pulled onto the highway. There was a black car two vehicles back that had departed after him at the airport. Coincidence? His training wouldn't let him make that assumption.

He was monitoring the black car, seeing if it was using other vehicles as blockers, when he smelled something foul, like he'd just driven past the city dump. And then he heard breathing behind him, just beyond his sight, and felt hot air clinging to the back of his neck like honey. Was this real, or another hallucination?

He adjusted the rearview mirror—only to find that the homeless man from the airport was riding in the back seat as if Sunday were his private chauffeur.

"The child can't save you," the homeless man said, as if the final wheeze of a dying man.

Sunday's breath caught in his chest. He spun around to look directly at the man, nearly running the car off the road.

There was no one in the back seat.

He turned on his hazards and pulled over on the right shoulder to double-check that the back seat was truly empty. The black car zoomed past.

What's wrong with me?

* * *

It was just before four a.m. as Sunday approached Tom Ferguson's house in Great Falls, Virginia, a Cape Cod–style home in an upper-class neighborhood of Washington elites. It was quiet, still too early for joggers or dog-walkers. No extraneous eyes.

He'd used the intervening time to clean himself up. He'd rented a cheap hotel room where he could shower, shave, and change into the new clothes—including comfortable sneakers—that he'd bought at an outlet mall. He'd also run a number of tedious surveillance routes to elude any would-be followers.

He parked facing away from Ferguson's house, and positioned himself right between two neighbors' houses so perhaps each neighbor would think his car belonged to the other neighbor's overnight guest. Leaning the seat back, he adjusted his side and rear-view mirrors so he could watch the house behind him. He half-expected to see the old man in the back seat again, but saw nothing. In the morning darkness—and exhausted—he settled in to wait.

Sunday knew that getting to Ferguson would be difficult. As head of counterterrorism, and soon-to-be deputy director, Ferguson lived with a security entourage. He would rarely be alone, and when he was, a team of men would be only a room away. His home was surrounded by a black metal fence with a single entrance gate. Deliveries were taken at the gate, and two men patrolled the grounds. All house staff would have been cleared by DOD.

There was a For Sale sign in the front yard. Sunday pulled one of the cell phones from the briefcase and did a quick search online. According to Zillow, Tom had put the home up for sale a week ago, asking $1.1 million—about $800,000 less than the asking price of similar homes in the area.

Why so low? Why such a hurry to sell?

Sunday checked the clock. How many hours of his life had he spent like this? Waiting.

He checked the back seat again, searching for an old man who wasn't there, yet each time he felt as though the old man would be there the second he turned away. He would feel the man's hands reach through the air, a breach of worlds, his fingers extended, cold and dead, to touch his neck.

Fuck, the paranoia was getting rich.

Am I going crazy?

Why am I seeing these things?

He still remembered the dreams of his coma. In the darkness of his slumber, there had been something more, something beyond. He remembered the black-eyed people who stood in the corners watching, waiting to bring him down into their pit. And yet they were also waiting for something else. For the coming of something else. A creature not of this world, one vast and huge, that hovered over the planet like a giant eye, pleased with what men had become because it was so far from what they should have been.

In the coma, he knew all this, *felt* its truth like a cold terror. In the darkness, even as he was split open and feasted upon by the children with black eyes, it was their master, their unseen overseer, who terrified him the most. The one whose voice he heard in his mind.

The coma had somehow protected him from the creatures, as if he were on pilgrimage to this place, not yet theirs to occupy. But with his waking, that master seemed to have emerged with him, following him back into this world, distorting the real, creating the unreal. Toying with his logic as if to show him that his science was shallow.

This must be madness. To be crazy, to know it, but to have no power to stop it. The bullet broke my brain.

Then, as if to prove the point, he saw the old home-less man again. He was pedaling down the street on his rusty bike in the darkness, his knees high and awkward like a bug. And as he passed the car, he stared at Sunday with empty sockets, his eyes hollowed out of his skull as if by a scoop. In his hand, by the handlebars, dangled a human eye. Sunday's eye. John knew it.

Sunday turned around in the seat and watched the old man bike out of sight.

He was losing it. His ability to distinguish real from imagined was gone. And he wanted to weep, because he was afraid to go on like this, but far more afraid of what would happen to him if he died.

Dawn came, and a black SUV pulled up outside the gate at Ferguson's house. A few seconds later, the garage door opened and another black SUV pulled down the drive. The gate opened, and the waiting SUV tailed the vehicle from the home.

Ferguson was being escorted to work.

Sunday didn't follow.

He watched as the two-man security detail that had patrolled the yard retreated now into the house. With the boss gone, they'd likely grab a cup of coffee. They'd still watch the front, but via a security camera, from the comfort of a couple of chairs.

Around ten-thirty, a garbage truck lumbered up the street like a dirty dinosaur. Sunday timed its pace. At each house, the truck would pause for ten to twelve seconds—just long enough for the worker on the back to jump off, grab a bag from a bin, and chuck it into the back of the truck. Then they would move on to the next house.

He waited for the truck to pass, reversed into a driveway, then pulled behind the garbage truck as if he was being a patient driver. When the truck reached Ferguson's house, he pulled over and parked such that he was shielded by the truck from the view of the cameras on Ferguson's gate. He quickly jumped out and walked to the rear of the truck. The worker grabbing garbage gave him a curious look.

Sunday pulled out a fold of hundred-dollar bills.

"Two hundred bucks for that bag. A hundred more to keep your mouth shut."

By the time the garbage truck moved on, John Sunday had already driven away with Ferguson's trash sitting in his back seat.

Sunday checked into a dingy Best Western. If this was their best, he didn't want to see their worst. He dumped the bag of garbage onto a tarp he'd purchased from a hardware store, then put on some disposable gloves he'd bought along with the tarp and went fishing.

He sifted through used Keurig coffee pods, empty cans of soda, the remnants of fast-food sandwiches, half a dozen banana peels. The food of men bound to surveillance or security. He dug through junk mail—a flyer for a pressure washing company, a pizza deal with free garlic rolls, a company promising hydro-blade sculpting so you could lose weight and look good in your bathing suit. He found a receipt from a sandwich shop, another from an online bulk store.

That last receipt was interesting because of the amount: $12,423.13. Apparently the company sold freeze-dried food in bulk. Ferguson had bought pouches of cheesy lasagna, pouches of chicken noodle soup, pouches of potato pot pie. Entire pallets' worth of canned goods and boxes of noodle bowls. Sardines in cans, Chicken of the Sea, hot and spicy noodles. Cans of Vienna sausages and Dole fruit bowls. Black beans, baked beans, green beans.

And toilet paper... he'd bought two full pallets containing twenty cartons each, each carton with ninety-six rolls. Someone had some serious plans for their ass.

Clearly, these purchases were not for the house. Tom Ferguson had put his home on the market—he wasn't planning on being there much longer. Certainly not long enough to use nearly two thousand rolls of toilet paper.

Wherever he *was* going, he was obviously planning on being there for a very long time.

That night, the dreams were even more real.

He dreamt he stood on a hill, beneath a black sky littered with inky filth, and as he looked down at the rocky ground, a dark black root broke through the surface like a tentacle. Waving in the wind, it sprouted black flowers, which oozed with rank white pus. Sunday realized the flowers were winding about a wooden post—a post from which a man dangled, though Sunday could only see his feet.

The flowers opened their dark petals, and larvae danced within.

Sunday turned then and saw a crowd, many of them on their knees and shrouded in cloaks. They looked up at him with black, hollowed eyes.

And in the center of the crowd was Kat. They had encircled her. She screamed, her voice as distant as it was in the cave, and Sunday moved toward her. He had to save her.

He had taken no more than two steps before the rocky ground swallowed his feet and calves, and he was planted into the earth.

He was forced to watch as she was consumed by them, devoured by teeth and claws. And as she was torn apart, he heard the cry of an infant.

CHAPTER XXXVII

Caesarea Philippi
63 CE

It was nightfall, and Longinus stood at the foot of Mount Hermon. This place would have been beautiful had man not tainted it. A natural spring here fed the Jordan River, its cool water a respite for many, and trees filled the air with the scents of lemon and fig.

But then the Romans had come, and now two temples and a large theater stood at the base of the rock, all devoted to the worship of the god Pan. Statues of the nature god and other pagan deities hid in hollowed-out niches like stone bats.

The centurion crossed through a crowd of writhing people. The ceremony was about to begin, and hundreds had come on this warm night to pray, to offer sacrifices, or to be sacrificed. As the sweat of their bodies caught the torchlight, they looked as if they burned.

Here, at the Cave of Pan, behind the Temple of Augustus, was where the fertility god retired during the winter. His worshippers hoped to awaken him from his retreat and bring the new spring with him. But Pan was not interested in the seasonal desires of men, nor the needs of his crops. He could only be enticed from his cave with the most tempestuous forms of debauchery and decadence. And blood.

So it was that beneath the full moon, musicians played and men and women danced, a slithering sea of pale naked flesh. The sweet aroma of spring was overcome by the tart smell of sex. Some wore the skull masks of goats and rams as they penetrated women on all fours, their heads swaying, their bone horns splitting the air.

Longinus passed a naked man wearing a white death mask, the eyes concealed beneath the plaster, fornicating with a goat. The animal squealed in fear or pain, but it was tied too tightly to flee, and the man soon ejaculated within. A circle of onlookers watched the spectacle.

The centurion continued on through the wine and song and dancing.

A naked woman with an ample bosom and thick nipples approached. "May I taste your cock?" she said as she wiped something unseen from her lip.

"It, like me, searches for another," Longinus answered.

Scorned, the woman left to find another willing to slice between her legs.

Longinus knew that the real festivities had yet to begin. He closed his eyes and prayed to Yeshua that his journey here would be fruitful. He was certain he was the only one in this place voicing such a prayer to the Nazarene.

He joined a procession of a half dozen young men and women who walked slowly to the accompaniment of tibia and drum. They lined up near the swirling waters at the mouth of the cave, where three priests in white robes stood. With the sounds of the instruments in his ears, Longinus could scarcely hear their prayers.

The first in line stepped forward. She was young and plain, no more than twelve years old. She stood on the marble lip at the edge of the waters and shed her white robe, revealing her pre-pubescent body. She appeared thick with wine, as her eyes and head swayed to the rhythm of the flute.

The priests said a prayer, and she dropped feet first into the swirling water.

She tried to surface, but the current was strong. The eddy dragged her around and slammed the back of her head into a rock. She surfaced briefly but made no sound, or if she did, no one could hear it over the drum. By the second time she had circled the pool her fate had been sealed. The current had bashed her against the rocks once more, and she was a lifeless lump of bloody, wet flesh.

The others followed, one by one. Those who were beaten against the rocks on the surface had been rejected by Pan. Those who disappeared beneath the water and were drawn down into the mouth of the underworld, had been accepted as payment.

When Longinus's turn came, he didn't wait for the priest to finish his pagan prayers; he simply jumped straight into the water.

The current was strong, seizing control, slamming him into the rocks. He hit his head, and blood poured from his forehead into his eyes. Then, as he flailed toward the middle, the current pulled him down. He tried to surface but could not.

If Longinus had learned one thing from his curse, it was that dying *hurt*. Every time was excruciating. The pain was so powerful, so overwhelming, that no matter the outcome, he was always afraid. There was always a primal fear to dying.

This time his chest filled with water. He gasped for air, and instinctively he panicked. His lungs filled to the bursting point, and his heart seized in his chest.

He sank deeper into the darkness of the water, dead for many minutes, but his mind was still aware. He knew he was dead, his arms and legs no longer responding. But in the murky brown cold water he had to wait for the brain to finally sleep.

Eventually, the familiar black washed over him again.

* * *

His eyes opened. His cheek was wet and cold. He thought for certain the allotted time had passed, and he would clear the slime that covered him after the three days of his death, and again he would reveal a new face.

But this time, something was different.

Normally he tasted the flavor of raw meat—that was the taste of the coating that usually cloaked his face. But now he tasted something earthen and wet. His eyes opened, and saw he was lying on the muddy bottom of a pit. The sound of rushing water was all around him, as if he was near a waterfall, but the sound came from above.

He looked up. Some sixty feet above was a swirling pool, hanging in space above him like a cloud. Somehow, in the bottom of this pit, he was beneath the pool, but was not underwater.

He got to his feet and stood before the mouth of a wide cave. It was too dark to see into, but from within he heard the howl of the wind and the cry of what sounded like thousands of animals, a steady wail. *The baying of wolves?* No, this was different. More like the howls of humans.

The shadows before him moved, congealing like ink in water. And he heard a voice. A deep tone that seemed to vibrate from within his own skull.

"The one who cannot die. The curse of the Christ."

The presence was inside his mind, seeing all the thoughts within that were or had ever been.

"Do you know why I come?" Longinus said aloud.

"We do. But you shall not find what you seek."

"I bring a message of salvation for my wife, and you shall not stand in my way."

"We smell the blood of the Christ within you, child of dust. But you do not possess enough to breach this gate."

"My wife. Where is she?"

"Kept from you, lest you soil her with your words more than those here stain her with their seed."

"Bring her!" Longinus demanded.

Suddenly the ground lifted and the earth and mud clamped down on Longinus's calves. The mud melted into his skin and coursed through his veins. A stalagmite rose behind him and the earth and air pressed him against the rock, his arms spread wide so he took the shape of a crucified man. Rocks jutted through his wrists and feet, pinning him such that he hung there suspended.

"Centurion, your inability to die does not preclude you from pain."

Invisible hands tore the flesh from Longinus's face in sheets, like he was being peeled. He screamed and writhed upon the rock, but could do nothing to stop it.

The room filled with watchers, their eyes sunk deep into the hollows of their skulls, black and wide as an insect's.

"You have been tricked, centurion. Sent on a fool's task by the messengers of the way. They have sent you here to be rid of you. They know you cannot cross into this world without the key."

"Where is this key?" Longinus screamed through his pain.

"Peter of Capernaum holds it. It appears he has denied you as well."

"Please… my wife." Longinus sobbed.

From the mud walls, a naked woman emerged, sideways, such that only one side of her face was visible. It was pale, drawn of color, and dangled loosely. Then she turned, and he saw her fully. The skin of her face had been split down the middle, leaving her eyes dangling on either side of two flesh curtains. And in the middle of it all was a third dark eye, as if something hiding within had claimed her as transport. A creature that occupied.

"Licinia…" He sobbed. "What have they done?"

"No, what has *he* done!" barked the voice. "Do you think we choose this way? Are *we* not his children?"

The watchers with the dark eyes gathered around Longinus to stare upon this eternal walker of the way, crucified upon the shores of hell. As they surrounded him, the voice tethered his mind, blocking any struggle or question, claiming him, pushing him into the corners of his own body, to bear witness and endure.

"You have killed the child of the one. For that, you are ours. Time here has no clock. We shall play with you until we tire. And you can thank your God for allowing it."

CHAPTER XXXVIII

Kat sat at the dining table, watching Mara struggle to down a spoonful of vegetable soup. Her nausea had returned, and she was as pale as wool.

Kat's bleeding had subsided, but according to her ultrasound, her placenta still covered her cervix, which meant that when it came time to deliver, she would most certainly need a C-section. The doctor had also told her that if the bleeding started again, she would be hospitalized full-time. That scared her. If she proved to be a "difficult" patient, she feared they'd just kill her and the baby and move on to the next woman with a number on her gown.

What happens when I give birth? Stay here to raise it? No way. I'm only here for one reason. And when the baby is done, so am I.

The cafeteria had grown far more crowded than it was when Kat first arrived. They'd even added more tables to keep up with the growing population. In her first week here, Kat had counted forty-three women. Now there were nearly two hundred, and new girls arrived daily. They seemed to be coming in from all over the world. Most were Middle Eastern, likely Syria or

Iran, but there were also Pakistanis, Indians, Asians, and Africans. All of child-bearing age, of course.

Were they abducted? Taken from their families like Mara had been? Prisoners of war?

And why were there so many? How many little Jesus babies could they need?

The nuns had also organized the seating, arranging girls based on their week of pregnancy. There were six girls in Kat's group, including Mara. The other girls were just numbers. Sitting directly across from Kat was a dark-skinned African woman. 6726. They'd never spoken—they weren't allowed to, and probably didn't even speak the same language. But Kat had often watched her. Round and plump, she would always devour her food as if each meal were her last. She seemed fine being here, content, as if being here was actually an improvement over her previous life.

After breakfast the dark nuns, the Disciples as they called themselves, stepped toward Kat's table, staves clenched tightly in hand.

"Stay," Ulga said, gesturing with her staff for them to remain seated.

A change?

Change is bad.

When the rest of the girls in the cafeteria were escorted back to their rooms, the girls at Kat's table remained, looking around nervously.

The side door opened, and Grand Mother stepped into the dining hall. Kat's hair stood up on her neck.

Grand Mother was not physically intimidating—she was no more than five-four—but her gait was menacing. One leg was shorter than the other, resulting in a hulking lumber, like she was crawling over rocks to come for you.

"Look at you," she said as she approached the table, using the warm soothing voice she usually reserved for reading the evening gospel. "My *special* children." She beamed. "I have a treat for you."

The Disciples rounded them up and led them out through the side door—a door Kat had only seen the nuns use. They passed through a hallway filled with window frames fitted over huge LCD screens that showed images of the sun shining over a beach. Speakers piped in the sound of waves crashing on the shore, and the fainter sound of a choir singing a hymn. They stopped at a set of double doors and waited for the familiar sound of locks clicking open. Then they stepped through into an area that looked like a hospital ward.

Grand Mother led them to an observation window that looked into another room. "There," she said, pointing.

The women moved closer. At the center of the room, on a pedestal in a glass chamber, as if it were on display at a museum, was the porous rock Kat had seen from the dig. The one that had come from the clay jar.

"The sponge used to clean the Christ," Grand Mother said. "The code of the Christ is locked within. It is from that, that we have seeded you."

Seeded? They pulled DNA from the sponge?

"Come. And see."

Oh my God. I thought I was carrying the cult man's baby. What is growing inside me?

As the nuns led them onward, she worked through the science in her mind, trying to convince herself that there wasn't some mutated thing inside her now feeding off her umbilical. She knew scientists had pulled DNA from the powdered bones of Neanderthals far older than the Christ. That DNA had been inserted into frog eggs and mice. They'd even done work with DNA from woolly mammoths. But this...

Could two-thousand-year-old DNA be preserved well enough to successfully fertilize a human egg? Perhaps if the sponge was insulated somehow. It had been kept hidden, sealed in the jar. And the cave was cold, like a refrigerator.

Could it work?

That was why they needed so many women. As *insurance.*

They stopped at another observation window, this one overlooking a room with three babies in bassinets and three others in playpens. Two women moved around the room, caring for the babies.

Grand Mother beckoned to one of the care workers, and the woman wheeled a sleeping baby in a bassinet closer to the window. The baby was beautiful, just lying there peacefully on his back.

"So precious," Grand Mother said. "This gift of life given to us by our Father. These are the children who have come *before* the way of the rock. They have paved the path for us, showing us how to farm with the seeds of the Father. *This* child shall grow to be a great warrior. A defender of the faith. And when he dies, he shall rise again."

With a smile, Grand Mother turned and strode onward, and the flock dutifully followed. They left the medical area, passing through a locked door into a hall with many doors on both sides. A bulletin board on one wall was filled with children's drawings, and Kat glanced at it as they passed. One rough crayon drawing showed a woman lying on a table and a man holding a knife standing over her. The woman had blood dots on her chest and X's over her eyes.

Grand Mother stopped at one of the doors, waited for it to unlock, then led the group into a classroom. A young teacher stood at the front of the room, a dozen children before her, all between the ages of about five and twelve.

"Hello, children," Grand Mother said.

"Hello, Grand Mother," the class answered in unison.

"I have a special treat," Grand Mother said, gesturing toward the women like she was a host on a game show. "The mothers."

The children let out a simultaneous "Ooohhhh."

"Who would like to touch them?" Grand Mother asked.

The children raised their hands with great glee.

Grand Mother clapped her hands with delight, then turned and nodded at Ulga.

"Lift your gowns!" Ulga shouted.

Lift my gown? Kat looked over at Mara. *For children?* None of them were wearing any underwear.

"Lift!" Ulga barked, moving closer to Kat.

Some of the women reached down and rolled their gowns to expose their bellies and breasts. Mara slowly followed, and then, feeling the weight of the collar around her neck, so did Kat.

"All right children," Grand Mother said, as if she were about to hand out cookies. "Single file."

The children lined up, and one by one they came forward and awkwardly planted a kiss on each woman's round belly. Two boys snuggled in deep with their cheeks, like they were nesting. Another boy lingered over Kat, rubbing his cheek against her bare flesh just above her pubic line. Then he turned and faced her belly button.

"The hour comes," he whispered, the heat from his mouth upon her. He kissed just above her pubic hair.

Kat shivered as his wet lips and words touched her flesh.

When the children were finished, the women lowered their gowns and were escorted back to their rooms.

That night Kat lay in bed, wondering what was inside her. Before lights out, Grand Mother came over the loudspeaker to read the evening passage, which, for the first time, was from Revelations. Normally her voice was gentle during these readings, but tonight it was tense and precise.

"The revelation from Jesus Christ, which God gave him to show his servants what must soon take place!"

CHAPTER XXXIX

Only a few people occupied the Tombs when Sunday walked in at just before seven. The bar across from Georgetown University had a permanent gloss of spilled beer that had soaked into the wood and floor, giving everything a permanent stickiness and the smell of stale hops. The walls were decorated with vintage war recruitment posters with slogans like "Men Wanted."

As Sunday pulled up a stool, a bleached-blond college girl with a face caked with makeup sauntered over from behind the bar. She smiled, sizing him up. He wasn't a professor, she surely deduced that much, not with the eye patch. Perhaps she was wondering if this older, dangerous-looking man might show her a thing or two.

"Hi," she said, moving her tits into proper viewing position. "What can I get you?" She had a slight Chesapeake accent.

Sunday smiled politely. "Bud, bottle."

"Sure." She grabbed the beer from the ice bin, popped its cap, and slid it over.

"Is it usually this quiet?" he asked.

"We got a late-night happy hour. Two for one 'til one. This place will get plenty crazy in a few hours. Stick around," she said with a coy smile.

He nodded, tipped his beer, and took a swig. It was honey on his throat, his first taste of alcohol in the six months since the cave, and it brought back memories of the quest for the deeper high. For the first time since he'd woken, he felt the stir of that beast from within.

He grabbed a booth in the corner. At just after nine, as promised, the party began. First came herds of frat boys, like packs of loud dogs. Then came the gaggles of sorority girls, who spent a considerable amount of time looking down at their phones or taking selfies. There was a bevy of others, stragglers and oddballs. All of them young, all of them loud.

At around ten thirty, Sunday watched a tall brunette stroll into the bar with a shorter blonde. The brunette and her friend got a table, and the blonde went off to fight the traffic at the bar, already a stumble in her stride. The brunette, left alone, nibbled at her thumbnail. She was nervous, uncomfortable here, as if her father would be disappointed if he were to see her in such a place.

One of the frat boys seized his opportunity. He strolled up, leaned against the high-top table and spoke to her. He was big, with wide shoulders and a thick neck—perhaps a football player, maybe a wrestler. Easily two seventy, with arms like flanks of rump roast. He was drunk, which made him confident. Sunday couldn't hear his words, but he could imagine well enough. The girl tensed at his presence and said nothing.

It wasn't until her friend came back, two beers in hand, that the brunette spoke. Whatever it was she said, the frat boy recoiled. He shook his head, pointed at them both, and informed them loudly, over the noise of the bar, that they were both female body parts, before returning to his pack.

At just after eleven, Sunday saw that the blonde friend had been drawn into the lure of a group of boys in a far corner. She flirted drunkenly, while the brunette sat alone, bit her nails, and checked her phone. Something was on her mind; she didn't want to be here. Perhaps her friend had dragged her out, or perhaps she really had wanted to go out and party, only to realize that alcohol and boys and loud music weren't going to solve whatever it was she was trying to escape.

When she got up and went to the bathroom, she took her phone with her, and Sunday noticed that the frat boy who'd previously pressed his luck with her rose and strolled past her table. As he passed, he subtly dropped something into her bottle of beer.

Son of a bitch.

Sunday leaned back in the booth. He had been hoping she'd leave her cell phone behind on the table. But perhaps there was another opportunity here. One he hadn't anticipated.

He paid the tab to the bartender, who said she was disappointed he wasn't staying. She got off at three. He stepped outside, away from the incessant noise of the bar, walked down the street, and tucked into a back alley where he could watch the door.

As he stood there, the sounds of the bar drifting into the night, he thought he saw someone in the shadows of another alley across the street, watching him. The man's face was pale, even in the darkness, and his dark eyes glinted with reflected light. Sunday wondered if the man was real. He just couldn't be sure anymore.

Twenty minutes later, the brunette stepped out of the bar alone.

* * *

Eve McAllister crossed 36th Street, bound for her apartment on M Street. She paused on the sidewalk across from the bar and looked back, wondering if her friend would even notice her absence. Fucking Samara. Sam had ditched her, and now here she was walking home alone.

I mean what the hell? She was supposed to help me meet a decent guy, and instead she hangs on the first guy who shows her any interest. I swear to God the second she gets a drop of alcohol in her, her fucking pants drop so fast...

She felt her mind starting to spin. She'd only had three beers, which she'd nursed over the course of two hours, but she felt far drunker than she should have been.

You're just tired.

She walked to the top of the stairs, the ones made famous by *The Exorcist*. It was a place where college kids took pictures making it look like they too had fallen down the steps, like Father Karras in the film. Their descent mocking his, or perhaps predicting their own. Yet as Eve stood at the top of the steps, her head spinning, she felt like she might tumble for real.

She just wanted to go home. Down the stairs, along M Street, past the muddy waters of the Potomac, and to her apartment. And her bed. She'd had a long day. Truth was, she'd had a long few months. And none of it made any sense.

First there was the car accident. She remembered the tow truck plowing into the side of her car. She could still hear the screeching of metal, could see the sparks, could feel the slamming of that unstoppable metal force. Until that moment she had felt so in control of her life, steering wheel in hand—and then in that moment she realized it had all been merely an illusion, that it was actually mindless physics that dictated her existence without care or compassion. She remembered drowning in an exploding airbag, and then nothing. Blackness.

When she woke in a hospital bed, her daddy was there, ragged and tired and unshaven. He sobbed, and wept, and scooped her into his arms and held her. He hadn't held her like that since she was a little girl. A baby so safe in her daddy's arms. Then he did something she had never seen him do. He dropped to his knees in front of the bed, and he prayed. He thanked God and swore his allegiance and love to God for what He had done. For bringing back his baby girl.

When she had enough energy, she slid her legs off the bed and moved slowly toward the bathroom. It felt like she'd never walked before—like her arms and legs had just been reattached to her body. It was after she used the toilet, when she went to wash her hands, that she saw her face in the mirror over the sink.

An unfamiliar face stared back at her.

Before the accident, she'd had curly brown hair and green eyes. Her cheeks were round and her lips full. Now she had straight black hair, a button-like nose, a less-defined jaw, and her eyes had turned brown. She was a completely different person.

At first she thought someone was playing a joke on her—that someone had somehow replaced the mirror with a TV monitor and was playing back an image of someone else. Or there was an actress on the other side pretending to be her. Miming her movements like on some TV prank show. Looking back now, she was amazed how long it took her to put the puzzle together. She supposed it was just so unbelievable, and her mind desperately sought rational solutions.

But the reality was, *it was her*. Which made no sense. The laws of man were supposed to be firm. But she could see the truth of it, could tell she was in there, behind those new eyes, as if her mind was trapped in a high tower and looked out now through two window slits.

She wondered what had happened to the old her. The old face.

She reached out and touched the glass, and for a moment, it felt as if the person staring back at her would reach through and grab hold of her fingertips. That this person who did not look like her had crawled through some distant realm to get here now just to stare back at her. A mirror child of another world, another set of circumstances and time, a seed hatched in a slightly different place that grew different branches but bore the same fruit.

It truly made no sense. And she fell to the bathroom floor crying, her mind unable to wrap itself around the unknown.

That was months ago. In time, she'd adjusted. She still didn't *understand*, but she'd accepted that this was who she was now. The same person, but with a different face.

Her father had explained that her transformation had been achieved through a secret CIA program designed to rebuild injured soldiers quickly. Code name: EVE. He said she could never talk about it or ask questions. He even made her promise.

It was a good story. But it was a lie.

Before she left for college, she'd come home drunk. And her daddy was angry and she was still drunk and she threatened him with the only thing she could: his love for her. She said she was going to go to the press and talk about the CIA program. He said that would get her killed. She said she didn't care, that she already felt dead inside, and then finally, he crumbled, confessing that a single man had given her a blood transfusion that had returned her from the dead.

Daddy then told her more things she didn't want to hear. Things she still couldn't accept about the man who had resurrected her.

And then this morning Daddy called and told her that she needed to be ready to leave at a moment's notice. Because the man whose blood coursed through her veins was coming… and he was going to bring about the end of the world.

That was why she'd wanted to go out and get drunk—so she could forget all about Daddy's call and his stupid plans. But as she'd looked around at all those jocks and frat boys, she knew she didn't want to be there. If the world really was going to end, then couldn't she at least be with a real man? She was going to be holed up underground somewhere for God knew how long. Couldn't she at least have some heaven on earth before it all went to hell?

She started down the stairs. The *Exorcist* stairs. She felt increasingly unsteady, and feared she was going to finish the trip with a somersault that cracked her skull. She also had the vague feeling she was not alone.

She stopped, looked back up the stairs, and saw a shadow standing at the top, staring down at her.

She quickened her pace, trying to get to the bottom before she fell. But another figure appeared at the base of the stairs. He started up.

Nothing to do with me. Just someone going up the stairs, she told herself.

"Fuckin' cunt."

She knew that voice. That shape and size. It was the frat boy from the bar. And God, she hated that word. Second time in one night. But she hated even more that he was inches away from her. Too close.

Eve contemplated trying to run back up the steps, but she was drifting dangerously to one side, like she was about to topple.

Oh my God. I've been drugged.

She turned, and another boy, this one just as big as the other, was coming down the stairs toward her. The two boys grabbed her, one on each side, and escorted her down the steps. She felt something sharp pressing into her side, but it didn't matter. She was losing feeling anyway. Her limbs drifting away like sails on ships moving in opposite directions.

At the bottom of the steps they dragged her behind a construction dumpster and threw her down onto the ground. She felt only a dull, distant pain as her elbow hit the pavement. One of the boys cut at her shirt with a knife, tearing it away from her body. Then he did the same to her bra straps.

She felt the night air and was vaguely aware she was exposed.

"Hold her!" the frat boy shouted.

The other obeyed, pinning her arms up over her head and pressing down on her wrists.

But she was no longer there. Her eyes drifted listlessly in her skull like dice rolling across a board.

She felt tugging between her legs, heard the ripping of fabric, and then the frat boy climbed on top of her as if he was getting on a motorcycle. She could smell stale beer in his breath, ripe and hot on her neck.

Then things changed. Very quickly. There was a thud, and she looked up at the frat boy, tried to focus. He hovered over her for a moment longer before collapsing next to her, motionless.

And there in the darkness above stood a man with an eye patch, clutching a brick.

The other boy dropped her arms and scrambled to his feet. A knife flashed in his hand, and he jabbed at the other man's abdomen.

If Eve had been more aware, she would have seen the man with the eye patch moving in a flurry of precise motion. He deflected the knife with the brick while he grabbed hold of the boy's wrist with his free hand.

Then he slammed the brick into the back of the boy's knuckles like a nineteenth-century Puritanical teacher scolding a mischievous student. Bones snapped, shattered, and the knife dropped.

The man swung the brick like a bat into the inside of the boy's right kneecap, and the frat boy toppled forward like a puppet that had lost a vital string. But even as he fell, the man swung the brick upward, an uppercut that struck the frat boy's nose. His head was flung backward and blood sprayed.

The frat boy fell to the ground. The man tossed the brick aside and reached down to help Eve.

She felt him lifting her up. Carrying her. Her mind drifted, unconcerned. She only hoped this man was taking her someplace safe.

* * *

Outside the small brownstone where he knew she lived, John Sunday fished through her small purse for her keys. He had been worried a passing car might see him carrying this girl over his shoulder, and the driver would call the cops, but only one car passed them, and the driver was looking down at his phone.

He unlocked the front door and carried her into her one-bedroom apartment. He'd already been inside, while she was at classes and the gym. He'd already gone through her closet, and kitchen cupboards, and desk drawers. He'd found receipts for the bar up the street, saw that she visited on weekends with some regularity.

He laid her gently on the bed, and she rolled over, her right breast falling free of what remained of her bra.

Sunday pulled her cell phone from her back pocket. He pressed her thumb onto the pad to unlock it, then opened her email and found her father's name in her contacts. He took out his own phone and emailed her a phishing file. He attached that file to a photo he found on her phone—the girl and her father posing in front of the Lincoln Memorial—typed a quick "Miss you. Love you," and pressed send.

He then pulled up her browser history. Most of it was ordinary stuff, but she'd done a number of searches on someone named "Josef Belac." Whoever that was, the girl seemed awfully interested in him. Her searches on him included key words like "DNA," "genetics," and "history."

Who is Josef Belac?

He returned the phone to her pocket, gently pulled up the covers around her half-naked body, and left the keys on the counter before he left.

* * *

When Tom Ferguson opened the email from his daughter on his phone, he smiled. Ever since the change, he felt he'd been losing her. That she'd been drifting away. And after he'd called her to tell her that He was coming, he was worried that she might do something stupid. Get too drunk. Try drugs. Sleep around. Live like she was about to die. Because, well, she just might.

And he wanted her to be clean enough for Heaven, because he wasn't sure what was coming.

He knew she hated him for what he'd done. Bringing her back, only to tell her it would all go away again. That the end was coming. So her email was a nice surprise.

But when Tom Ferguson opened the attachment from his daughter and read her note—that she did love him—he smiled even wider.

Not because he believed she had suddenly forgiven him. No. He didn't believe that.

He smiled because he knew John Sunday had hacked his phone by hiding an encrypted file in an email sent by his daughter. And now Sunday would follow the bread crumbs wherever Tom left them.

CHAPTER XL

Caesarea Philippi
63 CE

Longinus coughed up brown water from his gut. He gagged for air, hurled again, and looked around.

He was on the shore of the Jordan River, not far from the cave where he had gone in. It was night. What night, he did not know.

He vomited again, brown river water and stomach bile. He wiped his mouth, rolled over on the muddy bank, and looked up at a full moon shining through the clouds. He lay quietly, and from up the river he could still hear the tibia, the songs of the naked masses.

He had been in Tartarus for what felt an eternity. But here, it seemed no time had passed.

He looked down at his naked body. He was covered in a stitching of red scars, the reminders of their claims upon him, as if he'd been broken apart and then pieced together again and again.

How could God torture him and his wife so, while Longinus had given so much of himself for Christ? How could those souls be lost, kept so far from the light? They had been cast out because their God did not want them. Their bodies were twisted and broken, and worst of all, occupied. Dark creatures used their bodies as chariots, bending their flesh to fit their own, controlling their minds with voices that drowned out reason and love and forgiveness. It was their way. As if these creatures had been made for only this purpose, to feed on the dead like flies drawn to rotting meat.

This was the fate of the abandoned dead. And no one came to save them.

What kind of God would do that?

CHAPTER XLI

While Sunday kept an eye on the tracking program that was following Tom Ferguson's cell phone—Sunday was by no stretch of the imagination a computer genius, but technology these days made it almost as easy to be the watcher as it was to be the watched—he also searched the Internet for whatever information he could find on Josef Belac.

Josef Belac was born sometime around the year 1900, the seventh son of a seventh son, and rose to become the head of the powerful Belac banking family based out of Rome. He invested widely in military, medical, and infrastructure. He made deals with kings, built railroads, funded wars. But despite his influence, it was said that he lived his life as a ghost, extremely reclusive and rarely seen. When he died in 1987, his net worth was estimated at nearly one trillion dollars, in today's money. But his fortune was never seen again, hidden in trust funds that were never made public.

Why had the girl been looking into this man?

While he searched, the tracking program updated constantly, showing where Ferguson's phone had been and where it was going. For the last four hours, it had been somewhere over the Atlantic, and then over Spain. It finally stopped in Rome.

Rome?

What are the odds?

Sunday picked up his duffel and drove to the airport, where he paid in cash for the nine-and-a-half-hour flight. On board the plane he watched a bad movie, ate small portions of processed food that reminded him of the bunker, and sought to alleviate the boredom with a soldier's best friend: sleep. Thanks to the hum of the Triple-7's engines, he was quickly out.

But it was not a restful sleep.

It never was.

This time he dreamt of darkness. And horses. Or what he thought were horses. The darkness was thick, almost as thick as the darkness in the cave. But he was on a shore, and in the distance was a crumbling castle.

He saw them in the night. Hundreds of them, like Indians circling the wagon train.

And they galloped full speed toward him.

They did not make the noises of men, or even of horses. Instead he heard only the constant, incessant chirp of crickets.

Then he saw them. Pale, washed of color, as if they were things that burrowed deep beneath the earth. They were neither rider nor beast—they were both. These twisted creatures rode the broken bodies of men and women, but those men and women had been absorbed into their flesh such that the creatures sprouted from them.

In the dream, Sunday felt as if he was reliving an ancient battle, one that had played out long ago, or perhaps one that would happen one day in the future. He felt as the soldiers or peasants of old must have—that he was about to endure the wrath of a superior force. Enemy hordes rode down upon him, shaking the Earth, prepared to slaughter everything in their path.

But then he realized he was not alone. There was someone else there, with him, in the dream. Someone he was supposed to be protecting. But how could he save them from such a massive army?

Then he heard it. The cry of an infant in the darkness. And the screams of the one he sought most: Kat.

He saw her there, clutching the baby in her arms, the horde descending upon them. She called for him, but it was too late—the masses washed over her, burying her.

John screamed.

Then the screeching horde descended upon him as well, and he was slammed to the sand. As before in the coma dream, they split him open, but this time only one crawled inside his flesh, occupying him. He felt as if he was still in the coma, hidden in the distant recesses of his own mind, somehow aware of the outside, but being driven by something else. All that he was, all that he had been, had been consumed by this thing, and he could only ride along, a passenger in the back seat of his own mind, observing its dark intent from the shadows.

He woke with a start. Through the window beside him, the sun was rising in the distance over the clouds. Pink fingers reached out toward him.

It was then he knew. These were more than dreams. More than hallucinations.

These were visions.

CHAPTER XLII

Caesarea Philippi
Two Weeks Ago

The little rental car struggled up Highway 99 through the valley of Mount Hermon in the Israeli countryside. Josef Belac had the window down as he drove, and the warm air blowing past him somehow felt cool as it kissed the scars on his face. He drove past green pastures and desert scrub, all of it beneath the shadow of the mountains. Under the shadow of the mountain king.

He pulled into the parking lot of the visitor's center, got out, and stretched. The car was too small, too cramped for his long legs, and he regretted not getting a bigger vehicle. Or someone to drive him, because his mind wasn't as clear as it used to be. He knew he drifted more and more these days, his thoughts merging between old and new, which made distinguishing time and place difficult. A year would pass, and it would feel more like a week. By Monday afternoon it was already February, by Friday winter again. He would get in the car to start a journey and would find halfway through he couldn't remember where he was going or from where he had left.

He approached a map of the site posted outside the visitor's center. Like him, the site had changed much over the years. Once there were Roman temples here, framing the cave and the source of the Jordan. Then came time and earthquakes, and now there were tour buses and a little shop that sold T-shirts. And he had to pay twenty dollars for an entrance ticket at the gate. *A gate? That's funny.*

An older tourist and his chattering wife came up behind him to look at the map of the nature preserve. They wore matching red shirts with crosses on the back that read "He Lives." She was reading the highlights of a brochure to her husband like he was six.

"This is where the sacrifices were performed," she said as she pointed to the cave. "Where they threw in the bodies. Can you believe that?" Her tone implied Christians would never commit such atrocities.

They began their ascent up the stone steps, their eighty-year-old bones clogging the path to the top. Belac would be behind them now, stuck behind their failing bodies. His mistake.

He sighed heavily behind them, impatient with their slowness. He understood that they were old, but he was much, much older. His first death was at age forty-six, and thus he was always reborn at that age. Then he aged like everyone else, only to die and be reborn again as a forty-six-year-old. His last death was thirty-three years ago, so he appeared to be seventy-nine, but really, who was counting anymore? Numbers were just numb mockeries shouting into the eternal pit of his existence, as useful as measuring inches in space.

The old lady ahead of him continued to talk as they climbed—about Kathy back home, who had gone to France, and how *she* wanted to go to France, and maybe that could be their next trip, but it really depended on in if they could sell the van…

He fought the desire to hurl her off the cliff. He would grab her by the collar of her red T-shirt, clutch the top of her fanny pack that sat atop her enormous ass, fling her over the side, and watch her flail the eighty feet down and smack with a pleasing thud at the bottom. The impact would split bones and insides, and her husband's look of shock would certainly be worth the price of admission.

Instead he simmered and looked skyward. The stone path led beneath the remnants of stone statues of Pan and goats nestled in the rocky ridges like they were waiting for something. When he placed his hand on the stone wall to help guide himself, he could feel them within. The vibrations of their voices, their cries.

The old lady in front of him stumbled and started to fall. Longinus reached out, fast for a man his age, and grabbed her by the back of her arm, catching her. She turned to him and smiled.

"Oh, thank you sir. God bless you."

He smiled and nodded politely.

At the top of the ridge stood a father with a boy of no more than ten. The child clutched his father's hand. It made Belac think of the many children he had fathered. The ones who were of his seed, but not of his loins. They were his, certainly, in the genetic sense, but they still felt as foreign to him as his own changing flesh. For decades he had been using his seed to fertilize the eggs of many, because he knew that one day they would provide the knowledge he would need. So he looked upon his children as his own, but with the same indifference one might expect from a parent fish or ant, creatures that hatch thousands.

He did, however, remember that moment in 1944, truly like it was yesterday, when he first realized the "seeds" she had spoken of were DNA. It was Oswald Avery, a man he'd never met, who had used the two words that suddenly made everything clear. Though Avery didn't know it, it was Belac's foundation that had funded Avery's research into heredity. And when Avery published, that investment had proved worth it.

Transforming principle.

There it was. The two words, the little genetic light bulb. Suddenly Belac knew that Christ had a plan. That He had understood "transforming principle" two thousand years ago just as Belac now understood how infections spread or how the Earth was round. The Christ had had the seeds hidden with the intention of being found again. He *wanted* to come back. He wanted to be resurrected. This was His plan all along. So overnight Belac became, silently, one of the largest funders of global DNA research, human genome mapping, and genetic editing.

In 1984, they successfully took Belac's DNA and implanted it into a woman, an Irish prostitute, and his first child was born. Up until then, his seed had been too weak, and thus he'd never, in all these centuries, and through all his lovers, been able to father his own child naturally. It turned out the reason was lead. If he hadn't died his first death at the edge of a Roman's sword, he would have likely been dead within two years anyway, from lead poisoning, courtesy of Roman aqueducts. It had tainted his insides and reduced his sperm count. But modern doctors were able to find ways around that. And so came Silas, his firstborn.

Now there were dozens of his children spread around the globe, his code swimming in them all, and his powers thus transferred. He could have created more, but with each child the risk increased that one would one day attempt to overthrow him, or that they would leave behind a genetic footprint that an outsider could link to him.

So he had stopped at seventy-two.

It was all just practice for the real thing, anyway. Once they found the sponge, preserved as he had known it would be, pulling the DNA from the remnants of Christ's dried fluids would be easy. And indeed, the DNA proved to be ample—and flawless. No radiation or moisture intrusion. Void of human contaminants like Spanish flu or bubonic plague. And it possessed a remarkable ability to completely regenerate itself, due to a certain gene that could endlessly self-renew, similar to one found in hydra and jellyfish.

All those years it sat in the dark, just waiting for the light of day to be rekindled.

He looked out across the preserve. It was peaceful here. Big blue sky, a clear view to heaven. The Jordan bubbled peacefully below and would eventually lead to a nearby waterfall. Families picnicked near the water.

He turned and looked to the grotto, where a chain barred tourists from entering. When he first came here, the cave was the source of the Jordan, the swirling water its headwater. Since then, the landscape had been changed by earthquakes, and now there was only a spring-fed pool in the cave floor and the broken and faded white marble remnants of the Roman temple, left behind as if someone else would pick up the pieces.

Soon, he thought.

He had come here many times over the years, for Licinia was here, in these stones, in these rocks, and of all those he had loved, none rivaled his first. He felt close to her here. He *was* close to her here. It wasn't like the humans who would plant a gravestone for their dearly beloved in some random spot on earth. No, here he could actually hear her screams in the wind as it rustled the flowers, catch hints of her weeping in the cooing of the pigeons that lingered and stared. She was in this place, buried so deep beneath rock that no machine could dig deep enough to recover her.

He kneeled in front of the cave. Others noticed, and no doubt presumed he was a man of God, a tourist for the Lord, who revered this as the place where Jesus told Peter he would build his rock. But that was not why Belac knelt. He prayed instead to the stone statues above, the ones with horns and hooves. He wanted them to see that he was close.

And that he would soon join them.

CHAPTER XLIII

Kat, Mara, and two other girls sat alone at the cafeteria table under the watchful eyes of the Disciples. The side door opened and Grand Mother again hobbled toward them.

"There are many followers of the way beyond these walls. Come," she said.

Oh God. Here we go again.

Kat, Mara, 6714, and 6723 were led by the Disciples through the inner sanctum, but instead of turning toward the medical lab and children's classrooms as before, they went to a bank of elevators that took them to an underground parking garage.

A bus awaited them, and the women were escorted to the back, past a walled partition, into a part of the bus where the windows had been blacked out. Clearly the Disciples didn't want the women to see where they were going.

They rode in silence, a Disciple next to each woman, along roads they could not see.

An hour later, the bus stopped.

"Up!" Ulga shouted.

The women stepped off the bus, only to find them-selves on a desolate road in the middle of a desert. Kat squinted in the white-hot sunlight. It was the first time she'd seen or felt the sun in eight months. Hot wind swirled sand along the blacktop.

Is this it? Is this the spot where they kill me?

The bus pulled away, leaving the women and the Disciples on the side of the road. Only the shifting sands seemed to know their location.

No one said a word. The Disciples just stood qui-etly, as if waiting.

A few minutes later, a Gulfstream flew low over the horizon, glimmering in the sun like golden water, and landed on the empty highway. It taxied toward them and came to a stop, and the side door opened, stairs descending.

A man appeared in the doorway and looked out at the huddle of women. He wore a wide-brimmed hat and sunglasses, like a tourist on vacation, but Kat could still see who he was.

This was the man from the video.

"My children," he said, arms extended. He waved as if welcoming them home.

The women climbed aboard and were escorted down a narrow shiny row of leathered elegance. The man sat in a large chair at the rear of the plane and spread white caviar between his forefinger and thumb.

"Come," he said as he slurped a finger full of cav-iar. "Fear not." His deep voice was soothing, but his words had the opposite effect on Kat.

The women sat, and a Disciple sat next to each, just as they had done on the bus. The window shades were lowered.

"Look at you," the man said as he spread another rung of fish eggs on his fingers. He was strong, his arms as thick as a goat's neck. "Carriers of the Christ. Birthers of the way. You have been chosen for this by God himself."

"To do what?" Kat asked. A bold step.

The man turned to her and smiled, a mound of small eggs balanced precariously on his fingertips. It was then she saw the cracks in his makeup. It appeared that he was covering up not wrinkles, but scars. Dozens of them.

"Ah, the American." He smiled. "With the return of the Christ comes the fulfillment of the Lord's complete vision for man."

"What vision?" Kat asked.

Ulga started to rise to stifle such insubordination, but the man raised his palm ever so slightly, and the burly woman sat.

"To return to the light," the man said. "Look at what we have become. Are we not consumed with vanity, and greed, and violence? Has man not failed? First in the garden, then at Golgotha? God has turned His back on us. And we devour ourselves in His shadow. So we must appeal to His grace. We must bring back the son whom we struck from this earth, because of which God has abandoned us to our machines. And when the son returns, mankind shall witness the one true God, and in His overwhelming light, our judgments and wars shall end. And God shall remember us then and turn back and shine His brightness upon us. A fire that lights the way, but also must burn. And this is right. And it is just. And it is my gift to you."

He toasted her with the finger full of caviar, then slurped it into his mouth, the eggs popping between his teeth.

Kat's mind tried to parse his tangle of words, decode his Biblical rhetoric, but it all boiled down to one clear thought:

This guy is fucking crazy.

CHAPTER XLIV

Rome, Italy
64 CE

Longinus sat on horseback on Palatine Hill and watched as the city burned. As the fire roared into the night sky, the people scrambled frantically below, running from flames, running from fate.

After he'd drowned, the beasts of hell had made him a proposition, and accepting its terms was the only way in which he could escape. Find the key, unlock the gate, and he would be reunited with his beloved. Until then, she would suffer.

He had taken the deal. And then he'd surfaced again, his face once again changed, although the scars of hell still seared his flesh. With a new identity, he returned to Rome, stepped off the path of the followers of the way, and resumed the only role he'd ever really known: soldier. He arranged for forged papers that stated he had shown great valor with the IX Legion in Britannia against the revolt led by the Iceni queen, Boudica—and one look at his face would confirm to anyone that he bore the scars of battle. Thanks to the papers and his skills with a sword, he had found a place on the palace grounds as one of the emperor's personal bodyguards.

Much had changed in the city. Much had not.

The new emperor, Nero, had returned the treason trials, had murdered his wife with his bare fists, and had married a man. In a way, Longinus found it comforting that, even as he spiraled through time, the insanity of men remained constant.

Though it was night, it was miserably hot. He removed the crested helmet from his head and wiped the sweat from his brow. Below him, the flames roared and people wailed.

Hotter for them, he thought.

Nero was a fool who wanted nothing more than to be worshiped, wishing to be an actor instead of an emperor. He sang and danced and monologued. Then, suddenly, he was possessed with a singular vision to build a great palace, with a great statue of himself. But there was no money, so Nero sulked around the palace, choosing monologues in which he would weep.

Late one night, Longinus had gone to the emperor's bedside and whispered in his ear. It was a most unusual and dangerous act, but Longinus did not possess the fear of punishment that would plague a normal soldier.

"Emperor," he whispered.

Nero shot up in the bed, stammering.

"What? What is it? Do they come?"

"Nay, Emperor. You are safe."

Nero collected his thoughts and turned.

"Who are you to wake me?" he barked.

"I am the man who comes to you with a solution on how to build your Golden House."

Nero started to speak, then stopped. "Continue," he said.

"To build your home, you need land. And nothing clears land faster than fire."

"What are you saying? That I burn my own city?"

"Not you, Emperor. But the cult that lives with the Jews, near the Circus Maximus. Those who follow the Nazarene. They pray to their God for this Babylon to fall."

"Treason," he spat through breath tainted with sleep.

"Aye, but what if their prayers were answered with fire? Your duty would be to punish such traitors, and the land would be cleared. And then?"

Nero nodded. "My palace…" He smiled. "What is your name, soldier?"

"Longinus. And I am loyal to you, Emperor."

It was Longinus who set the fire himself. Three nights later, dressed as a beggar, he descended into the city under the cover of darkness and set the fire at a shop near the Jew slum.

Now, hours later, he need only watch as the smoke and flaring ash spewed toward the heavens. A little girl cried and screamed in search of her mother.

And Longinus hoped God was watching.

CHAPTER XLV

For once, John Sunday didn't stand out. The Ospedale Britannico—a post-war, peeling-copper-domed hospital off Via della Navicella on the outskirts of the city—was an inpatient hospital that specialized in retina and eye care, so a man wearing an eye patch fit right in. As he strolled through the hallways, no one gave him a second glance.

He had already checked the hospital from the outside, assessing its access points. Now he took an elevator up to the top floor. There was apparently some construction going on to repair the ceiling, and a whole section of the floor had been cleaned out so the crews could work. Sunday strolled casually to one of the windows, hoping no one would bother him.

One of the workers, a burly bear of a man, shouted from the scaffolding.

"*Posso aiutarti?*" he called down. "*Non puoi essere qui!*"

Sunday had no idea what this guy was saying, but he got the gist. He just smiled, acted lost, put his hands in the air, and said one of the three Italian words he knew.

"*Scusami.*" He was pretty sure he had used that correctly.

He returned to the elevator and went back down one floor, where he spent the rest of the afternoon hiding in a bathroom stall. Only when it was after hours and he was sure the construction crew had left did he return to the top floor. He went straight to the window from which he could see what he had come here to see.

Across the street was the Basilica di Santo Stefano Rotunda—the Basilica of Saint Stephen's Rotunda. Or Saint Stephanie. He wasn't sure about the gender. Remembering some Spanish from his high school days, where the 'o' ending was masculine, he decided Stefano had to be a dude.

He checked his watch. It was just after eight thirty. The Rotunda stood like a black fortress in the night, its old brick absorbing even the light from the nearby streetlamps.

Sunday had come here because Ferguson was supposed to come here. Courtesy of that file Sunday had sent through Eve's phone, he was able to access everything on Ferguson's phone—including his calendar, where Ferguson had set up a meeting at ten p.m. at this location.

Six cop cars blocked the two roads that crossed near the church, and a dozen more cop vehicles, marked and unmarked, sat in the parking lot, which had been closed off to the public. Several security teams walked the grounds, including two teams with Belgian Malinois. That was a lot of security here for just Ferguson, even if he was a future deputy director. And if there was this much *visible* activity, there were sure to be that much more that Sunday couldn't see, including snipers on the surrounding rooftops. In fact, there was likely a team on the roof of the very hospital in which Sunday stood.

At just before nine, a black Land Rover rolled up to the main security checkpoint set up outside the church. And so began a processional of black Land Rovers, all of them pulling up to the church and unloading men in suits and women in black evening gowns. Security people quickly whisked them inside.

Twenty minutes in, Ferguson stepped from one of the Rovers and was escorted inside. Still Sunday waited.

The last vehicle to arrive was different. A black Mercedes van. A security team stepped out first, followed by three nuns dressed head to toe in white. Then a gray-haired man in a dark Armani suit.

The nuns all bulged around their middles.

Are they pregnant?

The nuns wore white veils and form-fitting coifs. But there was something familiar about one. Her movements. She rubbed her hands across her plump belly as if warming the baby.

Kat?

He couldn't tell for sure. He couldn't tell at all, to be honest. It was just a feeling. And lately he'd been seeing a lot of things that weren't there. Then she was gone. Disappearing inside like a white phantom to oversee its own funeral.

His plan had been surveillance. See who Ferguson was meeting with. Now he knew he was going to have to go down and get a much closer look.

He turned to move off the floor, but just as he did, a light came on over the elevator doors. Someone was coming to his floor—and he was certain that whoever it was, they weren't here to talk.

CHAPTER XLVI

Having grown up a Jew, Ayelet's time inside churches had been somewhat limited. But because she had been raised in Jerusalem, she was never far from a Christian relic, or church, or monument, and she often found herself lingering outside, curious of the ways of this cousin religion spited by her own. When she joined Mossad, that interest was noted, and she spent a year studying Christianity, specifically Roman Catholicism. She'd studied all her saints, remembered all her vows for mass, and even had her rosary.

So as she stepped over the threshold of St. Stefano's Rotunda, she already knew there was no church like it in the world. She'd studied it, seen pictures in books.

Those pictures didn't compare to the real thing.

Her breath caught in her throat as she looked at the frescoes on the walls of the circular room. Frescoes of horrible beauty. Hundreds of years old, fading and peeling, depicting the early Christians being tortured.

There was a man lying on a table, rivulets of blood pouring from his body as his arms, belly, chest, and thighs were hacked apart with a blade. Behind him were the dead or dying, stacked like wood, reminding her of the mounds of withered bodies from the concentration camps that occupied permanent acreage in every Jew's mind.

There was a woman whose breasts had been hacked off, and yet she looked skyward, a smile upon her lips as if she knew something her murderers did not.

There was a dead man peering from beneath a giant stone block, the heavy rock pressing down with such weight that his intestines unfurled from his sides like coiled pythons.

There were Christians being force-fed molten lead, boiled alive in pots and pools, and a woman split down the middle with a horseman's axe as if the executioner were peeling apart a piece of fruit.

This was art celebrating murder, and horror, and the disembowelment of human beings. In the modern world, it would be exploitative, but the weathering of time made it sacred. A pulling back of the curtain to reveal the suffering of the devout. This place, this church, was a testament to those who had died. To those who had stood up to the Romans who had slaughtered them with such joy and abandon.

Ayelet felt a renewed kinship with the Christians, a common bond of suffering, discrimination, and affliction. It was part of what drew her interest to the religion in the first place.

Egin made the rounds, shaking hands with the powerful people in the room. Then again, everyone in this room was powerful. Ulrich Amon, a Danish billionaire who owned the largest telecommunications company in Europe, Asia, and the Middle East. Martin Seere, a British weapons manufacturer who supplied numerous government and private armies around the world. Andrew Aim, a cybersecurity software developer who built the communications platforms for US spy satellites so ground crews could talk to their birds in space. And Tom Ferguson, of course, future deputy director of the CIA.

All of them had been photographed as they came into the church by the surveillance crew Mossad had in place in the apartments across the street.

Egin came up behind her and placed his hands on her hips.

They had met, curiously enough, at a church. As she left St. Maria in Trastevere, a church near the Tiber, she passed him in one of the pews, where he kneeled beneath the saints, prayer in mouth. Their eyes met, and she moved on. Out in the parking lot, she had a flat tire. After a time, he exited the church and offered to help. As a man of means, he could have had his driver change the tire for her, but to her surprise, he did it himself. She thanked him and offered to pay. He bartered for a cup of coffee together.

And so they sat and talked, within sight of St. Peter's. That was where she told him that her husband had cheated on her. That she was tired of boys. That she wanted a man.

But now, her skin knew this man's touch was not true, and she shivered beneath his breath as his lips touched her neck.

"Are you all right?" he whispered near her ear.

"It's just this place," she said as she studied a painting where a strange device was being used to divide a man in half. She turned to him. "Why are we here?"

"Trust me." Egin smiled, his green eyes like biolu-minescent plankton.

He escorted her to her one of the pews, then ad-dressed the room.

"Ladies and gentlemen," he said. "Please take your seats."

It would seem Egin was the man they had come to see.

"Thank you," he said once everyone was settled. "Thank you for coming. Our Father will be here short-ly. Until then, I can answer any questions you may have."

Several hands went up. He looked around the room and pointed.

"Brother Andras," he said.

This was not what Ayelet had expected. Egin was not merely one of the guests among the crowd. He was leading them.

"Are we still on schedule?" asked Andras, a man as bald as a skeleton, even though he otherwise looked to be only in his thirties.

"Yes. Our most promising candidates are healthy at thirty-four weeks."

Another hand, this one belonging to a man with drooping jowls.

"Brother Buné."

Buné seemed to look past Egin, at Ayelet. "And what if there is… a disruption?" he asked, his French accent thick.

"There should be none. But if there is an unfore-seen circumstance, we are prepared to go early."

"What then?" asked another man.

"Re-read your Scripture, brothers and sisters. The trumpet will sound, the dead will be raised, and we shall be changed. 'The day and hour no one knows, not even the Angels of Heaven, nor the Son, but only the Father. Therefore, you must be ready, at all times, for the Son of Man is coming at an hour you do not expect.' Thanks be to God."

The crowd nodded and said in unison, "Thanks be to God."

Egin stepped into the aisle, revved like a minister in a tent in Southern Mississippi. "And I say thanks to you. You are the chosen. The anointed. Over the years, Father has opened your eyes, shown you the way that is true, the miracle that is the Son of God who lives and breathes in us today. And because you carry the burning flame of God upon your brow, those who are alive, those who are left, will be caught up together in the clouds to meet the Lord in the air! And the path we take to reveal the way will bring this world back into the Kingdom of Heaven. Thy kingdom come, thy will be done."

"Amen," said the crowd.

Ayelet looked around. What exactly were these people expecting? The end of the world? This room held some of the most powerful and intelligent leaders on the planet. Could they all believe that... what? That Jesus was coming back to smite evildoers, like a Biblical Superman?

A verse from her mandatory lessons suddenly popped into her head. It was from Matthew, or at least she was pretty sure it was. *And this gospel shall be proclaimed throughout the whole world as testimony to all nations. And then the end will come.*

Egin turned to the corner of the room, where a gray-haired man stood, flanked by three nuns dressed all in white. Egin stepped toward him and kneeled.

"Father," he said, bowing his head.

"*Optio.*"

Ayelet didn't recognize this man. In a room of famous billionaires, the only one to whom Egin bowed was a stranger.

The gray-haired man in black stepped to the altar, leaving the nuns in the shadows. He clutched a tattered, dog-eared red Bible in his hand.

"Children."

"Father," the crowd said in unison.

"You, my disciples, have seen the miracle that I have brought to you."

The crowd was full of nodding heads.

"Some of you I have come to, in a time of need, as a messenger to burn out the sin of your heart and heal your wounds with the word of the Lord and the blood of my body," he said. He turned to Egin. "Others of you have grown from my seed and know well the path of the way." He held his Bible high in the air. "But both of you are born of me. It is John who wrote, whoever feeds of my flesh and drinks my blood has eternal life, and I will raise him up on the last day. And so it is with you. The last day comes, and I have given you the flesh from which you have fed, the blood from which you have drunk, and in return the life I have given transcends time. For us all, the path is true. The way is marked for the Christ to return. And our mission here, our final blessing, comes to fruition."

He turned to the nuns and gestured with a simple wave of his fingers for them to step forward. "Come. See the way."

The women stood in front of the altar, white and pure, even their faces pale, as if frosted with snow. To Ayelet's shock, they lifted their veils and bandeaus, slowly unbuttoned their habits, and disrobed completely, exposing their thick mounds of pubic hair, their ripening breasts, and their fertile, plump, pregnant bellies.

What are they doing?

Egin stepped forward. "Please," he said to the crowd, a salesman showing off the newest model of Fords. "Approach."

One by one, the masses stood and walked toward the naked nuns, kneeled before them, and kissed their swollen bellies. Some whispered, some prayed. One woman even wept. The nuns just stood there like mannequins, the cold of the rotunda hardening their nipples and stirring the goose bumps on their flesh.

Soon it was Ayelet's turn. Egin stood by the end of the pew, waiting.

Is he expecting me to go up there? To kiss a nun's naked belly?

When she hesitated, he took the back of her arm and forced her to rise. He squeezed her arm tightly, painfully so, but it was what he said that chilled her to the bone.

"Convert, Jew. And when He returns, perhaps you will join us in Heaven."

CHAPTER XLVII

Before the elevator arrived, Sunday moved toward a pile of tools, grabbed a hammer and a crowbar, and tucked behind a concrete support beam.

With a soft ding, the elevator doors opened, and three men armed with MP5s stepped out. They weren't beat cops. They moved across the dark floor with skill, men trained to kill.

He'd have to wait for them to get closer. Their weapon was as effective at six hundred feet as it was at twenty. His—a hammer and crowbar—didn't provide quite the same range.

The men fanned out across the room, navigating the labyrinth of scaffolding. Sunday could tell by their movement patterns that they already knew someone was here. They weren't checking the floor—they were searching it.

One of the men crept within five feet of Sunday's position. The floors were covered with plastic tarps, laid there to protect the carpet, creating a plastic whisper beneath the men's boots—and allowing Sunday to know exactly where they were.

He tightened his grip around the crowbar, stepped around the post, and swung down like a serial killer in a slasher movie.

But instead of hitting the gunman, he hooked the barrel of the rifle, pointing it toward the floor. Sunday had only a half second before the man brought the rifle back up, and he used it—swinging the hammer in his left hand, striking the spot between the man's right eye and the bridge of his nose. The handle reverberated in his palm as the hammer shattered nasal bone.

As the man dropped to a single knee, crying out, Sunday swung the crowbar back through, wielding it like a samurai sword, into the man's raised knee. The kneecap burst beneath the blow, and Sunday half expected the patella to fly across the room like a bone hockey puck.

The other two men opened fire.

Grabbing the MP5 from the man on the floor, Sunday dove back behind the cover of the post. The rounds ripped into the concrete beam. Sunday felt to make sure the weapon was ready to fire, the weight was good, and then he came around, using the post as cover, and put a quick double-tap in each man's head. Four shots total, two to each man's skull.

They dropped onto the plastic tarp, almost as if Sunday had courteously laid it out in advance to help in tomorrow's cleanup.

The entire fight to live or die, as with most, was over in seconds. But the gig was also up. More men would be coming.

* * *

All Kat could do was stand, naked, and allow these men and women, these strangers, to kiss her bare belly. She was a cold statue being fondled by pilgrim's hands, the pins in the gold collar about her neck already rigid—a warning, a message, that someone held the switch that controlled whether she lived or died.

And then she saw a glimmer of hope. Tom Ferguson was here. He could save her!

He approached like the others, a smile hidden in the recess of his lips, and looked her in the eye. He knew her. He recognized her. And yet he said nothing. He simply kneeled before her naked body and kissed her belly.

He was with *them*.

She was theirs now. All of her. And more approached, more cold hands upon her skin, grasping her and embracing her belly, more coarse faces rubbing across her navel, more soft lips wet upon her.

She felt a series of strong kicks inside that almost doubled her over. A swift movement in her belly, as if the child within knew it, too, needed to flee.

* * *

Sunday peeled the bulletproof vest off one of the dead gunmen, then collected the extra clips from his belt and tucked them into a side pouch. He looked to the elevator, contemplating. If he went down, they'd be waiting in the lobby. The same would go for the stairwell, even the fire escapes. These men would know to cover their exits.

He looked up at the scaffolding.

Picking up the crowbar again, he slung the rifle strap around his shoulder and started to climb. At the ceiling, he jammed the crowbar into a sheet of freshly hung drywall and pried. A chunk, the size of a man, dropped to the floor below. Some worker would be pissed, but given the dead men scattered on the floor below, Sunday figured that worker would probably get the day off anyway.

He looked into the roof space. The drywall had been installed onto two-by-fours, which could support his weight, unlike the newer, and far weaker, aluminum framing. And there was enough space up there for him to move about, to crawl over the wood trusses. He snaked the crowbar behind his bulletproof vest, so it was tucked between his shoulder blades like a sword in a sheath, then took one last glance toward the elevator.

The light above the doors turned on again.

They were coming.

CHAPTER XLVIII

Ayelet approached the naked nuns in the center of the rotunda. She could feel the eyes of the men upon her. They knew. They all knew. Ayelet was on display as much as these naked women were. She too was being judged.

She met the eyes of one of the nuns, a white woman with pale, cropped hair. Ayelet nodded slightly, as if to say, *I'm sorry we both have to be here.*

She was prepared to kiss their bellies, as the others had done, but Egin had other plans for her. He pulled her closer to the man in the black suit, the man he called Father. In her ear, he whispered, "The men across the street, the ones taking pictures of us? They're dead."

She said nothing, but inside, she gasped. Her only hope of rescue had been severed. They knew who she was, they'd killed her team, and now they were going to kill her. Perhaps they'd torture her first, but they'd kill her eventually. Of that she had no doubt.

Egin placed her directly in front of the man in the black suit. His hair was graying and tattered, as if it struggled to grow. He wore heavy makeup, and visible beneath it was a maze of scars.

He reached out and stroked Ayelet's face as if she were four.

"My child," he said. "You have a choice. You can accept Jesus Christ as your Lord and Savior and repent for your denials as a Jew. Or you can die right now and find out which of us was right."

They seriously want me to believe in Jesus? Just like that?

"So… do I sign something?"

The man in black smiled, the grin of a man who knew something that she did not, like the smile of the woman getting her breasts hacked off in the picture on the wall. "There is more than that to following the way. Like those in this room, you too shall give. Everything."

"Do you accept Jesus Christ as your Lord and Savior?" Egin asked.

Ayelet looked out at the crowd. She was part of this now. Like the naked nuns. Part of the show. Part of the ritual.

"I do," she whispered.

Egin beamed like a groom on his wedding day as he looked toward the man in black.

The Father smiled as well. "Then let us begin."

* * *

Sunday crawled blindly and silently through the maze of studs, careful not to let anything clank or bang and give away his position. It took him a good five minutes of careful crawling to feel his way to the drop-off that was the elevator shaft. The elevator had gone back down to the first floor, probably loading up with more guys to come join the hunt for him.

He could wait for the elevator to come back up, ride it down, and then try and crawl out onto a lower floor. But that would leave him in the same predicament he was in now—trapped in a building where every exit was covered.

Instead he looked up, toward the top of the shaft just above. Although he was already on the top floor, there was another set of elevator doors above him—a rooftop access for workers. A steel cable on a pulley system hung down the center of the shaft, and he could pull himself up that cable, hand over hand.

The climb was only about ten feet. But he'd have also to lean out to grab the cable—over a shaft that dropped some sixty feet. Eight months ago, he could have done it, even with a ruck and another grown man piggybacking on him at the same time. But now, after the coma, he was half the man he'd been. He just didn't have the muscle meat anymore.

He also didn't have a choice.

He crawled to the edge of the two-by-four frame and reached out for the cable. But even as his fingers stretched to their limits, he was still six inches short.

He'd have to jump.

Fuck.

There was no point waiting. He took a deep breath, gathered his strength, rolled his neck like he was getting ready to step into a boxing ring, and leapt into the emptiness of the shaft.

He felt the steel cable first with his chest as he plowed into it. The impact almost knocked his hands away from the catch. But at the last moment he clutched the steel, only to slide, the friction of the cable burning into his palms, rough patches of unclipped metal shredding his fingers. He clenched and tightened instead of releasing, which was what his brain was telling him to do. It was either that, or the long way down.

He used his new sneakers to slow his descent, then locked his ankles and legs tight around the line, strangling it with his thighs like a jiu-jitsu hold to choke it out.

And then he climbed, a monkey on a vine, pulling himself slowly, tediously, hand over ravaged hand. Blood from his torn palms slicked the ascent.

Jesus, if I had just grabbed a pair of gloves off one of the dead guys...

He released one hand long enough to wipe some blood on his shirt, then performed the same operation with his left. He scooted and pulled, slowly rising, until he was hanging within a foot of the elevator doors.

He heard something in the darkness. Something below. Whispers. Like people were talking about him far below in the shaft.

What were they saying? The words were overlapping, talking over each other.

He runs?

No.

He comes.

He felt something fluttering at his leg, like a bat caught in the fabric of his pants, or something trying to pull him down into the darkness. But when he looked down he saw nothing, even as he continued to feel it clearly as ever.

But then he did see something far below, deeper, much deeper, what seemed like miles beneath the earth: a fiery pit. Wails and screams suddenly rose up the shaft, and the air sizzled with waves of heat. And as Sunday stared into the distant cauldron, in its glow he could see a large shape, like a giant spider, tentacled and vast, with horns upon its head and hands for its feet.

It was climbing.

And as it came closer, he saw that it was not a spider at all, but a tangled mass of humans, bound and stitched awkwardly together.

It's not real, he told himself. *Not real.*

Still the primitive drive responded, and he frantically resumed his climb, determined to escape this thing that was either there or was not.

At that moment the elevator began to move, and with it, the cable. It was pulling him up—but too fast. He was going to be fed into the pulley near the roof. His fingers would be chewed apart as badly as if he had stuck them into a garbage disposal. He slid down against the ascent, reversing as best he could, his hands boiling with pain. And then just as suddenly as it had started, the elevator stopped at one of the lower floors.

The combination of upward and downward movement had largely balanced out. Sunday was still just below the rooftop doors. Holding the cable with his knees and feet, he reached around to grab the crowbar tucked into the bulletproof vest. His hands were so bloody, the metal bar almost slipped from his grip, but he got it. He wedged one end between the metal doors, and pried.

The bar slipped in his bloody hands before he could give it a good push.

The whispers began again below. Different whispers. Human voices. The elevator was loading again. He was running out of time. If that elevator moved again, up or down, his hands were done. He'd just release and fall into the darkness, to be claimed by gravity, or whatever else was down there.

He readjusted the now-bloody crowbar, wedged it back into place, and gave it another strong pry.

The doors moved apart easily—like they had just been waiting for the proper finesse.

He pushed the doors farther apart, then adjusted his feet on the cable and bent his knees so he could spring. He took a breath... and leapt off his lifeline.

His chest slammed into the side of the ledge, knocking the wind out of him. His hands were slick with blood, but somehow he managed to hold onto the lip even with his bloody fingertips. He was dangling in free space.

As the elevator started again, he struggled to lift himself, to pull himself up out of the abyss, his already weakened muscles too tired from the climb, but he dug his fingernails into the ledge and lifted himself up, painfully, until he collapsed on solid ground once more.

He was in a rooftop access space that doubled as an elevator machine room. A blinking red light was the only illumination. He paused in the dim, strobing light to check the state of his hands.

They weren't good.

His fingers were shredded to flesh confetti. The skin on his palms lay in tattered flaps. In his left palm he saw what looked like an exposed white cord.

Fuck. Is that a nerve?

He looked around the room for something to bind his hands, but there was nothing. He settled for gently patting them on his pant legs to blot the bleeding. Then he got to his feet and very quietly touched the handle of the door to the roof. The cold metal felt good in his grip. He slowly opened the door just enough to see what lay on the other side.

As he'd expected, a sniper team was in position about forty feet away, watching the church and street below. He'd have to take them out. His plan was to drop down to the lower rooftop of an adjacent building, moving from roof to roof until he could find a way down to the ground. But the sniper team was in the way.

He looked down at the bloody crowbar in his palms and wondered if he had either the grip or strength to wield it.

CHAPTER XLIX

"Take off your clothes," Egin said, holding a pile of folded white cloth.

"Why?" Ayelet asked.

The crowd in the rotunda watched her intently, eager for the show to begin.

It was the man in black, the Father, who answered. "You must give up your life as a Jew whore. Accept Jesus Christ as your Lord and Savior and repent for your sins. Then, and only then, can you become like them." He nodded toward the three naked nuns. "Chosen."

"If I don't?"

"Then like Judah in hell, we will strip your flesh instead."

Ayelet looked again at the gathered crowd. She had been naked many times in front of strangers. In front of men she did not love. She had used her body as a tool, as a way to get what she wanted. In high school, she'd used it in a desperate grab for affection, for the attention she never received from her father. And when she was trained as an agent for Mossad, she learned to use it for a greater purpose—to gain intelligence for the homeland.

The secret, if there was one, was to detach. To fully disengage mind from body. The real Ayelet tucked away, somewhere deep inside her mind, like a little girl hiding in her room while her parents argued.

Now, again, she compartmentalized, sending little Ayelet back to her room. But the child was never really hidden, was she? The men were always there, being carried around with her, taking her as they pleased while inside her mind the little girl wept for the sins committed in the name of God.

She slowly unzipped the side zipper that held her little black dress together. Had Egin picked this dress because it was so easy to take off? Because he knew she would be doing this?

She gave a slight shimmy and let the dress fall, revealing her black bra and underwear. She reached around, unhooked the bra, and slid out of it as well. Then she rolled her panties to her ankles.

She could feel eyes upon her, icy stares, as she stood like the nuns, cold and naked.

"Come," said the man in black. He gestured with a wave of his fingers for her to step in front of him. "Bend."

She wondered if he had an erection. If this act had aroused him in the house of God.

She did as she was told, bending at the waist, as if performing a ceremonial bow.

The man in black raised a golden cup into the air and dipped it into the water of a basin beside the altar.

"Hear the words of our Lord Jesus Christ: 'All authority in heaven and earth has been given to me. Go therefore and make disciples of all nations.'" He poured the water onto her hair. It ran down the sides of her face and dripped off her nose and chin. "'Baptizing them in the name of the Father and of the Son and of the Holy Spirit, teaching them to observe all that I have commanded you, and lo, I am with you always, to the close of the age.'"

She stood back up, water droplets now rolling down her exposed body.

Egin smiled at her as if he'd just seen his bride for the first time. He handed her a simple folded frock. She dressed, as did the nuns.

Is that it? Is the show over?

A group of armed men approached. One of them whispered in the ear of the man in black. Ayelet was close enough to hear.

"He's on the roof," the man said. "He has nowhere to go."

The Father nodded to Egin, who turned and disappeared with the security team in tow.

Another armed man took Ayelet by her arm.

"Where am I going?" Ayelet asked.

The old man in black smiled, his teeth white and new. "You have been baptized in the name of the Father. And when you die, He shall judge if you have earned the right to wear His name upon your head."

* * *

Sunday opened the door that led onto the rooftop. As he stepped out, he was grateful the roof was made of soft, silent tar paper and not gravel that would betray his footsteps. He clutched the crowbar as tightly as his severed palms would allow, and moved silently toward the sniper team. Their attention was focused on the street and church below, not on what was behind them.

And then a voice shouted from behind him. "Drop your weapon!"

The words were in English, but with a slight Italian accent. And Sunday recognized that voice. It was a voice he would never forget.

The voice of the man in the cave. The man who had tried to end his life. And almost succeeded.

Sunday slowly pulled the MP5 strap off his shoulder and let the weapon drop. He released his grip on the crowbar and let it, too, slide from his mangled fingertips. He turned then, and saw him. The man who had shot him. The man who again pointed a gun at his head.

"Good to see you again, John."

Sunday was immediately swarmed by a half dozen men. Not the sniper team. Apparently a separate team had been waiting for him on the rooftop all along.

"Hands!" someone shouted.

Sunday did as he was told. Someone grabbed his wrists and zip-tied his bloody hands behind his back. He winced as their fingers pressed into his palms.

As he was escorted toward the elevator, he knew three things:

One, he was grateful this time he'd be taking the elevator car down instead of using the elevator cable.

Two, they wanted him alive for some reason. Otherwise they could have simply put a bullet clean through the back of his skull. With slightly better aim this time.

And three, not being dead was a problem. These men weren't connected to any organization, any government. They played by their own rules. Which meant whatever was about to come, would be painful.

CHAPTER L

Rome, Italy
64 CE

Longinus rode by horseback with a dozen Praetorian guards behind him, making their way through the burned streets. The fire had lasted a week, and there was little left but ash.

Before the fire started, Nero had gone to Antium, so as not to arouse suspicion. He had returned to act the role of hero, helping the thousands of refugees who had been burned out of their homes. He let some use the palace, even his garden, as shelter.

How noble.

As Longinus passed through a blackened slum, the houses charred flakes, he was bound for one in particular. He knew it was somewhere around here, because he had seen the signs of the fish scrawled in ash on the remaining walls—signs that led other followers to it. Signs that now led him.

It proved to be a nondescript house on the outskirts of the Caelian Hill. This area was not as badly damaged, and it had retained not only its walls but its roof.

Longinus climbed off his horse, stepped up to the door, and knocked.

A little girl with a soot-stained face answered. Upon seeing the centurion, she stepped back, wisely afraid, and her mother rushed to see who was there.

"Peter of Capernaum," Longinus said. "Get him."

The little girl and her mother both turned to look back inside the house. That was all Longinus needed. He drew his gladius and barged through the door.

There sat a dozen Christians, huddled together. Peter sat in the corner, a shaft of sun cutting across his face, as if the light revealed him after all.

"Simon Peter," Longinus boomed.

Another man rose to his feet. "I am he."

Longinus stepped toward the man, smirked, and ran his sword quickly through his gut. "You are not."

"Father!" the little girl cried, running to his side.

Longinus approached Peter. "You let this man die for you?"

"He acted without my word," Peter said.

"Yet it is your word that has brought us here. On your feet!" Longinus grabbed the old man by his robes.

An old woman, probably Peter's wife, rose to his aid, but Peter quickly cast her back with a wave of his hand.

"You sent me to hell," Longinus growled, pulling the disciple in closer.

"I showed the path you needed to take," Peter said calmly.

"Now I shall return the favor."

Longinus pushed the old man out the door into the arms of his men.

"What of the rest?" asked one of the Praetorians.

"Take them all," Longinus replied.

His men went inside and rounded up the others. As one was pushed past him, Longinus grabbed her by the arm.

"You are his wife?" he asked the old woman who had stood to help Peter.

She looked into his eyes. "I know why you do this, centurion. And we forgive you."

Longinus met her gaze. "But I do not forgive you."

CHAPTER LI

When John Sunday woke, he was on the floor, face up and naked, spread eagle, with his arms and legs stretched and chained. His first thought was that it was freezing.

After he'd been captured on the rooftop, he remembered being strapped to a gurney and given an injection. He vaguely remembered being put in the back of an ambulance. After that it was all a blank.

Now he was here. He knew this room. Not this particular space, but the concept and function of what was to occur here was quite well known to him. He'd been on the unchained side of this exchange many times.

It was cold to keep him awake. Nearby was a drain that would make it easier to clean the fluids that would pour from his body. The surgical lights in the corner could be aimed and ramped up to blinding levels. And on a wooden table to one side sat a locked box, which certainly contained his interrogator's tools of choice.

The door opened, and a man carrying a cardboard box stepped into the room.

"Hello, John."

The man who had shot him in the cave. A man whose name he did not know.

He unpacked his cardboard box slowly, heightening the buildup as he placed squeeze bottles of honey one at a time onto the tabletop, lining them up like golden brown showgirls.

Sunday had employed numerous weapons through the years to get a prisoner to cooperate. Lack of sleep, loud music, water torture. Threatening or killing family members, electroshock, suffocation, bone-breaking.

He'd never used honey.

The man moved over to the toolbox, a big wooden one, like the one Sunday's father used to keep in the garage. "Don't touch my tools!" his father would bark. The man opened the toolbox and pulled out a black, tasseled whip. He smiled, like a child rediscovering a toy, and let it dangle next to his hip, giving Sunday a clear view of the sharp metal prongs on the end.

Ah, that's more like it, Sunday thought.

His interrogator kneeled to study the side of Sunday's face. "I'm impressed, John," he said, assessing the damage to Sunday's vacant eye. "A bullet to the brain, and yet, here we are."

Sunday said nothing. It was best not to speak. He'd need the energy later.

The man stood and returned to his unpacking. He pulled a plastic tube and a clear IV bag from the cardboard box.

"Are you working with Mossad?"

Sunday didn't respond.

"Are you working with Mossad?" the man repeated, clearly and slowly, as he unfurled the tubing.

Still Sunday didn't answer.

The man pulled out a huge glass mason jar with a lid. Something was in it, but Sunday couldn't make it out.

"Do they know of our plans?"

The man turned, and in his hands were the plastic tubing and a squeeze bottle of lube. He flapped them in front of Sunday's face like he was waving his pecker.

"Lube or no lube?" he asked.

Sunday knew now what the honey was for. That plastic tube was going up his ass.

"I'm just kidding," the man continued. "We go in dry here. So let me fill you in on the specials of the day. We'll use the whip, of course. The razors on the ends make nice, clean, lacerations of the flesh. Then we're going to fill you with honey. You're going to shit like you've never shit before. That's where these come in."

He picked up the jar and held in front of Sunday's face. Hundreds of white, grub-like insects were crawling around on the inside of the glass. "Bot fly larvae. They love to burrow. Head deep into something warm. They've found bot fly larvae crawling around inside people's brains. Searching for answers, maybe. Makes you wonder, whose brain is it then? You can feel them beneath the skin, crawling through your blood, squirming deeper and deeper. And with all that crap and honey, they're going to drag your own shit into every opening you have."

He grabbed Sunday hard by the back of his head.

"Are you working with Mossad?"

Sunday again said nothing.

The man smiled. "That's what I was hoping you'd say."

CHAPTER LII

Ayelet sat naked and cold, bound to a chair, a hood tied around her face. The bag covered her eyes but did not blind her fear. It lay below, a quivering puddle, for she knew what was coming.

She heard the clicking of a lock and the opening of a door.

The hood was removed, and she found herself in a small room with gray cinderblock walls.

An older woman stepped in with an awkward, lumbering walk and a manila folder in her hand. She wore a plain gray frock—the woman looked a little gray herself—small round glasses perched on the end of her nose, and a wooden crucifix with a golden Jesus upon it dangling from her neck. She had the calm of someone who spent her afternoons baking cookies with her grandchildren.

She noticed Ayelet looking at her crucifix and scooped it up proudly, gently, like she was cupping water in her hands.

"Do you know why Jesus looks the way he does?" the grandmother asked. "With his flowing brown hair and blue eyes?"

Ayelet didn't answer.

"Because Christians so hated the Jews for what they did to Him, they tried to wipe out any idea he was a Jew. And so, here he is. Created in our image, not yours." She placed the cross back down on her chest and sat at the table across from Ayelet. "Does Mossad know about our plans?"

"What plans?"

"Does Mossad know?"

"No."

"Are you working with the CIA?"

"No."

"No?" She opened her folder and slid a photograph across the table. It was David Conrad, dead on a gurney in a morgue.

"Who else in the CIA knows about our plans?"

"I don't know."

She pulled out a photo of another man. He was unconscious or dead, Ayelet couldn't tell. And he was naked, bound by chains in a cell.

"Are you working with John Sunday?"

"Who?"

"Does Mossad know about our plans?"

Ayelet said nothing.

The grandmother leaned back in her chair. "In times like these, I turn to history." She tapped her head as if trying to load a thought. "I knock, knock my noggin' to come up with something fun. Something new. But the old ways never die. I don't want to spoil the surprise, but I want to show you what we're going to do to you."

She pulled a piece of paper from the file like she was producing an ace from a deck of cards. It was an old drawing of a man tied upside down to two wooden posts. He was naked, spread eagle, and two men were using a huge saw to cut him apart between his legs. The blade had caught halfway, stuck in the middle of his gut.

"Caligula most enjoyed this method. He would have this done while he watched and ate his dinner. Do you know what he called it?"

Ayelet did not answer.

The old lady smiled. "The appetizer."

CHAPTER LIII

John Sunday hung suspended over the floor, his body a limp container of blood, honey, and shit. He'd been torn apart with the whip, and pieces of skin and bloody meat lay scattered on the floor below.

He could feel the insects crawling on him, hundreds of them, burrowing into his blood, moving beneath his skin. They had found his tattered wounds and taken advantage of the gateways into his juicy middle. He could feel them sliding through his circulatory system. One was currently boring through his ear, tunneling straight through the canal, tickling deep within his head like a slithering feather. It scurried toward his brain, the real and the imagined insect both now within his skull.

He had tried to be the man born of Delta, hardened by battle.

But as he had been whipped, and the blades shredded his skin, he had cried out for mercy.

There was no mercy to be had.

The door opened, and his torturer entered the cell again. He kneeled, examined the bugs upon Sunday's body as if he were an entomologist, then plucked a fat, white burrowing larva from Sunday's side.

"Are you working with Mossad?" he said, rolling the bug between his fingers, toying with its mealy flesh.

"No," Sunday gasped.

The man shook his head and picked up the whip again.

"Please," Sunday said. "Don't."

The man took a smear of honey and wiped it across Sunday's forehead and down over his good eye, blessing him with the sign of the cross.

"Shhh," he said. "God is in the suffering."

* * *

Ayelet was suspended upside down, heels spread apart in the air. Two men examined her closely, enjoying the spectacle. One of them held a giant saw blade, the kind of vintage two-handled saw that might have been used by lumberjacks in an earlier time. The teeth were gnarled and twisted, with tips of rust. Small black tufts decorated some of the points.

It had been used before. And not on trees.

There was nothing left but to barter, as do all when the tool of the reaper is revealed.

"Please," she begged as the blood filled her skull. "I'll tell you. I'll tell you."

The old lady leaned against the far wall. "Does Mossad know about our plans?" she asked once again.

"They don't. They don't," Ayelet cried, snot and tears rolling up her forehead and onto the floor. "Please.

We tapped his computer and phone. But we have nothing! We don't know what you're doing!"

The old lady licked the outside of her teeth like she was savoring a meal, then nodded to the men. The man with the saw fed it into the space between Ayelet's legs. The other man grabbed the handle on the opposite side. They placed the cold teeth of the saw in the warmth of her mound.

Ayelet screamed as the metal touched her skin. *"No! Please! Please! Don't!"*

She flailed and kicked, but her arms and legs were bound tightly, and she was nothing more than a human sail in the wind.

She felt the beginning of the motion, of the saw moving between her legs, parting her with its teeth. This was it? This was how she was going to die? Everything she was, everything she'd ever be, to disappear down the drain that she now hovered above?

She closed her eyes and spoke in Aramaic, the words catching in her upside-down throat. A prayer of old. A prayer for the dying.

"May His great name be exalted and sanctified in the world which He created, according to His will. May He establish His kingdom, and may His salvation blossom and His anointed be near," she gasped.

The old lady leaned down.

"Oh, He is," she answered.

She looked up and nodded at the blade men.

Ayelet felt the saw teeth begin to tear, and she sobbed to Him who was not there to save her.

* * *

Sunday was in and out of consciousness. He'd lost a lot of blood. Even when he was awake, he couldn't focus, his one good eye now smeared with honey. The larvae crawled across his face, up his nostrils, into his ears.

"Please," he begged.

There was no one in the room to hear. And yet he implied to whom he spoke, for it was the overseer of all, the one he had denied, the one he had abandoned by his actions. A god he could not believe in, and yet here he bartered with it as if it held sway over the particles of the universe.

"Please," he said again.

In his mind he heard the voices. The whispers. And he felt something new upon him, touching him. A hand. Gentle. A soft stroke on the side of his chest.

He opened his eye, but through the honey smearing his vision, all he saw was a silhouette.

A child?

In a blue winter coat.

Who was this boy? Was it the child in the rain who watched his mother fade into a haunting memory? Was it him?

A voice parted his thoughts: *Save her.*

Sunday felt the child's touch, and the larval filth that crawled around, consuming his body, moved as one toward his chest. It was almost like they were racing, all closing in toward a single center point.

They burst from a wound in his chest as if he had vomited them, and the filthy pile landed with a splat on the stone floor.

A sound echoed from beyond the room.

Gunfire.

Sunday tried to focus, but he drifted again, and the darkness consumed him, and the child was gone.

CHAPTER LIV

Rome, Italy
64 CE

Longinus stepped through the door of the Carcer and looked down at the prisoner chained to the floor. With the prisoner were several guards, each holding a flagrum, and they'd clearly done a decent job of warming Peter up. He bled profusely from his face and chest, and his left eye drooped heavily from an assault of fists.

"Ah," Longinus said as he kneeled, careful to avoid the puddle of piss. "This brings back memories." He spoke in Hebrew so the guards would not understand. "You know what I seek?"

Peter nodded slowly.

"I shall end this suffering," Longinus said soothingly. "Tell me. Where is the key?"

"I don't know."

Longinus stood. "A faithful witness does not lie, brother. Ten years I spent preaching His word. All that time my wife suffered. And the entire time you *knew*! You knew if I reached the gate I would not be able to open it and bring her back."

"I told you the gate opens only for Yeshua," Peter said, trying to catch his breath from the beating. "And once opened, the earth would shake and only He could keep back what clamored within."

"No. *You* hold the key that would have opened her cage," Longinus said. "You hold it, and you hid it from me." He grabbed the old man by his hair. "Where is it?"

Peter said nothing.

Longinus looked toward one of the guards. "Unshackle him."

* * *

It was dark as Peter was thrown into the back of a wagon and hauled toward the palace on Palatine Hill, but the stars lit the landscape, and he looked out over the city of Rome. At the rolling hills. This seven-headed dragon.

He knew what was coming. Where this wagon led.

Three nights prior, he had thought of escaping with his wife. He had gone for a walk, longer than normal, and contemplated fleeing into the wilderness. And then he saw Him, waiting.

"*Quo vadis?*" his Lord asked. *Where are you going?*

"Home," Peter said.

"And soon you shall be," his Lord said. "And I wait to welcome you there."

Peter knew then that he must return. To this most foul city which he held in such contempt. This Babylon that he knew would fall, as would all the Babylons to come.

He knew he must return. Because his Lord expected him to die.

* * *

Longinus was waiting when the wagon pulled up to the palace. He dragged Peter off the cart and led him to the gardens.

"I had long wondered how my fate came upon me," Longinus said. "Why the Lord chose me to suffer in such a way. Then I realized. It was as we broke bread one night and drank wine to remember Him. 'This is my body, this is my blood.' Those words. It was his fluids that tainted my insides. Like a pestilence. Perhaps it is in all men, brother. A hidden disease of our own design that afflicts us all."

"Does good not have the same power to spread and grow within?" Peter asked.

Longinus smiled. "That garden has long since been consumed by weeds."

They continued into a courtyard. There, bound to a stake, was Peter's wife, Miriam. She was covered from head to foot in some kind of grease. Beyond her, lining a stone path, were all the other captured Christians, each bound to a similar post.

"Miriam!" Peter shouted. Two Roman soldiers stood guard next to her.

"My love," she said, smiling, as if her rescuer had arrived.

Peter turned to Longinus. "Please!" he begged. "She plays no part in this. It is between you and I!"

"And yet *my* wife suffers because of *you*..." Longinus said.

He gestured toward one of the soldiers guarding Miriam. The man lifted a torch that illuminated the garden path and moved back toward Miriam with the flame extended.

"No! Please!" Peter cried.

"This can end," said Longinus. "You can return to Capernaum and live out your days preaching the word with your wife by your side. Would that not better benefit God than this?"

Peter looked skyward, to the black satchel of sky, as if the stars were eyes that could blink an answer.

"I cannot deny Him again," he said, sobbing.

"So be it." Longinus gestured toward the guard, who lowered the torch.

"No! Wait! She has it! She has the key!"

"Peter, no!" called his wife. "Don't."

"Who has the key?" Longinus asked.

"I hold the knowledge of where the key is kept," Peter said, his head low. "But I do not keep it."

"Who does?"

"Mary. Of Magdala."

Longinus nodded. He knew the name. "Where is she?"

"She vanished into the wilderness, years ago. To hide from you. I do not know where. Please," he said. "Release my wife."

Longinus turned and nodded again toward the guard. The man lowered the torch.

Miriam's body burst into flame. She wailed, the sound rising above the crackling of flames and the screaming of her husband.

The guard then walked down the garden path, igniting all the others, until the path was illuminated with fires and thick with screams.

"Why?" cried Peter, looking to Longinus. "I told you what you asked!"

"Because you have denied God yet again."

* * *

Later that morning, before the sun had risen, Peter was dragged toward a cross that had been erected on a hill in the garden, overlooking the city. He was stripped, flogged again, and then strapped to the patibulum.

Spikes were driven through his wrists. He screamed in agony with each blow of the hammer.

He was helped to his feet, only so he could carry the wooden patibulum up to the stipe.

Peter looked toward Longinus, who watched. "Please," he begged. "I cannot die as He did."

"I have no intention of it," Longinus answered.

Peter was bound to the stipe, but was flipped, his feet nailed above his head. He hung there upside down, the blood from his legs and chest flowing into his skull.

By the time the sun rose, so much blood had already pooled behind his eyes that Peter could scarcely distinguish between the darkness and the light. As he died, his blind eyes grew wide, and he saw the things coming out of the earth toward him. People emerged from the mud, dark-eyed things that clamored toward him.

And in the distance he saw a man in a cloak, sitting upon a rock. A man he knew.

"Forgive me," he whispered, his voice weak.

Longinus kneeled next to him.

"Who comes to collect?" he asked.

But there was no answer.

CHAPTER LV

The next time Sunday woke, he was being half-carried out of his cell by two armed men dressed in black. A blanket was draped over his shoulders.

As he limped into the hall, he glanced into an open cell across the way. Though his vision was still blurred with honey, he saw what looked like two men cutting down a naked woman hanging upside down, soaked in blood.

They continued down the hall, passing several bodies, including what looked like a little old lady. He couldn't tell if any of the bodies belonged to the man who had tortured him.

As he stepped outside into the blinding brightness of the sun, his rescuers guided him toward one of two waiting helicopters. They were in the desert somewhere, judging by the sand the helicopter blades kicked up.

He was laid gently aboard the helicopter and ministered to by a medic. A short while later, an injured woman was laid down beside him, and the medic turned his attentions to her.

The helicopters lifted off, and Sunday wondered who had rescued them.

CHAPTER LVI

Kat woke to the morning bell, ready for Grand Mother's dramatic rendition of Revelations, which was being read with increased fervor morning, noon, and night. Instead, for the first time, the voice over the speaker belonged to someone else: Ulga. Her reading was excessively dramatic, her English choppy.

"They called out in loud voice, 'How long, Sovereign Lord, holy and true, until you judge inhabitants of earth and avenge our blood?'"

Kat rose, urinated, wiped, and saw dark red. The color of a crime. That was two days now. Heavy flow. Too heavy. This was the beginning of her end. The blood was a sign. Like the prophets and the parables, a foretelling of what was to come.

"Then each of them given a white robe, and they were told wait a little longer, until the full number of their fellow servants were killed..."

Am I going into labor?
It's too early.
Oh, God, what if I lose the baby?
What happens to me?

She was supposed to tell them about the bleeding. But what would they do?

Back in the world, she would have read about it, Googled for answers. Weighed her options. Gotten a second opinion. But here, she was in the dark, a pregnant peasant in the field of her master.

Mara sat on the edge of the bed and watched. Their eyes met. She knew. They didn't speak, and they didn't need to. Kat knew the girl would agree with her own assessment.

"They'll kill you. They'll take the baby."

A strange notion rose up to take the blood and wipe it upon the doorpost, to smear the crimson filth, as if to ward off the Angel of Death which she knew hunted her now.

Instead she stood and flushed, careful to hide the paper, hide the sin, as so many do.

The voice over the loudspeaker continued.

"I look when He broke the sixth seal, and there was great earthquake! And the sun become black as sackcloth made of hair! And the whole moon become like blood! And stars in the sky fell to earth, as figs drop from the fig tree when it is shaken by strong wind."

CHAPTER LVII

Tel Aviv

Sunday was sick of hospital beds. He'd only been in for two days, and already he was going stir crazy. But he was going nowhere. The skin on his chest, his legs, his hands, was stitched together like a leather purse.

A tan man in a white polo shirt and khakis stepped into the room. He had thick bushy black hair and needed a shave.

"Mr. Sunday, my name is Uri Greenlow," he said, taking a chair. "You're very lucky we found you."

Sunday nodded. "Yeah? Who are you?"

"I'm with Shin bet," he said. "I was friends with David Conrad. Would you like us to contact your employer? Someone at the embassy, perhaps, so they can send someone to retrieve you?"

"If you do," Sunday said, "you kill me."

Greenlow nodded. "Yes. So we assumed. You seem to be operating out of jurisdiction. But perhaps if you answer some of our questions, then we can continue to keep your presence here a secret from your employers. Who ambushed our team in Rome?"

"I don't know."

"Well, that's not a very good start."

"But I can give you a name. And everything I know about the CIA's involvement."

Greenlow nodded again. "That's better."

"Before I do any of that, I want your word."

"On what?"

"That if you go after them... I go with you."

Greenlow smiled.

* * *

Two days later, Sunday sat in a conference room surrounded by Israeli intelligence officials. A woman, the one who had been put into the helicopter with Sunday, was wheeled into the room in a wheelchair. Her face was black and blue, her cheeks were swollen, and she was wrapped in large swaddling bandages below her waist.

Greenlow leaned down and kissed her cheek. "You will receive the Medal of Valor," he said.

She nodded, but didn't smile. Sunday understood. A medal wouldn't make it all better.

She met his eye, studied the stitched lacerations across his face, his missing eye. They shared a look—a silent understanding of their shared abuse. For God. For country.

Greenlow cleared his throat and addressed the room.

"Thanks to information from Mr. Sunday," he said, "we believe the name of the man we're looking for is Josef Belac. We think he is 'the Father,' as he is known to his followers—who we now believe form a Christian apocalyptic terrorist group. They believe the end of the world is coming. And that Jesus is somehow returning. They are the ones who hit our team in Rome. They're likely also the ones who attacked a CIA team in the desert of Jordan. And CIA director Tom Ferguson is himself a part of Belac's church. Here's the problem: Belac supposedly died back in 1987."

He switched to another slide, this one containing a list of at least sixty company names.

"After his death, his vast fortune was never accounted for, but these are some of the holdings his bank had invested in. The ones we know of. Everything from cybersecurity firms to private military contractors that still operate today. The well is deep.

"So let me get this straight," interrupted a gray-haired man at the end of the table. He wore a light-green shirt adorned with medals and stripes, and the maroon beret tucked beneath the left shoulder strap of his uniform indicated he was Special Forces. "You're suggesting that a dead man is leading a cult that attacked our team in Rome?"

"No, I'm not saying he's alive—even if he faked his death, he'd be well over a hundred by now. But his cult lives on. And so does his DNA... in some very surprising places." He pulled up another slide, one that Sunday couldn't make sense of. "This shows the result of several DNA tests. Mostly taken from saliva samples as part of unrelated investigations. People like Ulrich Amon. And Andrew Aim and Martin Seere. We have a dozen more high-profile people like this, all of them in the basilica that night. And here's the interesting thing: *all* of these people appear to be related to Josef Belac.

Closely related. In fact, if we didn't know better, we'd say Belac fathered every one of them."

"That's impossible," said the Special Forces commander.

The woman in the wheelchair looked up.

"Impossible, but true," she said. "In the basilica, he called them all his 'children.' Said they had grown from his seed."

"Yes," said Greenlow. "It was that precise detail in Ayelet's report that led us to *this* place." Greenlow went back to the previous slide and pointed to one of Belac's corporate holdings. "BioGrail. It's a biotech company in Cairo that works with DNA, stem cell research, that kind of thing. They also house the world's biggest collection of human eggs."

Sunday looked up from his report. "Taresh's compound had storage containers full of frozen embryos. Thousands of them."

"And the nuns in the church were all pregnant," said the woman in the wheelchair.

"Wait. Hold on a second," said the commander. "What exactly are you suggesting? A dead man's DNA is being used to impregnate women?"

"We're not sure the women are pregnant with *his* DNA," Greenlow continued. "Mr. Sunday, would you tell the commander about what the CIA was doing in the desert?"

Sunday turned to face the commander. "We were searching for the body of Jesus Christ."

The commander raised one bushy eyebrow.

"I know how that sounds," Sunday continued. "But the portrait we found on Taresh had a gospel under the paint, claiming that Jesus's body is in a cave in Jordan. We didn't find a body, but we did find a clay jar, which they took from us when we were ambushed. Maybe it contained bones, or something else with Jesus's DNA."

"And maybe it was someone else's DNA altogether," Greenlow said, "and they just believed it was Jesus's."

"Let's take a step back," said the commander. "Let's pretend for a second that all of this makes any sense whatsoever, and that a bunch of nuns are now pregnant with little Jesus babies. How is any of that a threat to Israel?"

"Honestly, we don't know," said Greenlow. "What we do know is that when Ayelet and Mr. Sunday were interrogated, the only question they kept asking was whether Mossad knew about their plans. We don't know what they're up to, but we can't just let this lie without finding out."

The commander frowned, then nodded ever so slightly. "I agree." He turned to Sunday. "But I have to ask, what's your interest in this, Mr. Sunday? You've done your part, supplied us with a name. Why are you still involved?"

"I'm just trying to find someone."

Greenlow brought up a slide of Kat. "Kat Devier," he said. "She was with Mr. Sunday on the dig in Jordan, but she has since gone missing."

The woman in the wheelchair spoke up again. "I've seen that woman. She was at the basilica that night. She was one of the pregnant nuns."

CHAPTER LVIII

Hawara, Egypt
66 CE

First the wood had to be prepped. She had oak and cedar at the ready, but for this particular work, she had chosen fig. The wood was soft and pliable, and it had meaning to her.

Perhaps now this tree will bear fruit, she thought. *And the seeds shall drop.*

She had then prepped the plaster— in this case, a mat of papyrus laid one sheet on top of the other. The papyrus itself had been made by hand, from the center of the plant, including both the higher-quality "Augustus" paper and the slightly lesser-quality "Livia."

Then came the paint. She procured her pigments from stones and plants, grinding and mixing the petals, leaves, or rocks into the color she desired. Her kitchen and workshop was a library of stone, fruit, and flower. She preferred to heat beeswax before adding pigment, because it resulted in a lusher, more vivid color, but that meant she had to work quickly, since the wax would cool.

As she worked, Bathsheba, the na'arah, organized several of the planks of wood against the far wall. Between them was another row of stacked and ready boards. Each bore the portrait of a face. A man from Alexandria who had died from sickness. A woman from Antinopolis who had died during childbirth. And children. So many small faces.

The old woman had been tasked with bringing them to life again through her art. To allow the mourning parents to see their children again, and mourning children to see their parents. She felt her faces provided a good likeness of the deceased, although she had a tendency to make the eyes larger than they were in real life. That was deliberate. Large, wide eyes were the window in, to see the true light of one's being.

Bathsheba watched her master work. "Is it done?" the little girl asked in Hebrew.

"Almost," the old lady answered. Her hand was not as steady as it once had been.

"It doesn't look like you," Bathsheba said.

"No?"

"No. You're much older."

The woman smiled. "Yes. *Much.* But in my eyes, I will always look like this."

"When will you paint me?" Bathsheba asked.

"Hopefully, never," the old lady answered.

* * *

Later that afternoon, when Bathsheba had gone to the oasis to fetch water, the old woman swept the stoop. The desert wind sent clouds of sand swirling across the sky, and a rider suddenly emerged from it as if born of the earth.

He dismounted, his face covered by cloth to keep out the sand, and walked slowly toward her. A sword swung on his hip.

"Water?" he asked.

She nodded. "Inside."

She led him to a bucket and ladle in the corner. He slurped until his thirst was quenched.

Then he turned and looked around her house, stacked with paper and plants and baskets of colored rocks.

"You are the one who paints the dead?" he asked.

"I am."

"Then I have need of your services."

"You have lost someone?" She moved toward the kitchen to fetch a plate.

"I have," he said. He perused examples of her work leaning against the wall. "These are good."

"Thank you." She returned with a plate of olives and offered it to him.

The man looked down at the plate. He plucked a single olive and stared at it.

"I haven't had olives since my wife died."

"I'm sorry. Is that why you have come? Is that whom you wish me to paint?"

The rider nodded. "Indeed. But not because I wish you to paint her."

"No?"

"No." He squeezed the olive between his finger-tips, squashing it to pulp. "I seek the key so I can release her from the hell your God has kept her in, Mary of Magdala."

The old lady stepped back, away from him.

"*You*. You are the one who does not die? Whose face changes?"

"Yes," the rider said. "And I remember you. You were there that day I killed Him. You stared at me so. I remember those eyes. Why did you stare? Did you know then? Know he would curse me?"

Mary shrank back farther.

"*Did you?*" he shouted.

Bathsheba stepped through the front door with a bucket of water. As she carried it into the kitchen, she spilled some on the floor near the rider's sandals. "Sorry, sir," she said.

"Bathsheba," said Mary, "I need you to make a delivery. Antones is ready for his wife's portrait. Can you deliver it?"

"Yes," she answered. "Which one is it?"

Mary turned to the centurion. "If you give me a moment to send the child away, sir, I will give you what you seek. She is not part of this."

Mary took Bathsheba into the back room, where more paintings were kept. She fetched the portrait of herself and wrapped it.

Bathsheba looked up at her. "No," she whispered.

Mary stroked her cheek. "Be a good girl and do as I say."

Bathsheba pouted.

"Go," Mary said.

Bathsheba took the painting wrapped in cloth and tried to run past the centurion. But he stopped her at the door. Looked down at what she held. Took it from her, unwrapped it.

"You are good," he said as he stared at the face within the painting.

Mary's pulse quickened.

He handed the portrait back to the child, and she ran out the front door.

Mary took a handful of olives from the plate and plopped some in her mouth.

"Now give me what I seek," the rider said.

"There is nothing to give," she said, spitting two seeds into a bowl.

"I have run through many of your kin," he said angrily. "If you prove difficult, the suffering of your Lord will pale compared to what I will do with you."

"You have that power. No doubt. But all you do is free me to return to Him."

The centurion pointed toward the door. "Then what about the child? Shall I run her down as well? Does she hold your same resolve?"

"Patience. I will tell you what I can."

"So do."

"What you seek is a clay jar," Mary said. "Within the jar is the sponge that I used to clean Him, to wipe away the blood. To clean the wound that you opened with the spear."

"A *sponge*? What good to me is a sponge?"

"The sponge contains the seeds of Him. He told me that when man is ready, His seeds will be planted, and He will rise again." She popped another olive in her mouth and sucked on the meat.

"What does that mean?"

She smiled, lost in the memory. "I honestly don't know. His stories often had meanings I could not understand."

The centurion was clearly losing patience. "So where is this sponge?"

Mary spit another seed into the bowl and wiped her mouth. "I hid it. Many years ago."

The centurion rested his fingers on the handle of his blade. "Where?"

"That's what you're not going to like." Mary took two more olives and chewed on them. "Because that's the part you shall have to pry from me with that sword. But rest assured, centurion. All that will spill here shall be my blood."

"Many claim such boasts," said the centurion.

"Do you remember that day?" she asked as he drew the blade. "When the sponge was raised to my Lord's lips? Laced with something to dull the pain. And he refused it so he could suffer fully. Alas," she said, "I have not his strength." Pools of foam curled at her mouth as she continued to chew on the olives. "Tonight, I dine with my Lord."

She smiled as she collapsed to the floor, convulsing.

Longinus grabbed her as if to shake what he needed from her, but her own flailing beat him to it.

"Tell me!" he shouted.

But it was done. The old woman lay still, her fluids and spirit leaking from her.

Longinus walked around her house angrily. Without her, the key would be lost forever. His wife would suffer for eternity!

In a fit of rage, he grabbed her paintings and hurled them across the room. Pictures of the dead shattered and cracked. He knocked over paints and baskets of flowers.

And when he was finished with his fit, he sat, laid his hands over his face, and wept.

Why? Will this last forever? For all my days am I cursed to walk this Earth?

Never resting. His wife in a hell concocted by the very God he had come to praise. Was this God not the Devil as well, both halves of the same being, each one unable to destroy the other since they were the same?

He dried his eyes and looked around at the room. On the table where he sat were several sheets of loose papyrus with bits of writing on them. He picked up a sheet and thumbed through it. They appeared to be drafts of some kind of testament. These were clearly false starts, quickly discarded, but he could see what she intended.

She was writing down her story.

A painting sat on an easel beside him. The old woman had been in the middle of prepping the wood with paper. He picked at the plaster. There were layers of papyrus to it, stacked together like a codex.

The painting. The girl.

He raced to the front door and scanned the horizon. All he saw was sand swirling across the desert.

CHAPTER LIX

As John Sunday stepped out of the airport in Cairo, the dry, desert air cracked his sinuses to the point of bleeding. The hot air carried not only the sand of the desert, but the dust that chugged from Cairo's concrete factories, as well as the smog of two million cars. Women on the sidewalk held their head scarfs around their mouths, and the men used their coats to shield their faces from the desert's sting.

He took a cab, its Arabic music cranked high, only to find himself stuck in traffic almost immediately, a chorus of car horns chirping like birds in an urban jungle.

Too many people. Too jammed in. Too little sharing of the road we're all on.

It was the same story everywhere he went.

He hadn't been in Cairo since Kat. Not since they made love beneath a full moon that hovered over the pyramids like an eye without an iris. He remembered now the puff of her cheeks, soft like pillows. The curve of her leg, as it moved to the knee. The length of her fingers, the fine hands of a lady, yet caked in dirt and stained with mud. Yes, it was here that he had fallen in love with her and all her imperfections. The smile that turned her whole face red. The crookedness in her teeth.

He'd once, foolishly, asked if she'd ever wanted braces. "That's the way God made me," she replied. And he loved her more for it. For having the confidence to be swayed by no man's opinion. To accept herself for who she was.

With Kat, this city had seemed romantic. Mysterious. Now it seemed dry, barren. Fighting a desert that conspired to bury it grain by grain. He wondered if that had been the plot of the earth all along.

When his cab pulled up to the hotel, he checked in as Lucas Evans, the name on his Canadian passport, and took a rickety elevator up to his room on the tenth floor. It was a Tic Tac of a room, in a shitty hotel, with a view only of apartment buildings covered in satellite dishes. He couldn't see the pyramids, or the ferry boats for tourists illuminated like neon fish that navigated the Nile. He just saw people stacked on top of each other, their little satellite dishes their only escape, pointed toward the heavens, like eyes once were.

He threw his bag on the bed and knocked on the door that led to the adjoining room. A man with an athletic build and a salt-and-pepper beard opened the door.

"I'm Eichel," the man said. "Welcome to Cairo." He made polite eye contact with him by staring squarely at Sunday's one good eye. "You look about how I imagined."

"Better than dead," Sunday said as he stepped into the room.

"Not by much." Eichel smiled.

There were building blueprints taped to the walls of Eichel's room. Two other Shayetet 13 operators sat behind laptops.

"Sadat and Yimkur," Eichel said, gesturing to the two men. They barely nodded in response. Both looked like they hadn't slept in a few days.

This room had a more interesting view. The nine-story, desert-brown building across the street from them had a faded red-lettered sign over its main entrance: مختبرات BioGrail—or BioGrail Labs. Window AC units marked the lower floors, but the higher floors had only rows of smaller windows, no more than six inches wide. It did not look like a place where nervous couples would fidget in the lobby, waiting to hear if his sperm count was up to the task.

"There are no customers," Eichel said. "No one comes in off the street. But it has more security than your Federal Reserve."

He sat at a laptop, clicked on a mouse, and pulled up several live feeds of the building. The camera lenses were frosted with dust from the sandstorm.

"Five armed security guards in front. Two dogs. All that for a lobby no one ever walks into."

"What about at night?" Sunday asked.

"Shift change is at seven." Eichel pulled up video of the parking lot. "One hundred twenty-three employees for the day shift. One hundred and fourteen work nights. We ran all the plates as they pulled into the garage. Janitorial, security, doctors, lab techs. All legit. No records. No terrorist ties. Just regular people."

"What about deliveries?"

Eichel pointed to a loading area where several semi trucks and a bus were parked. "Trucks come in, pass through an x-ray scanner here in the alley, and are then searched by dogs. Tough to sneak in the back door. And we count at least thirty armed security guards on the grounds. We'd need to go in hard and loud, with more men than we got here. We're talking a shitstorm by Jewish Special Forces in the middle of Cairo."

"Why so many trucks?" Sunday asked. "What are they moving?"

"Supplies. Lots of them." He paused. "There's something else."

Eichel pulled up another camera view. This one used thermal imagery to show the heat signatures of people inside the building. There were bundles of warm yellow and red bodies moving back and forth, sitting and sleeping. More than a hundred of them.

"These are floors seven through nine," he said. "Way too many people up there. Not enough cars in the parking lot. And they don't come and go from those three floors."

"Who are they?" Sunday asked.

Eichel shrugged. "They're prisoners."

CHAPTER LX

The latch to their door unlocked, and Kat and Mara looked at each other, their faces white with fear. The evening cleaning ritual was not complete. The routine had been broken.

Broken was bad.

Ulga and two male guards stepped into the room.

"Come," Ulga said.

Kat considered pushing past them and running. *They know. They know I'm bleeding.* But she was frozen by the thought of collapsing in the corridor, burning alive from the collar.

Instead she stepped with Mara into the hallway. The other women were being removed from their cells as well and were being sorted into groups by male soldiers.

Kat and Mara were assigned to a smaller group and then led by guards down the corridor to a service elevator that took them to an outdoor loading area. There was a bus waiting, and dozens of women were being boarded.

Kat and Mara made sure to stay together.

"What's happening?" Kat whispered.

"Something's wrong," Mara whispered back. "We're evacuating."

Kat couldn't help but wonder if her Arabian knight was coming for her after all.

CHAPTER LXI

A knock sounded on the door connecting the two rooms. In an effort to show his gratefulness for being allowed to tag along, Sunday had taken a few hours of surveillance to relieve Sadat and Yimkur. Now it was his turn for a little sleep.

Little was right. He'd only been resting for half an hour.

Outside the window the light was fading faster than it should have been for the hour of the day; the sun was completely choked by the lingering sand storm. He could hear the grain grinding against the glass like grit trying to get in, trying to fill every corner of every room.

He rolled out of bed, lurched like a dead man across the room, and opened the door to the adjoining room.

He stood on the edge of a cliff, or within a cliff, looking down at a dark earth far below, radiating embers of heat. Hordes of naked, blind people climbed like spiders up the rock wall below the door, cackling and wailing. There were hundreds of them, then thousands, then tens of thousands. They crawled over each other, building in mass, a giant tide of crawling flesh.

They reached the threshold where John stood. He tried to close the door to seal them out, but the door wouldn't move.

A hand, its skin dead and peeling, grabbed the threshold and pulled itself up.

It was the child. The one in the blue winter coat. He stood before Sunday, jacket now tattered and smeared with mud and blood. Half the child's face was gone, and his eyes were black and empty. He opened his coat, revealing the outlines of creatures moving beneath his skin, pushing him forward. He lurched toward John on legs twisted and broken to bend forward at the knee, feet shuffling on the floor.

Sunday took a step backward and looked back to the bed. Kat lay there sleeping. Resting on her chest was a baby—so small, so new, like she had just given birth.

Hovering over them both was the child in the blue coat, possessed by the creatures within him. The child turned to a side table where a Bible lay open beside a red pencil. The child picked up the pencil and brought it down on mother and infant, repeatedly stabbing, wood entering flesh.

* * *

Another knock on the door. Sunday shot up in bed.

"We've got movement!" Eichel called from the other side.

Sunday rose and grabbed the door handle, then paused, leery of what lay on the other side. But when he opened the door he saw only the adjoining room. The real world.

"Look," Eichel said, pointing at his laptop screen. "They're all leaving."

Sunday shook off the dream and looked at the screen. Employees were pouring into the parking lot, getting in their cars, and driving off. And in one corner, a large group of women were being loaded onto a bus. Pregnant women.

"We need to follow that bus," Sunday said.

* * *

For once, traffic in Cairo worked in their favor. By the time they'd gotten into the team's sand-washed white Jeep Cherokee, Sunday thought for sure they would have lost the bus and its security entourage. But the roads were clogged, and the bus hadn't made it far ahead of them.

Eichel strained to see from behind the wheel. Like all the other drivers, he was blinded by the swirling sand that was sporadically illuminated by red brake lights. Sunday sat in the passenger seat, and Sadat and Yimkur were in the back.

They followed the entourage onto a ramp leading to the Six October Bridge. It, too, was snarled with traffic, but the lead vehicle pulled aggressively into traffic, and other motorists honked furiously as the bus pushed its way in even more aggressively. In Cairo, honking was a language.

Sunday fidgeted in his seat as they waited to merge. His mind was racing, even as the vehicles weren't. *Is Kat on that bus?*

In this traffic, in this storm, it was difficult to tail. The slithering blanket of dust that surrounded them was Cairo's version of a blizzard, and just as hard to see through.

"Closer!" Sunday barked.

Eichel shifted right and cut off a driver who honked a symphony at him. "How does anyone get anywhere in this place?"

Sunday checked the M4 rifle riding next to him in the space between the seat and the center console. He pulled his arm out of the seatbelt so he was free to grab the weapon without getting tangled.

The bus was now about a quarter mile ahead.

"You're gonna lose 'em," Sunday said. His mind was already playing out hypotheticals. If she was on board, how he was going to get her off?

"I fucking can't see!" Eichel barked. But he floored it all the same, suddenly switching lanes and clipping the bumper of another car.

As Eichel played leapfrog with the other cars, doing his best to close in on the bus and its security entourage, the desert sun faded, and the night did nothing to improve their visibility. But they gradually moved within a few car lengths. Was that too close? Would they be spotted. Honestly, who could spot anything in this?

The lead car took an exit ramp toward "26th of July Corridor." Everything in this city was named for a war or a revolution.

"That's the highway," Sadat said from the back. "Once they get on, they'll be able to move."

He pulled hard to the right in order to get to the ramp, scraping a taxi. The driver shouted and gestured. His window was rolled up because of the storm, but Sunday could imagine what he said.

Up ahead, brake lights lit up. The bus and the Rovers had stopped at the top of the ramp, even though they were clear to go.

"They're stopping!" Sadat shouted.

Sunday grabbed the rifle.

"We're pinned in place," Eichel said. Traffic blocked them in front and behind, and concrete walls hemmed them in on either side.

Four men, scarves around their mouths, cloaked in swirling sand, stepped from the rear Land Rover, wielding Beretta AR70s. They raised their rifles—

"Down!" Sunday shouted as muzzle fire erupted from the swirling plume of red dust.

Rounds pierced the windshield of the Jeep, spider-webbing the glass.

Sunday pulled the M4 to his shoulder in a single rapid motion and fired back through the remains of the windshield. He pressed the rifle barrel against one of the bullet holes in the cracked glass and fired again. Gunpowder choked the confined space of the cabin.

The attackers retreated behind a gray minivan and returned fire, shredding the Jeep's hood and engine block.

Sunday tucked low, opened the passenger door, and kicked it wide. He fired suppressive bursts through the gap between the car and the door. One of the shooters was knocked backward onto the pavement. The other three returned fire from behind the front of the minivan.

An elderly couple emerged from the minivan's driver's side and lay flat on the asphalt, covering their heads. Smart move.

Sunday and the Israelis dumped together from the Jeep, covering for one another as they moved to the rear of the vehicle.

In the chaos, the lead Land Rover and the bus pulled up the ramp and onto the freeway, leaving the other SUV to contend with their tail.

One of the gunmen stepped forward—and it was then that Sunday saw his weapon held a grenade launcher. A deep *whomp* sounded over the gunfire and the howling wind as the gunman launched an explosive.

"Grenade!" Sunday shouted.

He and the Israelis sprinted away down the ramp. A muffled boom sounded behind them, and the Jeep was lifted a few feet into the air, spitting plumes of sand from its undercarriage, before settling back down, its belly burning, tires blown.

The three remaining gunmen climbed back into their Land Rover and peeled off to rejoin their team.

Sunday and the Israelis covered their mouths against the choking sand, ran up the ramp to the old couple's minivan, jumped in, and floored it, with Sunday in the driver's seat. The vehicle shuddered and struggled up the freeway, as if unaccustomed to the weight of so many grown men. The steering wheel rattled in Sunday's grip and it felt like the tires were going to fly off. Still, he would have pushed the pedal all the way through the floorboard if it would have gotten him closer to that bus. *Closer to her.*

You don't know she's on there.

But she could be.

He whizzed through the lighter traffic of the expressway. The cars here were zipping along despite the storm, and he closed the gap to a half mile.

"Police!" Sadat called from the back seat.

"Shit," Sunday said as he looked in the rearview mirror and saw the flashing lights coming up fast. The last thing he needed was a delay.

Two patrol cars zipped up behind them, hovered for a moment in the red cloud, like UFOs, and then sped past.

"They don't want us," Sunday said.

The cop cars raced up behind the bus and its entourage, sirens now blaring. One of the cop cars tried to clip the tail of the trailing Rover in a PIT maneuver. But the back seat passengers in the Rover rolled down the windows and presented an assault rifle with the grenade launcher. The rifle fired succinct bursts, shattering the cop's windshield, then the launcher lobbed a grenade right through the broken glass.

A second later the remains of the cop burst through the windows, and the police car spiraled into a barricade and flipped right over it.

Sunday now had the minivan within cracking distance. Sadat and Yimkur slid open the side doors and crouched with their H&Ks to take out the Rover's tires. But the Rover swerved left and braked, and the minivan raced right past them.

"Fuck!" Sunday shouted. Now the Rover was behind them and *they* were the ones being chased.

Sadat turned around and fired behind them, but his shots went wide. The gunman in the Rover was far more accurate. He shot the minivan's rear tires, and rubber spooled from the treads and flapped against the asphalt, sending the van spinning toward a barricade.

Sunday spun the wheel back, his control limited. The van started to roll, and Sadat almost tumbled right out the open side door onto the road. He grabbed the plastic handlebar on the back of the passenger seat just in time, his head inches above the speeding asphalt, and hung on as the van righted itself.

Sunday slammed on the brakes as the Rover came up fast behind them. Yimkur hung out the open side door and opened fire.

The driver of the Land Rover took a round to the face. As his hands reached up to reattach his jaw, Yimkur shot out the two front tires. The Rover swerved, like it had been pushed, into a semi. It bounced off the tractor-trailer and spun wildly into the rear of the minivan on its way to flipping off the side of the road. The impact sent the wounded minivan sideways as well, and they slammed hard into a barrier wall.

Sand and smoke swirled into the open vehicle. Dazed from the impact, Sunday shook his head and pressed the gas again. *Come on. Go.*

The van whined and complained, but it moved forward.

He pulled back onto the highway, the rear tires flogging the asphalt. They had to be close to rims.

"Roadblock!" Eichel said, pointing. A half mile ahead, a wall of flashing lights illuminated a cloud of sand.

The remaining Rover and the bus weren't stopping. Instead the SUV pulled to the left and allowed the bus to lead. The cops on the line opened fire as the bus plowed right over the stop sticks and barreled through the cop cars. Rounds tore into the bus and blew out the front windows. They must have gotten the bus driver as well, because the bus came to a smoking stop. Or maybe that was because of the cop car now wedged beneath its front bumper.

Blasts of gunfire erupted from the windows of the bus, targeting the cops, who took cover and returned fire. The training Land Rover stopped beside the bus and joined in the vicious firefight.

Sunday pulled to the broken minivan into the median, two hundred yards from the smoking bus, and he and the team grabbed their weapons and raced up the road. Sunday was focused on only one thing: getting on that bus.

He ducked behind a car stuck in the traffic jam and fired, hitting one of the men from the Land Rover. The other two spun around to address this new threat from behind, but were met by Sadat's and Eichel's bullets.

The firefight with the cops was taking place on the driver's side of the bus. John moved quickly to the other side, to the door, and quietly pried it open, his sounds covered by gunfire. He crept up the bus steps and crouched behind the railing.

Two men were in the bus seats, firing out the window at the cops. Sunday popped up and opened fire. One tap. Then two.

Both men were dead without even seeing the man who pulled the trigger.

A round buzzed past his head, and he ducked back down. There was another gunman back there, toward the rear. Someone he hadn't seen. Staying low, Sunday peeked around the corner. Beneath the seats, he saw a dark-skinned pregnant woman, huddled on all fours, terrified.

Pregnant.

Jesus, he wanted to call out her name to see if she was here, hear her voice, but he stopped himself. If she answered, the gunman in the back could take her as a hostage. Use her against him.

He looked up at the mirror used by the bus driver to see the passengers. There, in the back, was the gunman. Or gunwoman. She was a large woman, perhaps

European, gun in hand, and she was surrounded by pregnant women.

I don't have a shot.

The woman was speaking. Saying something.

Prayers. She's praying.

And then he saw that she wasn't only holding a gun. In her other hand...

Is that a detonator?

Sunday raced back down the steps—and was thrown from the bus by a white-hot blast. Light engulfed him, and it felt like someone had driven screwdrivers into his skull. He landed hard on the asphalt and did an awkward shoulder roll that carried him onto the graveled shoulder.

He lay there a second, a minute. His ears hummed. Every muscle in his body throbbed.

Slowly he rolled to his side and looked at the burning bus.

Kat.

He considered running back in, but no one could have survived that. The smell of burning flesh drifting across the freeway confirmed it.

Please...

Eichel grabbed him by the arm and helped him to his feet. "We've got to go!" he shouted.

They ran back to the minivan and threw the guns inside. Sadat then tossed in an incendiary grenade, and a second later the van was engulfed in phosphorous flame.

Eichel shouted and waved the others toward a taxi that had pulled onto the shoulder. Through the window they could see the driver's frightened face. "La, la," he shouted in Egyptian as they approached. *No, no.*

Eichel pressed a wad of Egyptian pounds against the window.

The taxi driver assessed the handful of cash.

"Yes, come, come," he said.

The cab navigated the traffic jam and passed the burning bus, now being sprayed down by fire crews.

Sunday looked into the pulsating orange hulk and wondered if Kat had been on board.

CHAPTER LXII

Back at their hotel room, they checked all the cameras they had on the building across the street. It was completely empty now. No one in the parking lot. No one moving around the lobby.

"What's that?" asked Eichel. He pointed to Sadat's screen, which showed a faint scattering of heat signatures piled together.

Sunday leaned in. "Bodies." He started preparing to leave.

"Sunday, stop. If we go in there and the cops show, it'll be a problem," Eichel said. "Bunch of Israelis walking around a building in downtown Cairo?"

"That's why *I'm* going," Sunday said.

* * *

Sunday stepped out of the elevator onto the fifth floor of the BioGrail building, fanning his shotgun like he was dusting a crop. He moved down a white, sterile hallway past windows that looked into empty laboratories, their microscopes and centrifuges unmanned.

Another window looked into a room of bassinets, like a NICU unit at a hospital, but the beds were empty, the babies gone.

As he continued his sweep, he came to a hallway of what were clearly prison cells. Each room was furnished with two bunks, a toilet, and a washbasin. Every bed had a Bible laid out on it, with a small red pencil at its side.

Sunday kept moving.

He came upon a changing room with benches and teak wood floor mats, like a locker room minus the lockers. At the far end was a set of double doors. Locked. He pressed the shotgun against the hinges. Two blasts later, he pulled the doors open to reveal a large public shower.

He was immediately hit by the smell. Like pesticide. He brought his shirt up over his mouth.

Then he saw them, and nearly gagged.

In one corner were dozens of dead women, children and babies, huddled together in a mass, stacked on top of each other like little bundles of pale corkwood.

They'd been gassed.

Jesus.

Tears ran down Sunday's face as he looked through the women's bodies, many of them pregnant.

Please don't let her be here.

He moved body after body, searching. When his lungs burned from the lingering gas, he stepped outside to get some fresh air, then went back to search some more.

By the time he was done, his eyes were bloodshot and his lungs felt like they'd been scraped with steel wool.

Kat wasn't there.

His stomach churned, threatened to erupt. He raced back to the hallway with the cells, ran to one of the toilets, and vomited.

He leaned against the commode, collecting himself, wiping the remnants of puke from his mouth with the back of his hand. As he sat there, his gaze went to the Bible on the nearest bed, and the little red pencil next to it.

Why would they have pencils? Prisoners don't get pencils. They could use it as a weapon.

He stood, and went over to the Bible. It lay open, a passage underlined in red. Curious, he went to the Bible on the opposite bunk. It lay open to the same page, the same passage underlined.

He moved to the next cell. Again, both Bibles were open—same page, same passage.

He looked up. There was a speaker in the ceiling, along with the black globe of a camera.

They were being told what to read. What to underline. What to study.

Sunday read the underlined passage. It was from the Book of Matthew.

When Jesus came to the region of Caesarea Philippi, he asked his disciples, "Who do people say the Son of Man is?"

They replied, "Some say John the Baptist; others say Elijah; and still others, Jeremiah or one of the prophets."

"But what about you?" he asked. "Who do you say I am?"

Simon Peter answered, "You are the Messiah, the Son of the living God."

Jesus replied, "Blessed are you, Simon son of Jonah, for this was not revealed to you by flesh and blood, but by my Father in heaven.

And I tell you that you are Peter, and on this rock I will build my church, and the gates of Hades will not overcome it.

I will give you the keys of the kingdom of heaven."

Sunday's earpiece crackled in his ear.

"We found something," Eichel said. "One of the semis parked outside left while we were gone. Thermal picked up heat signatures in the trailer. They look like pregnant women."

Sunday's mind raced with hope.

Maybe the bus was a diversion. Maybe those woman were meant to die, like those in the shower.

Maybe the truck has the precious cargo.

* * *

The Israelis had run the plates on the semi, but so far, there had been no visual on it. Sunday's mind was doing somersaults, so to occupy himself, he re-read an element of the passage from the Bible he'd taken from the prison cells.

"And I tell you that you are Peter, and on this rock I will build my church, and the gates of Hades will not overcome it. I will give you the keys of the kingdom of heaven."

Sunday had seen similar language before, in the gospel written beneath the mummy portrait: *When my word again sees the sun, my body shall be rekindled, and the gates of this rock will be opened. And then I shall return to the kingdom of man.*

Both passages mention "gates," Sunday thought. *And rock. What rock?*

He scanned the Bible passage again.

"When Jesus came to the region of Caesarea Philippi, he asked his disciples…"

Caesarea Philippi? Where's that?

Sunday looked it up. Caesarea Philippi was near the base of Mount Hermon in Israel, in the Golan Heights. It had been named "Caesarea" because Herod the Great had built a temple there to honor Caesar. Herod's son, Philip, later added his own name. Today it was a nature preserve, a site where tourists went hiking, but at one time it had been a site where pagans worshipped Pan, the mischievous devil often seen playing a flute. It was said that cult worshippers were cast into a whirlpool at the entrance to a cave considered to be the home of Pan. If the victims disappeared into the water, the god was considered to have accepted their offering. If, however, blood appeared in the nearby springs, the sacrifice was thought to have been rejected.

Cult worshippers?
Gates?
Was this what they believed?
The cult worshippers were cast into a whirlpool…
God, that's it.
The women were to be sacrificed.
And if Kat was still alive, she was with them.

* * *

"We got a hit on the truck's plates!" Eichel said, listening on a pair of headphones. "Egyptian police found a semi abandoned two miles outside the Rafa border crossing." He turned to Sunday. "They're going through the tunnels."

Sunday nodded. Hamas had an entire subterranean interstate system crossing from the Gaza Strip to Israel and Egypt. They used it to smuggle everything from cigarettes to soldiers.

And now it seemed they were using it to sneak women into Israel.

To Caesarea Philippi.

CHAPTER LXIII

Kat and Mara rode in the dark, jostling each other in the back of the semi like cattle. There were six of them total, all pregnant. Armed men in khakis and Kevlar sat next to them.

Kat knew she was bleeding. She could feel the warmth, then the cooling as the blood pooled and congealed beneath her.

After the truck, they were moved to a set of waiting cars. They rode for a short time, then got out and were escorted into a tunnel. They emerged into the daylight and were put onto a tourist bus. As Kat climbed aboard, she laced her gown between her legs.

What will happen if they see the blood?

Armed soldiers moved down the aisle, strapping the women's wrists to their seats with leather cuffs bound to the armrests. One of the soldiers stopped by Kat, hovering over her.

Oh God. He knows.

He pulled something from a holster on his hip, and she felt a quick prick on her bicep.

Was that an injection?

As the soldier moved on to the next woman, Kat felt cold coursing from her bicep toward her neck like an icy river.

And then she felt something she had not felt in a long time.

Peace.

CHAPTER LXIV

Sunday and the Israeli team stood at the fenced border south of Rafa and watched as a Blackhawk helicopter skirted over the desert sand toward their position. It landed on the Egyptian side of the fence, and Sunday and the men climbed aboard.

Sunday put on a pair of headphones and nodded to Uri Greenlow. "Anything?" Sunday asked.

"We've got four sniper teams tucked in the hills around the site," Greenlow said. "Park has only been open for about an hour. So far, only about a dozen tourists. Not much traffic in the parking lot, no pregnant women." He raised an eyebrow. "What exactly are you expecting here? These women to be executed in broad daylight?"

"No," Sunday said. "It could be at night."

* * *

The semi lumbered down Highway 99 toward the kibbutz of Snir, a little neighborhood where the locals grew avocados and raised cattle and worked at a factory that made cleaning supplies. On this morning, the town was filled with Israeli police.

The trucker turned off the main highway, which in this rural section of Israel was still a country road, and stopped at a police barricade.

An older cop stepped toward the trucker with the swagger of years. "Need you to turn around," he said in Hebrew to the young, sweating man behind the big rig's wheel. "We got a situation at the factory."

"I got a delivery," the trucker answered.

"Factory is closed. Turn around."

The trucker shifted in his seat like he was adjusting his crotch, and closed his eyes.

* * *

From the Blackhawk, Sunday looked out over the land. The nature preserve was nestled in an arid region filled with trees and scrub. In the distance, on the other side of Mount Hermon, were the Golan Heights.

The chopper landed seven miles outside the reserve. Beneath the shifting shadows of the blades, Sunday and the team switched over to a pair of waiting SUVs and began the journey down Highway 99 toward the police staging area in Snir.

* * *

The sniper team in the woods watched as a tour bus made its way down the highway toward the nature preserve.

"Bus," whispered the spotter tucked beneath a thistle bush.

"Copy," said the sniper.

The bus pulled off the main highway and stopped in the parking lot of the tourist center. The doors opened and an older man stepped off, a brimmed hat upon his head. He squinted in the sun and put on a pair of sunglasses.

"Visual on target," said the spotter.

The older man looked toward the woods, as if staring back at the sniper team.

A man in Kevlar, rifle slung over his shoulder, escorted a woman off the bus.

"We got a pregnant woman," said the spotter.

* * *

The big rig trucker, his eyes closed, mouthed the Lord's Prayer under his breath. His body rigid and wet with sweat, he leaned back in the seat.

The cop pulled his gun.

"Get out of the cab!" he shouted.

The trucker released the trigger he had been holding, wired to the fifty thousand pounds of explosives he carried in his trailer.

A second later, the trucker, the rig, the cop, and everything else within a thousand feet was fire and burning metal.

* * *

"What the...?" the spotter said as a fireball filled the sky. The sound of the explosion came to him a second later.

The words had barely escaped the spotter's lips before a fifty-caliber round tore through the back of his head.

The sniper heard the round whisper through the brush like a copper wasp, but he never heard the crack of the shot, because a second round blew his skullcap clear into the thistle bushes.

* * *

Five miles away, Sunday heard what sounded like a rumble of thunder and watched as greasy black smoke plumed into the sky. There'd been an explosion, and it was burning a lot of fuel. It was followed by Greenlow's frantic voice from the front seat. He was radioing the sniper teams.

None answered.

* * *

Kat squinted in the sun as she got off the bus, the sedatives like sludge in her skull. She looked skyward, toward the top of a cliff some eighty meters high.

The six women were shackled together and led up narrow stone steps. On one side of them was a sheer rock wall, on the other a steep drop-off. It had rained recently, and cocoa puddles filled every depression in the stone. Rock doves flicked their blue-gray heads in the niches along the ridge, watching the women with cold, orange eyes, cooing as if welcoming them.

Kat's feet were as heavy as the stone steps she climbed. She was a walking dream, here in this quiet place that smelled of lemon and fig. She was only faintly aware that sometime during her drugged transport, an IV had been attached to her forearm. It now dangled off her like a remora on a shark.

CHAPTER LXV

Longinus, now known to the world as Josef Belac, waited by a surgical table at the mouth of the limestone cave. Silas Egin stood next to his father, and beside them both was an IV stand with two bags of clear fluids that hung like limp liquid sentinels.

The women crested the steps, and the soldiers who escorted them forced them to their knees.

Longinus gestured, and a soldier lifted one of the women back to her feet and brought her forward. An African woman. She stared with big, wide eyes, as if amazed at this alien world of men. Egin strapped her down on the table with a series of leather belts and attached the IV to the open port in her arm.

Longinus pulled a clean steel knife from a sheath on his hip. The blade was long and straight, like one used to skin animals.

At the sight of the knife, the African woman wept. She had no doubt known violence in her village and in her dreams. It spoke in a universal tongue, and whether she believed in hell, she must now know it was here all the same.

"Shhh," Longinus said, wiping the tears from the woman's dark cheeks. "There is nothing to fear."

He nodded to Egin, who was warden of the IV pole. Egin released the drugs from the bag and checked the drip chamber.

Thirty seconds later the woman on the table closed her eyes.

Longinus sliced into her belly, the blade moving easily through her dark skin and red muscle. Fishing around with his bare hands, he found the baby, a bloody, jellied ball, and pulled it from her womb. He held it up, then turned it toward Egin, who gently kissed the child on the head.

Even sedated as they were, the kneeling women who watched wept and wailed. They were witnessing their own fate. The big blue sky was spotted with only a few tufts of clouds, hardly enough to obscure the vision of the God to whom they all now prayed.

Longinus carried the infant to the cave's murky brown pool. He kneeled and lowered it into the dark water.

"Bless this child," he said.

It disappeared into the pool. The sacrifice was complete, the child accepted.

Longinus waited, but nothing happened. There was no sign that either the god of light or the god of dark was real.

What did I do wrong? Is the DNA not enough?
Am I merely insane?
Please.

* * *

As soon as the SUVs pulled into the parking lot, Sunday climbed out and scanned the area. A rock rabbit stared at him from beneath a tangle of vines, its small eyes judging. Sunday checked his M4 and looked toward the path that led up to the cave. It threaded along a narrow ridge, a steep canyon wall along one side.

He hadn't even taken his first step toward the path before a round tore through Sadat's head. The rock rabbit darted away, his sentry complete. Sadat never had a chance.

Sunday ducked behind the SUV and returned fire.

* * *

Longinus heard the gunshots. But they didn't matter.

"Another," he said.

The first woman had already been removed from the surgical table and dumped unceremoniously on the rocky ground.

One of the soldiers grabbed another woman by the arm and lifted her to her feet.

* * *

"I repeat! Heavy fire in the woods around the preserve!" Greenlow shouted into a radio.

Rounds chewed into the SUV's hood and blew glass across the pavement. Sunday and Eichel were pinned down behind another SUV about twenty feet away.

"Chopper. Two minutes!" he shouted to them, using his fingers to clarify.

A rocket-propelled grenade whistled through the air, and Greenlow and the four men beside him were engulfed in a wave of heat and fire.

* * *

Sunday's ears rang with a high-pitched hum. Greenlow and the others lay split and smoking near the charred SUV, and he and Eichel were sure to be next. If they stayed here, they were sitting ducks, just waiting for the next RPG.

"Visitor's center!" Eichel shouted.

Sunday nodded.

Eichel laid down covering fire, and Sunday moved quick and low toward the building. When he reached a half-wall, he covered behind it and reciprocated with suppressing bursts up toward the mountain, toward no target he could see.

Eichel started forward, but as he passed the safety of the SUV, a round spun through his spine and dropped him. He rose to his knees to try and continue the run, but was met instead with another round that blew off the right side of his face.

He collapsed onto the black asphalt that would become his grave.

Sunday was alone.

He raced toward the glass double doors and pushed into the cold silence of the visitor's center. If there had been tourists here, they'd fled. All that was left now were carousels of postcards and brochures encouraging visits to other historic sites across scenic Israel.

He couldn't stay here. He had to go back out.

He had to see if Kat was up there.

* * *

The old man stroked Mara's shaved head as she was strapped to the table. She stared up at him, deeply dazed.

"Do you give your child so that it may save the world?"

Mara felt tears rolling down her cheeks and a wiggle in her vein as someone adjusted the IV port in her arm.

"Please, Father," she cried, her mouth numb.

The old man pulled the blade from its sheath. In her mind it was a viper in his hand.

"As you wish," he said.

CHAPTER LXVI

Sunday peered out of the visitor's center toward the ridgeline. He could see a cluster of people on the cliff. Beyond it, the faint roar of a returning Blackhawk reverberated across the clouds in the wide blue sky. As it came into view, a series of Hellfire missiles shot forth, and the tree line ignited in a tidal wave of smoke and fire.

Sunday knew now was his chance. He ran from the visitor's center and raced up the stone steps.

Even through the drugs in the IV, Mara distantly felt the blade slice her open, the hands penetrating her insides, and most of all, the baby leaving her womb. She lay there, bleeding out, a pulp shell, the meat plucked from within.

Yet before she faded, or perhaps after, she saw her father standing over her. She knew it could not be, but he seemed real enough, and she needed him to be there. He took her hand in his, as she had done for him, and she knew what she wanted.

To be home with him again.

Longinus lowered the small blue infant into the pool. For the briefest of moments the child floated, and then it disappeared into the murkiness.

Still nothing.

Longinus raised his head skyward, as he had so many times over the course of his existence. *What do you want?*

He turned and gestured for the men to bring him another.

They would try the American woman this time.

From the top of the stairs, Sunday could see several men standing around a group of women on their knees, and one woman strapped to a surgical table. He recognized two of the men. One was Josef Belac. The other was the man from the cave. The man who had tortured him.

And then he recognized a third figure. The woman on the table.

Kat.

He raised his M4 and dropped his finger down over the trigger, but before he could fire, shots rang out from the stairs below him, and a bullet whizzed past his head. He ducked behind a rock, and more rounds struck its surface. He turned the rifle to face the new threat—a dozen men racing up the stairs toward him —and opened fire.

Then he brought the rifle quickly back around and squeezed the trigger, killing the man who stood over Kat.

The bullet hit Egin square in the bridge of his nose, bursting the ocular jelly out the front of both irises, sending pieces of his green eyes leaking down his cheeks. Blind now, his brain reeling from trauma, he could not see what was about to come, and for that he had regret.

He fell to the rock and lay there in the darkness, wondering if he would wake in three days. In the distance, he heard his father's voice yelling... but there was something else, too. The rising sound of locusts, like white noise in his dying ears, and as he felt hands clutching at his body, he wondered who was coming for him.

"Get the women!" Longinus shouted to the soldiers. "Get them into the cave!"

Two soldiers grabbed the ropes that bound the women and dragged them to their feet. Three others returned fire.

As the Blackhawk roared over the reserve, the door gunner opened fire with the M240-H, shredding the soldiers at the top of the cliff, throwing flesh from bone.

The women were rushed into the recess of the cave, but in the chaos, Kat had been left strapped to the table, hooked to the IV, the drugs coursing through her veins.

She struggled to keep her eyes open, her lids fluttering, and then saw only black.

As Sunday fired down on the men below, the cliff rumbled, a deep tremor from the core of the earth itself. The rock pigeons took to the skies in a flurry, and Sunday fell forward, the ground shaking beneath his feet.

Inside the cave, the brown pool bubbled, swirled, and steamed, a festering soup. A sonic burst erupted from beneath the water, and the ceiling of the cave was blasted skyward, spewing rock and dust in a huge plume.

The shock wave rippled across the preserve, knocking men to their knees, burying them in clouds of dust.

The mountain had woken.

The Blackhawk shuddered in the sky, and the pilot flicked frantically at the control panel that was now black.

"Six-one going down!" he cried into the headset.

"Pull up. Pull up," replied a robotic voice in the cockpit, as if it too did not wish to die.

The overhead rotors and tail rotors slowed and stalled, and the pilot instinctively lowered the pitch to go in for an autorotation landing.

At that moment the shock wave hit, a blast of hot air, and the helicopter spun like it had been thrown.

"Going down! Engine failure! Brace yourselves!"

The tail rotor caught the side of the cliff, spinning the chopper hard into the rock face, and the Blackhawk fell like a dying metal beast to the ground below.

The canyon shuddered again as a giant blast of quivering dark light shot skyward from the blown-out roof of the cave. It twisted the air around it like a stream of jet fuel fumes a hundred feet wide and miles high, creating a hole through the few white clouds above, pulsing and screaming like a giant horn blasting into the heavens.

The ground quaked, angered, as if earth and sky were separating.

"Kill them," Longinus said. "None must survive!"

The soldiers raised their weapons and opened fire, killing the three pregnant women on their knees in the hollow recess of the cave.

Sunday emerged from the dust cloud and raced up the stone steps. Kat lay still on the table, in a white gown covered in blood. He disconnected the IV, tossed the line, and felt for a pulse. But with all the tremors he couldn't tell whether she still had a heartbeat.

On the ground next to her was the man who had tortured him. Although he was dead, his eyes blown clear from his skull, he looked up with a wide smile as if he knew something Sunday did not.

Sunday turned to deal with his remaining threats. Crossing along the rock face that led into the cave's stone mouth, he moved past the edge and fired two clean shots, killing the last two soldiers, who toppled onto the pregnant women they themselves had just killed.

That left only Josef Belac.

The old man didn't even look up. He had stepped into the rippling water and was watching the pool swirl around his feet as if collecting him.

"What did you do?" Sunday shouted.

Belac finally met his eye—and smiled. "What God would not."

Sunday fired, a double-tap to the forehead, knocking Belac into the swirling pool. His body sank as if sucked down a drain.

The bullets nestled in Longinus's brain like eggs in a nest. The swelling and trauma choked his thoughts, but a silhouette still filled his fading vision.

She surfaced next to him in the water. Her hair was gone, her eyes and lips sealed with flesh, her ears removed. She collected him in the muddy waters and held him tight against her.

Then she dragged him down into the abyss, from which no light is born.

Kat lay lifeless, her lips parted, on the blood-soaked surgical table. Sunday felt for a pulse again.

Nothing.

No...

He leaned down over her mouth.

Is she breathing?

The earth rumbled yet again, and the sky turned dark with ash and rock. Waves of heat rippled across the canyon, and the air filled with the rank odor of sulfur. Sunday, his rifle slung over his shoulder and Kat in his arms, somehow kept his feet. He was carrying her down the stone steps, scanning the hillside, looking for threats.

When he reached the bottom, he carried Kat into the visitor's center and laid her gently on the floor.

She sat up, her eyes wide and panicked, the drugs still lingering.

"I've got you," Sunday said.

She looked at him as if uncertain who he was.

"You're safe," he whispered.

Tears pooled in her eyes. "Is this real?"

"Yes."

He wanted to reach out and hold her, but the distance between them was still so great, and he was afraid she wouldn't reciprocate. That she would reject him.

She didn't. Even as he hesitated, she smiled and reached out, and he felt her gentle touch upon his cheek as she traced the scars on his face.

CHAPTER LXVII

The car pulled up to a chain-link fence off a rural road in a valley of Carrol County, Maryland, and Eve McAllister stepped out. She had no bags, no possessions.

"Good luck," the driver said as he pulled away, no doubt racing toward his own family.

Good luck? Good luck with what? The end of the world?

There was a gate in the fence. It was locked. A rusted *No Trespassing* sign hung from the metal links.

Eve pulled out her phone. It was dead, even though she'd charged it on the car ride over.

She felt it first in her knees, a wobble in her bones. Then it rattled up through her belly. The gravel on the roadside rolled and shook, like kernels of corn in a sizzling pan. A distant wailing sound came from the sky and blew the leaves of the trees. The woods around her erupted with the deafening chatter of crickets.

The car stopped down the road, a quarter mile away. The driver climbed out, looking skyward.

Eve looked down at her cell phone again, habit, but the screen was still blank. She shook it, as if an image would appear like a message in a Magic 8-Ball.

The air was filled with a bitter smell, like the pulp of a toxic plant.

The driver screamed. Eve looked up from her phone and saw him flailing wildly as if swatting at bees. Still screaming, he collapsed to his knees.

What is he doing? Is he bowing?

"Eve!" a voice shouted.

She turned. On the other side of the fence, her father raced down a gravel walkway toward her. He pulled a set of keys from his pocket.

"It's going to be okay," he said, panting. "We have what we need. We're going to be okay." He hurriedly unlocked the padlock and cracked open the gate the length of the chain. "Hurry! Squeeze through!"

Dark clouds unfurled across the sky like a black roll of carpet. Eve looked back down the long road. The driver was on his feet now and racing toward her, full speed, more of a gallop than a run.

"Dad?" she said.

* * *

Tom Ferguson pulled the gun from his holster, but not quickly enough. The car's driver had already done the same, and had fired off a single round. It spiraled through the crisp country air and struck Eve in her chest.

She fell where she stood.

"No!" Tom screamed. He shot the driver in the stomach. The man fell to his knees, but not before getting off another round, striking Tom in the throat.

Tom fired again, hitting the driver's face, and he fell backward onto the gravel.

Tom held his hand to his neck to stay the blood. He squeezed through the gate and dropped down beside his daughter.

"Eve!" he cried.

But the blood bubbling through her chest would be her final sound.

Tom kneeled before her, his only true church, and clutched his throat to hold back the pulse that dribbled through his fingers.

He had wanted only to bring her into the safety behind the gate. To the world he had built for them in the bunker beyond. To the place that would keep them together as the earth around them crumbled.

He had just wanted to protect her. To keep her safe.

He died holding his little girl in his arms.

CHAPTER LXVIII

Sunday moved through the parking lot, rifle at the ready. Kat stayed close behind, where he could shield her from attack. The aftershocks continued, and the sky was black as pitch, even though it was only a little past midday.

Sunday knelt by Eichel's dead body. Reaching into the man's pockets, he pulled out keys and a cell phone. The phone's screen was dead, despite his taps to resurrect it. He tossed it aside and leaned into the SUV that had not been blown up. He found the right key, stuck it into the ignition, and turned it.

Nothing. Not even a spark of life or a knocking from a bad starter.

A deep bellow sounded somewhere up on the ridge, as if a lion purred at the touch of daylight. The plume spiraled skyward, a wave of black fire, swirling and churning the clouds overhead. Sunday felt as though an alien planet had been brought forth into this one. A Venus upon this Earth.

"What's happening?" Kat asked.

"I don't know," he said honestly.

He opened the trunk and retrieved two nine-millimeters and a handful of clips. He tucked it all into his belt, then handed Kat a bulletproof vest. "Put this on."

They walked down Highway 99, bound for the small kibbutz where black smoke from a smoking semi curled into the roiling sky. When they passed an abandoned car, Sunday put Kat in the back seat.

"Stay here," he said. "I'll go for help."

She clung to his hand for a moment, but she was already fading, exhausted.

He continued forward alone.

As he approached the kibbutz, he heard screams. He tightened his grip on the M4.

He found the source of the dark plume—the metal skeleton of a semi that burned and crackled. All around it were the husks of charred people, still burning from within like orange embers. He moved on, past empty houses, many with doors left open as if the residents just dropped everything and ran. But he didn't see another soul—though he heard their screams.

And then he found them. Following the sounds, he turned down a side street, and there they were, not a hundred yards away.

It was a collective slaughter.

The people of this town were attacking each other and themselves. Some hacked at their neighbors with kitchen knives. Some convulsed on the asphalt, grinding their foreheads into the rocky grit. One man, his beard stained with blood, chased after an old woman with a hammer in his hand. As he caught up to her, he repeatedly sank the hammer into her skull.

Why? Why are they doing this?

But Sunday knew. Something had come over. Something had *crossed*. That something now filled the sky like a plague, draining the rivers of men, and he felt it. He knew it was here, because he had known it before, and it hung upon him like the cold that had crept in with the vanquishing of the sun.

He backed away slowly, quietly. He had to get back to Kat.

* * *

He heard screams. Kat's screams.

A crowd of men had surrounded the car where he'd left her. Apparently she'd locked the doors, but the men had broken a window and one was attempting to crawl inside.

Sunday fired as he ran, taking out the man who was halfway through the window.

The rest of the men turned toward Sunday and charged. They moved faster than he expected, and without fear.

He fired repeatedly until they all lay dead. Then he dropped the clip and reloaded.

He pulled the man's body out of the car's window, reached in, and opened the door.

Kat lay on the floorboards, face down.

"Kat!"

She slowly raised her head, her face white, her eyes wide with shock. He helped her out of the back seat, her pregnant body cumbersome to move.

She paused as she looked around at all the bodies on the street. Then she looked at him.

"What's happening, John?"

Sunday's attention was drawn by a dull roar—the sound of people—growing louder, closer. He turned, and there they were, racing down the street toward them, men and women screaming like some ancient army crossing a battlefield, fifty strong.

"Go!" he shouted.

Kat needed no further convincing.

They ran off the road, through a field, into a playground. Beyond it there was nothing but open land. Nowhere to hide. In the center of the playground was a small metal yellow castle playset with a slide. Sunday led Kat to it, helped her up the steps, and tucked her into a corner. Sunday took a knee at its entrance, and from there he had a perch, as feeble as it was.

He checked his ammo. Two clips. Thirty rounds each.

He took cover behind the metal frame of the play castle wall, near the painted face of a clown wearing a crown, and as the mob crossed the field, he opened fire. Cool, calculated shots through the head of each approaching man or woman. They continued pouring down upon the castle, not distracted by the gunfire. They moved as if a hive or pack, driven like primal hunters.

A few were able to climb the stairs of the playset, but he shot them off. Fingers jutted between the metal rungs and grabbed at Kat's hair and clothes. Parts of their fingertips peeled back, revealing jagged bone nails that had sliced through the flesh, claws revealed. Kat screamed as they tore into her back.

Sunday turned and fired, a round whizzing over Kat's head at a man climbing the wall to try and pull her over the side. More tried to clamber over the top, and he shot them off.

And then it was done.

Bodies lay on the sand, on the grass of the playground, and on the asphalt of the road.

Sunday helped Kat down the stairs and led her through the field of dead.

She spoke no more that afternoon. She walked like a blood-stained ghost, eyes wide and hollow, hands clammy despite the creeping cold. The black sky above was a reminder to them both that the world they knew was gone, swallowed by a creature neither of them had yet to see.

They left the village and drifted toward the mountains, away from people, and eventually came across a small farm. The farmer's naked body had been pinned to the barn doors with sixteen penny nails. Crucified.

From within the barn came the tapping of hooves. Sunday pulled back the doors, rifle at the ready, and found a white horse spotted with black, its breath clinging in the cold air around its nostrils. It looked at them with skittish eyes, its walnut-sized brain keenly aware that a predator was somewhere near.

Sunday found a saddle and prepped the horse.

Inside the house, Kat removed her white gown, and wiped away the blood. She sobbed as she sponged in the tub, using the water that remained in the toilet tank, the crimson reminder of Mara washing down the drain. Her own bleeding continued, the flow heavy, and she searched for some kind of pad that could absorb it. The best she could do was some dishtowels from the kitchen. She bundled them together, and wearing the farmer's underwear, packaged the whole thing together with duct tape around her waist.

She dressed in a man's woolen thobe she found in the closet. On the dresser near the bed, she spotted a small burgundy Christian Bible, and though it was in Arabic, she tucked it into her front pocket before she slid the bulletproof vest on over it.

They took jackets and blankets, and canned goods, and an old Winchester, and two boxes of ammo from the barn.

They stepped out onto the porch, the clouds above thick with darkness. The night had become permanent, and snow had begun to fall, in a place where snow rarely came. Despite the cold, they heard crickets chirping in the distance. Beyond that, carried like thunder, the cold wind blew.

When they were ready, Kat rode the horse, and John led it. She felt the baby kicking inside, as anxious to flee as they were.

As they climbed the snow pass, toward the wilderness of ancient Babylon, the Bible whispered to Kat. The readings of Revelations, which she had heard over and over these last months.

"And she gave birth to a son, a male child, who is to rule all the nations with a rod of iron; and her child was caught up to God and to His throne. Then the woman fled into the wilderness where she had a place

prepared by God, so that there she would be nourished
for one thousand two hundred and sixty days."

They disappeared into the mountains, far from
man.

AVAILABLE SPRING 2020

THE END OF DAYS
IS JUST THE
BEGINNING.

jamesholmesauthor.com

THE
LAST
TESTAMENT

JAMES HOLMES

ACKNOWLEDGEMENTS

We are nothing but what we give. These people believed in me, guided me, gauged me and for that I am eternally grateful.

Aaron Tucker
Amber Lyda
Arleen Eutin
Brian Shields
Chantal Watts
David Sirak
Jim & Gunn Loyd
Nancy Alvarez
Racquel Asa
Vanessa Echols
Editor David Gatewood
Cover Designer Adam Hall
Interior Designer Kevin G Summers
Marketing WattsYaReading@gmail.com

And to my wife and children:
Hannah, Harrison, and Hailey.
I am nothing without you.

ABOUT THE AUTHOR

James Holmes is a journalist who has been writing for television for twenty-five years. He's covered the dark side of human nature for so long he needed a fictional outlet to come to terms with where we're going as a species.

He wakes at 1:30 every morning to write and in this caffeinated haze, his literary monsters are born.

He and his wife homeschool their three children.

The Last Disciple is his first novel. The sequel, *The Last Testament*, will be available 2020.

Made in the USA
Coppell, TX
22 January 2022

72082207R00229